Gangsta Twist 2

Clifford Spud Johnson

www.urbanbooks.net

Urban Books, LLC
78 East Industry Court
Deer Park, NY 11729

Gangsta Twist 2 Copyright © 2011
Clifford Spud Johnson

ISBN 13: 978-1-60162-548-9
ISBN 10: 1-60162-548-0

First Mass Market Printing March 2013
First Trade Printing August 2011
Printed in the United States of America

10 9 8 7 6 5 4 3 2 1

This is a work of fiction. Any references or similarities to actual events, real people, living or dead, or to real locales are intended to give the novel a sense of reality. Any similarity in other names, characters, places, and incidents is entirely coincidental.

Distributed by Kensington Publishing Corp.
Submit Wholesale Orders to:
Kensington Publishing Corp.
C/O Penguin Group (USA) Inc.
Attention: Order Processing
405 Murray Hill Parkway
East Rutherford, NJ 07073-2316
Phone: 1-800-526-0275
Fax: 1-800-227-9604

Dedication

This book is dedicated to Devin N. Johnson and Denver J. Johnson two of the main reasons why I continue to strive for perfection. I love the both of you with all that I have and I hope that though I have missed a large part of your lives I am making you proud to call me your father.

Love forever,
Daddy

Chapter One

Taz, Sacha, and Mama-Mama were sitting in the waiting area of the emergency room at Mercy Hospital. Taz sat dazed as he stared at the wall without saying a word to anyone. Sacha sat next to him, trying her best to console and comfort her man, while Mama-Mama, Taz's mother, was on the other side of the room silently praying.

Taz couldn't believe that fool, Cliff, had actually shot his child. His daughter Tazneema was currently in surgery fighting for her life all because of his arrogance. *If I hadn't chosen to goad Clifford on, my child wouldn't be inside of that damn operating room,* Taz thought as he continued to stare at the wall.

"Please say something, baby. You're really scaring me," Sacha told Taz as she gently rubbed his back.

Taz turned toward his fiancée, smiled sadly and said, "I'm here, Li'l Mama, but I'm damn sure not all right. This shit is killin' me."

"I know, baby . . . I know. But Tazneema is going to be okay. You have to keep the faith, baby."

"Faith? *Faith?* Faith is for Mama-Mama, Li'l Mama, not me. All my life I've vowed to protect that girl. When I lost her mother because of my cocky-ass attitude, I swore to never let anything ever happen to my Baby Girl. And years later, look what the fuck I've done. Once again, my cockiness has gotten another loved one hurt. I'm tellin' you, Li'l Mama, I'm a cursed man. You really might want to take some time and think again about marrying a nigga like me!" he said angrily.

"That's nonsense, boy, and you damn well know it!" screamed Mama-Mama from across the room. "God has a plan for us all. It is not your fault what happened today. It's that damned Cliff's! So don't you dare beat yourself up behind this, Taz. And sure as I know God is good, He's not going to take my grandbaby away from me."

When Taz saw tears streaming down his mother's face, he quickly got to his feet and went and held her in his arms. As they were hugging, he said, "I can't lose her, Mama-Mama! She's all of MiMi I got left. I can't lose my Baby Girl!" he cried.

"She's gon' be all right, baby. She's gon' be all right," Mama-Mama said as she held on tightly to her only child.

After Taz seemed to have regained some of his composure, he sat back down in his seat and resumed staring at the wall.

Sacha, still confused about everything, had a lot of questions running through her mind. *This may not be the right time, but I need some answers,* she thought to herself. Then to Taz she said, "Do you feel like talking, baby? It might help a little."

"Talk about what, Li'l Mama? How I'm gon' murder Cliff? Do you really want to talk about somethin' like that? 'Cause that's the only thing that's on my mind right now, other than my Baby Girl."

She knew not to even go there with him, so she said, "You're right. I don't want to talk about any of that nonsense. Why don't you tell me about MiMi?"

Taz stared at Sacha's beautiful face for a moment, and once again gave her that sad smile and said, "All right, Li'l Mama. I should have told you this story a long time ago, but for some reason I chose to keep it to myself. If you're goin' to be caught up in my cursed life, you might as well know the entire story." He shook his head from side to side as he began:

"What seems like a million years ago, I was a wild youngsta with a two-year-old daughter.

MiMi was my everything. We'd been in love with each other ever since we were in junior high school. I guess the first sign of my curse was when I messed that girl's life up."

"Would you please stop with that 'cursed' stuff? You are not a cursed man, Taz. God!" Sacha said sternly.

"Whatever! Anyway, I got her pregnant when we were in the tenth grade, and she had to miss the rest of our tenth grade year as well as our eleventh because of the baby. She had plans on becoming a doctor. She actually wanted to be a brain surgeon. I used to laugh at her, but I could tell by the determined look in those beautiful brown eyes that she was going to accomplish every single goal that she had set for herself. And I fucked it all up. Once Tazneema was born, her family flipped out on her and refused to give us any help. They actually put her out! Can you believe that shit?! I was so mad that for a minute I thought about doin' somethin' to them. But, as usual, Mama-Mama came to my rescue and let MiMi move in with us." Taz smiled at that memory and continued.

"Since Mama-Mama had spoiled me so much, I had no choice but to drop out of school so I could get my hustle on. I couldn't let my mother be the breadwinner for me and my family. I would have felt less of a man. Even though I was just a seventeen-year-old, I had to step up to the plate. So, like everybody else in the city was doin' in the late eighties, I started slangin' rocks. But somethin' about being a dope boy just wasn't cool with me. I was small time, and I didn't like the fact that I was destroying my people. So I quit the dope game after a few months and got some of my closest friends together and formed the crew."

Sacha smiled and said, "The crew, as in Keno, Bob, Bo-Pete, Red, and Wild Bill?"

"Yeah. My plan was simple. Since a bunch of dudes from Texas and Cali were coming to the city, gettin' rich off of the dope game, I came up with the smart-ass idea that we should just sit back and let those niggas make the money. Then we would come in and jack them for their easily earned dividends. With the li'l money I had from the game, I bought us some guns, and we quickly put my plan into effect. We was jackin' every nigga we even thought had some money. We were young, and murder was something that I never even gave a thought about. Can you believe that shit? Here I was, robbing niggas for a living and I wasn't even thinkin' about takin' a nigga's life. Young, dumb and arrogant as hell. Yep, that was me.

"Anyway, after a year of this, we had came up pretty damn good. We all had cars, and we even had our own apartments. I saved a nice chunk of change so MiMi could enroll in college. I was determined to help her become a brain surgeon. As far as I was concerned, she wasn't goin' to fail because of me. She was proud of me, yet she hated what I was doin' in them streets. She understood though, because hell, I didn't know much of anything else. All I had was my high school diploma, and that wasn't shit. See, after I dropped out of school, MiMi made me promise her that I would go back so I could get my diploma. I kept my word and went back to school, but I was still robbing any and everybody with chips.

"Everything was goin' just fine, until the day my stupidity finally caught up with me. Some Crips from California set up shop on the East Side, and as usual, they were slippin'. You see, niggas come out here from out of town and think since we're from Oklahoma we're some straight country suckas. And to tell you the truth, most of them dope boys in the city are exactly that . . . suckas. All they want to do is get plugged in with Cali niggas and try their best to be just like them. That's how we got all of this damn gang-bangin' in the city now. Anyway, once we found out where them Crips niggas was gettin' money at, we quickly came up with a plan to get at them fools. The lick went just as smoothly as the rest of them had. But, you see, I was so cocky that I never anticipated any retaliation from any of our victims. That's why we never wore any ski masks over our faces. After all, most of the niggas we were jackin' weren't from here anyway.

"A couple of weeks after that particular jack, the word around town was that those Cali niggas were lookin' for me and my crew. I was confident that no one knew where any of us lived, so we decided to lay low for a minute until those clowns got tired. That was my second mistake. It took them a li'l over a month, but somehow they finally found out where my apartment was. I was at the store gettin' some fish and shrimp for MiMi, because she loved her some seafood." he remembered fondly. "By the time I came back to the apartment building, I heard my daughter crying. I ran up the stairs as fast as I could because I knew that something was wrong. When I made it to my apartment, I saw that the door had been kicked in. I dropped the bags I was holding and ran inside of the apartment with no gun or nothin'. All I was thinkin' about was MiMi and my Baby Girl.

"The first thing I noticed when I entered the apartment was Tazneema crying. For some reason, that's what I remember most about that day;

the way my Baby Girl was crying. When I saw MiMi lying on the floor with three bulletholes in her chest, I screamed as I ran and held her dead body in my arms.

"After a few minutes, a strange calm came over me. I gently laid my MiMi back on the floor, grabbed my daughter out of her bassinet and took her into the bedroom and fed her a bottle so she could calm down. I then grabbed the phone and called Keno, and told him what had happened. After I hung up with him, I called Mama-Mama and told her that she had to hurry up and get over to my apartment before the police did, so she could take Neema over to her house."

"By the time Mama-Mama had come and left, the crew had arrived just before the police did. They asked me all types of fuckin' questions. For a minute I thought they thought I did that stupid shit. When the homicide detective told me that I was going to have to go downtown to the police station for more questioning, I lost it. I told them that they could all go to hell 'cause I wasn't goin' any fuckin' where. My girl was dead, and those niggas had to die. You see, I wasn't prepared for murder before, but after they took my MiMi from me, my murder game became the most vicious that Oklahoma City had ever seen. Not only did I get those Cali Crip niggas, but almost every other jack we put down after MiMi's murder resulted with a murder being committed. I didn't give a fuck about anything anymore. All of the money I made I gave to Mama-Mama for Neema. I kept what I needed for survival, but I had to make sure that Mama-Mama was straight financially, because I knew I was walking around on borrowed time. My niggas rode with me, and we all made a pact that, no matter what happened, if anything happened to any one of us, the rest of the crew would ride until we were either dead or in jail for the rest of our lives. So murder was my game, and that was the only thing that kept me sane. If I didn't kill someone at least twice a month, I started to feel as if I had somehow betrayed MiMi. That's how twisted my thinking had become. MiMi was my everything, and without her in this world with me I didn't give a damn about anyone other than Neema, Mama-Mama, and my niggas."

"What stopped you from that insane mission you were on?"

Taz smiled and simply answered, "Won. He came into my life because a friend of his had heard about this crazy-ass crew in the city, robbin' and killin' everything in their way. This friend then set up a meet for me and Won. That was the day that Won gave me a brand-new way of thinking."

"What did he say at that meeting, baby?"

"He told me that it was time for me to stop killing and to start living for my seed."

"So, Won is the reason that you stopped killing and robbing people?"

Taz thought about Sacha's question for a moment, and then said, "Yes and no. You know what we do, so you know that I've never stopped doin' my thang. But the senseless killings stopped. The only time I've had to take a life since then was to ensure the safety of me and the crew—not counting that time that fool tried to jack me and you at the club. My anger has subsided over the years, Li'l Mama, but believe me, the hatred is still in my heart. I lost the woman of my dreams, and I will never be able to have her back. That pain still lingers deep within me, and I honestly feel that it will never go away completely."

"That's natural, baby. You were deeply in love, and that love got cut short. But, Taz, you have to stop this madness. You can't let what Cliff has done turn you back into that monster you once were. It'll ruin you this time, baby," Sacha wisely said.

Taz shook his head slowly and said, "If God wants that fool to remain breathing, He has to spare my baby's life. 'Cause if Neema dies, so will Cliff. That's real talk, Li'l Mama."

Sacha stared deeply into her fiancé's eyes, and knew that he meant every word of what he had just told her. Before she could say anything, the crew finally arrived.

Keno was the first to enter the waiting room. He walked straight up to Taz and asked, "How is she, dog? Why the fuck didn't you call us as soon as you got here? Who did this shit?"

Taz got to his feet and said, "First off, calm down, my nigga. Neema's still in surgery. We're waiting for the doctors to finish up with her now. Her nigga Cliff shot her. He was trying to blast me, and Neema pushed me out of the way and took the hit for me, dog. Some straight move shit, for real. I didn't call y'all 'cause I haven't even been thinkin' straight, G. That's my bad."

"Who is this nigga? 'Cause he gots to go!" Bo-Pete said vehemently.

Taz smiled and said, "Remember that nigga that used to try to holla at Sacha? He somehow got Neema to fall in love with him. Not only did they become involved with each other, the nigga got my Baby Girl pregnant!"

"*What?* Come on, *G*! That's some straight up soap opera shit," Red said as he stepped closer to Taz.

"Yeah, I know, but it is what it is, dog."

"All right, *G*. Where can we find this clown-ass nigga? You stay down with Mama-Mama and wifey while we go handle this nigga real quick like," Wild Bill said in a deadly tone.

Mama-Mama, who had been silent through all of this, stepped over to them and said, "You will do no such thing, Billy! I want each one of you to sit down and wait this out here with Taz, Sacha, and myself. Do you understand me?"

Keno gave Mama-Mama a hug and said, "Mama-Mama, you know we love you and Neema as if we were all family. We can't let this clown get away with this. We gots to go."

Tears fell slowly from Mama-Mama's eyes as she said, "Keno, you boys have been family to me for a very long time. Just because we're not blood-related doesn't mean a thing to me. Out of all of these years, have I ever asked any of you for anything? Have I?"

"No, ma'am," Keno answered with his head bowed.

"Well, I'm asking y'all for something now. Will y'all please leave this alone, at least for the time being? My heart wouldn't be able to take it if anything else happened to someone I care for. Please, baby. Y'all sit down and help us through this rough time like families are supposed to. Please!"

Red, Keno, Wild Bill and Bo-Pete each took turns hugging Mama-Mama and reassuring her that they would stay and do as she asked them to. They all sat down and resumed waiting for the doctors to come and tell them whether or not Tazneema was going to live or die.

The room became silent, until Taz's cell started ringing. He pulled his phone off of his belt clip, checked the caller ID and answered it. "What's up, O.G.?"

"What's up, Baby Boy? Look, I was out of line the last time we spoke. This shit is really getting hectic for me. You have to understand that everything we've been doing is for a very important reason."

"Yeah, I feel you, O.G., but right now I got a lot of shit on my plate. That shit with you is like way on the back burner, for real."

"What's up out that way, Baby Boy?" Won asked curiously.

"Neema got shot."

"*What?* When did this happen? And why in the hell haven't you called me?" Won screamed.

"My mind is on a million and one different things right now, O.G. I can't think straight enough to take a piss, let alone think about callin' you and lettin' you know what's what."

"I understand, Baby Boy. Look, I'll be on the next thing smoking. I should be there some time tomorrow. How is she?"

"She's in surgery now. We're all here waiting and praying that everything goes her way."

"How's Mama-Mama?"

"You already know how she gets down, O.G. She's put everything in God's hands."

"Is Tari there?"

"Nah. Shit, I haven't told her either, and she works in this fuckin' place."

"So, y'all are at Mercy?"

"Yeah."

"All right, let me get my flight shit together. We'll talk some more when I get into town."

"All right, O.G."

"Your boy Bob will be flown into town in a couple of days. Magoo has everything set up out east. By the time I get there I'll have all of the details."

"That's cool. At least something is goin' like it's supposed to."

"Hold your head, Baby Boy. Everything is going to be all right."

"I hope you're right, O.G. I hope you're right. Out!" Taz said, and closed his phone.

Keno stared at Taz with raised eyebrows and asked, "What's he talkin' 'bout?"

"Bob's straight, and he should be home in a day or so."

"That's cool. That it?"

"Basically," Taz answered as he reopened his phone and dialed Tari's home number. When he didn't get an answer, he left a message quickly explaining what happened to Tazneema over at Mama-Mama's house earlier. After he was finished, he turned toward Sacha and asked, "Are you straight, Li'l Mama? Why don't you go on back to my spot and get some rest. I'm not tryin' to have you gettin' sick on me or nothin'."

Sacha shook her head no and said, "If you think I'd leave your side right now, you're out of your mind, Mr. Good. I'm going to be standing right next to you when they come out here and tell you that Neema is going to be just fine."

Taz smiled that sad smile and said, "Okay." He sat back down and started thinking again about how he was going to kill that nigga, Cliff.

"Taz, tell me some more about what happened to you and the crew after you hooked up with Won."

"You really want to know it all, huh?"

"Yep."

"All right. After meeting Won, he took me out to L.A., where he gave me what he likes to call my complete makeover. He taught me a lot of things about the game, and how wrong I was playin' it."

"Like what?"

"Everything. But the most important lesson to me was to make sure that I never shit in my own backyard."

Sacha smiled and asked, "Meaning?"

"Meaning, never do dirt in the city you live in. That has been a rule that I've sworn never to break. That's why I told you that you would never have to worry about any of my actions puttin' you in any jeopardy. Other than that, everything else was basic common sense really. He told me that I should get healthy and maintain a strict habit of exercising. In order to be thorough, he wanted me and the crew to be trained properly."

"Trained? Trained for what?"

"In order for us to be effective in what we do, we had to be able to be as fluid as possible. By it being six of us, we had to become accustomed with each other's moves, and be able to watch each other's backs so we would always be able to maintain our safety during missions. So, for one year after our meeting, me and the crew worked out seven days a week, and went to the shooting range daily to get familiar with various types of weapons. We went out to the country and practiced all types of simulated jack moves and stuff like that. Won told me to call him back when I felt that we were ready."

"Ready for what?"

"To get rich! I called him a year later and told him that we were in fact more than ready. After that, everything is pretty much history. I kept my word to Won, and in return he kept his word with me. He made each of us richer than we could have ever imagined. We stuck to the script he laid out for us, and everything fell into place just like he said it would. I owe that man my life, Li'l Mama. He's been like a father to me. But enough is enough. I want out. I'm ready to live my life with you and put all of this shit behind me now."

Sacha smiled at that comment and said, "Have you told Won that you want to quit?"

"Yeah, and he told me that we're not finished yet. We're almost there, but not yet."

"What is that supposed to mean, Taz?"

"Right now, Li'l Mama, all I'm worried about is my seed. Everything else has to hold up. Won's comin' out here tomorrow, so I guess we'll talk more about that shit then."

"He can't make you keep doing something that you no longer want to do, Taz."

"Don't worry about that, Li'l Mama. No man has ever made me do somethin' that I didn't want to do, and I ain't gonna let that shit start now."

Before Sacha could respond, Tari came running into the waiting area with her face flushed a deep crimson. She stepped straight up to Taz and asked, "How is she?"

"I don't know. We've been waiting here for hours and no one has came and told us shit," Taz said seriously.

"I'll be back in a minute," Tari said as she stormed right back out of the waiting area without saying a word to anyone else in the room.

Taz smiled and said, "Tee is 'bout to go the fuck off!"

Keno smiled and said, "I bet she finds out somethin' for us."

"They done fucked up! That white girl is 'bout to go on the warpath for real!" Red said from the other side of the room.

"Red! Watch your mouth boy!" yelled Mama-Mama.

"Sorry, Mama-Mama," Red said sheepishly.

Everyone laughed, and for a minute the tension inside of the room seemed to have eased up a little . . . just a little.

Ten minutes after Tari had left the waiting area, she came back with a smile on her face. That smile made Taz's heart rate increase dramatically as he stood and stared at her. He was so nervous that he could barely speak as he whispered, "How is she, Tee?"

"She's all right, Taz. She's all right. The doctor is on his way here now so he can tell you exactly what's been going on. But he did confirm for me that she is okay, and that she should make a full recovery."

Mama-Mama clapped her hands together loudly and screamed, "Thank you, Jesus! I Thank You, Lord! I knew You would keep Your gracious hands on my grandbaby! I knew it!"

Taz was feeling so numb that all he could do was stand there and smile. Tari put her arms around him, and they shared a tight hug. "My God! What the hell happened, Taz?" she whispered into Taz's ear.

Taz pulled himself from her embrace and said, "Later. I'll explain everything later on. Right now, I need to see my Baby Girl."

A doctor came into the waiting area, stepped toward Mama-Mama and said, "Hello, ma'am. Are you a relative of Tazneema Good?"

"Yes, yes, I am. She's my granddaughter. And this young man right here is her father," Mama-Mama said as she pointed toward Taz.

Taz shook the doctor's hand and asked, "Can I see my baby, sir?"

The doctor shook his head no and said, "I'm sorry, Mr. Good, but not tonight. Tazneema is going to be just fine, but she's been heavily sedated and she won't come out of it until early in the morning. We had to remove the bullet out of her back because it traveled much farther than we had originally anticipated. She's going to have a nasty scar, but she'll definitely make a one hundred percent recovery. I suggest that you all go on home and get some much-needed rest. Come back bright and early, and I'm positive Tazneema will be in a much better state than she is now."

"Thank you, doctor! Thank you so very much!" Taz said, relieved. He then turned toward everyone inside of the waiting area and said, "Come on, y'all. Let's bounce. You heard the man. My Baby Girl is gon' be all right!"

"I know that's right, my nigga! Let's get to the crib so we can kill some of that liquor of yours. I don't know about y'all, but my ass needs a drink!" yelled Bo-Pete.

Mama-Mama grabbed her purse from her seat and said, "I'm spending the night at your house, Taz. I want to be here with you bright and early in the morning."

"Okay, Mama-Mama. Anything you say."

"Shoot! I think I'll have me a strong dose of whatever y'all gon' be drinkin' too!"

Everyone started laughing as they filed out of the waiting area. Everything was going to be all right, or was it?

Chapter Two

Clifford parked his CLS 500 Mercedes in the parking lot of the Oklahoma City Police Department and turned off the ignition. He couldn't believe what he had done. He shot the woman he was in love with. Even though it wasn't intentional, he knew it was still his fault for trying to shoot Taz. "God, help me!" he said aloud as he stepped out of his car and walked inside of the police station. He went to the front desk and asked a police officer, "Who do I speak with about a shooting?"

A small overweight police officer asked him, "Where did this shooting take place, sir?"

"Out in Spencer."

"And how long ago did this happen?"

"About thirty minutes ago."

"Do you know the person who did the shooting, and was anyone shot?"

"Yes, on both accounts. My girlfriend, Taznee-ma Good, was shot, and I am the person who shot her," Clifford said somberly.

"Would you please have a seat, sir, while I get a detective for you to speak with."

Clifford gave the officer a nod of his head and went and sat down in one of the chairs in the hallway. While he was waiting for a detective, his mind was steady racing. *Was Tazneema all right? And if she was, was their child going to be able to survive this type of trauma?* These were the questions running through his mind as he patiently waited for the detective. *Please, God, let her be all right! I don't care what happens to me, just let Neema and our baby be all right!* he prayed silently.

After a few minutes, a slim brown-skinned detective came from behind the closed doors, walked directly up to Clifford and said," Hello, sir, my name is Detective Bean. Would you step this way, please?"

Clifford stood and followed the detective to an office. Once they were inside the office, Detective Bean motioned for Clifford to have a seat while he went and sat down behind his desk. "Now, I've been told that you have some information about a shooting. Why don't you tell me about it."

Clifford sighed heavily and said, "About forty-five minutes ago, I accidentally shot my girlfriend, Tazneema Good. I went over to her grandmother's home out in Spencer, so I could be introduced to who I once thought was my girlfriend's brother. But it turned out that the person I thought was her brother was actually her father. His name is Taz Good. Taz and I have a mutual dislike for one another."

"Wait a minute. I thought you said that you went over there to meet him."

"I did. You see, it's like this, we already knew one another. Taz got involved with a woman that I was kind of involved with." He sighed again and continued. "To make a long story short, the woman decided to leave me alone and mess with Taz. Ever since then, Taz and I had a slight beef with one another. Anyway, I met his daughter, and we became very close—so close in fact that she's pregnant with my child. She didn't know that I knew Taz, and she wanted us to meet each other. When I got to her grandmother's home and Taz saw who I was, he went ballistic. He started yelling at me and Tazneema, talking about how I didn't care about her, and how I was trying to get back at him for taking Sacha away from me. He was very irate and was not trying to hear anything either Tazneema or I had to say. He even went so far as to threaten me."

"What did he say?"

"He told me that he would kill me before he let me be with Tazneema."

"Okay. What happened next?"

"I took his threats literally and felt like my life was in danger. I pulled out my weapon. I pointed it at Taz and told him that I loved Tazneema. He smiled and tried his best to get me to shoot him."

"What exactly did he say to you?"

"He told me to go ahead and shoot him 'cause, if I didn't, he was going to kill me."

"And?"

"Tazneema yelled for me not to do it, but I was scared and I feared that Taz would in fact live up to the threats he was making. So, I pulled the trigger. Just as I did, Tazneema screamed and pushed her father out of the way. By doing so, she was hit instead of her father. I don't know where the bullet hit her, but I watched as she fell to the floor. Taz got off of the floor and grabbed her in his arms while I turned and ran outside to my car."

"And then you came straight here to the station?"

"Yes, sir. I know that I've committed a crime, and I had no other choice but to come and turn myself in."

Detective Bean nodded his head for a moment and said, "I respect that, sir. For the record, please give me your full name."

"Clifford Nelson."

"Place of employment?"

"I'm an attorney for the firm of Whitney & Johnson here in the city."

"An attorney? Well, I guess my next question won't need to be answered. Since you're an attorney, is it safe to assume that you have no criminal record?"

"That's correct."

"Since you've come and turned yourself in to the authorities, I'm going to try my best to make this situation as bearable as I can for you, Mr. Nelson."

"Thank you, Detective."

"Excuse me for a moment while I go speak with my captain. You can help yourself to some coffee if you'd like. It's not the best in the world, but it's strong and hot," Detective Bean said as he pointed toward his coffee pot on a small table behind his desk.

"No, thank you. I don't drink coffee."

"All right. I'll be back in a few," said the detective as he came from behind his desk and left his office. While on his way toward his captain's office, Detective Bean stopped at another detective's desk and said, "Wally, have we received any calls from any hospitals concerning a shooting within the last hour or so?"

"Yeah, we got two. One of them was from Mercy, and the other one was from St. Anthony's. What's up?"

"Do me a favor and check and see if the victim at either of the hospitals is a female by the name of . . ." he pulled out his notes that he had taken while Clifford was telling his story, found Tazneema's name and continued, "A Tazneema Good. If it is, make sure that you get right back at me, okay?"

"Gotcha, Frank."

Detective Bean then stepped briskly toward the captain's office and knocked on his door. After being told to come inside, he opened the door and entered his superior's office. He quickly told the captain what Clifford had told him, and asked, "So, what do you think? Should I book him now or what, sir?"

"Book him for what? We don't have any grounds to actually arrest him yet. Wait until you can confirm whether or not this Tazneema woman has actually been shot. Then we'll go from there," said the captain.

"Gotcha, sir," Bean said as he turned and left the captain's office.

As Bean was walking back to his office, the detective that he had asked to check on any shootings stopped him. "Looks like there is a Tazneema

Good over at Mercy, Frank. Gunshot wound to her upper torso," he said.

"Has anyone been sent over there yet?"

"She's still in surgery. The nurse I spoke with told me that they didn't know how long she'd be in the operating room."

"Thanks, Wally," Detective Bean said as he made an about face and went back toward the captain's office. He once again knocked on the captain's door, and was told to enter. Bean stuck his head inside of the door and said, "We have confirmation on Tazneema Good, sir. One gunshot wound to her upper torso."

"How is she?

"She's still in surgery."

"All right, read Mr. Nelson his rights and let him go."

"Let him go?" Detective Bean asked, shocked.

"That's what I said. He's not a runner. He'll be okay."

"Are you sure, Cap?"

"Trust me, I know what I'm doing. Let him know that after we get a statement from Ms. Good, he'll be hearing from us."

"But what if she dies, sir?"

"Then he'll definitely be hearing from us. Give him the not-to-leave-town speech and let him go, Frank."

"All right, sir." Detective Bean closed the office door and went back to his own office. As soon as he stepped inside, he said, "I'm going to have to read you your Miranda Rights, Mr. Nelson."

"So, I'm being arrested?" Clifford asked nervously.

"Not at the moment. We have confirmed that Tazneema Good has indeed been shot. She's currently in surgery over at Mercy Hospital."

"Do you know how she's doing?"

"Not at the moment. After I've finished reading you your Miranda Rights, you'll be free to go. I have a complete statement from you, so once we interview Ms. Good you'll most likely be hearing from us."

"I understand," Clifford said somberly. He sat back in his seat and listened as the detective read him his Miranda Rights. After the detective was finished, Clifford asked him, "How much time do you think I'm facing, Detective?"

"Honestly, it all depends."

"On what?"

"On whether or not Ms. Good lives or dies. If she lives, then you're looking at a shooting with intent charge. Since this is your first arrest, a judge may be lenient. You might come out of this with some probation and community service because of the unique circumstances of this situation—that is, if things went exactly the way you say they did. But if she dies, then it could mean a lot of time, Mr. Nelson."

"I understand. But what I don't understand is, why are you all letting me go home now? I could run away if I chose to."

Detective Bean smiled and said, "We don't think you're the running type, Mr. Nelson. After all, you did come and inform us of your crime. But, for the record, let me tell you that it would be in your best interest not to leave town," Bean said sternly.

"I won't, Detective," Clifford said as he got out of his seat.

"Go on home and try to take it easy. We'll contact you after we've had a chance to speak with Ms. Good."

"Okay. Thank you, Detective," Clifford said, and left the detective's office. As he walked out of the police station, he gave a sigh of relief. He was happy as hell to still be a free man. *If I was still the same man I used to be, I might not have come and turned myself in to the authorities*, he thought as he climbed inside of his car. *At least I'm not going to jail tonight,* he thought as he started his car and pulled out of the parking lot of the police station.

Chapter Three

The next morning, Taz, Sacha and Mama-Mama got up early and went straight to the hospital. When they arrived, two nurses escorted them to Tazneema's room. Tazneema was lying in her hospital bed sleeping when they entered her room. Taz smiled when he saw that his baby was breathing on her own without any medical equipment. *She's going to be all right,* he thought as he stepped closer to the bed. He bent over and kissed her on her forehead and said, "You're going to be all right, Baby Girl. You're going to be all right!"

Tazneema slowly opened her eyes, smiled and said, "Hi, Taz."

Tears welled in Taz's eyes as he said, "What's up? How are you feeling?"

"Tired."

"Yeah, you're going to have to stay off your feet for a minute," he said as he wiped his eyes.

Tazneema saw Mama-Mama standing beside Sacha and said, "Hi, Mama-Mama."

Mama-Mama came to the bed, grabbed Tazneema's hand and said, "Hey, baby!"

Tazneema waved at Sacha and said, "Well, it looks as if the whole gang's here, huh. I feel kinda important."

"You are important," Sacha said as she stepped up to the bed and stood next to Taz. "You gave us all quite a scare, young lady."

"I know, but I'm fine." Tazneema turned her head toward Taz and asked, "What happened to Cliff? You haven't done anything to him, have you?"

Taz's smile turned into a frown as he said, "Nah, not yet."

"Please don't do anything to him, Taz. He was scared. You pushed him into trying to shoot you."

"So, you're sayin' this is *my* fault?" Taz asked angrily.

"What I'm saying is, there isn't any reason for you to hurt him. I'm all right, and we should let this all go."

"Don't worry yourself 'bout any of that stuff right now, Neema. You need to be getting some rest so you can hurry up and get back on your feet. Taz ain't gon' be doin' nothin to that boy," Mama-Mama said sternly. She gave Taz the eye. "Ain't that right, boy?"

"Yes, Mama-Mama," Taz answered without looking in her direction.

Before Tazneema could speak again, there was a knock at the door, and Keno, Bo-Pete, Red and Wild Bill all entered the room, each holding a dozen red roses in their hands.

Keno smiled and said, "Look at my niece, all laid up looking all pretty like."

Tazneema smiled brightly and said, "Stop it, Uncle Keno! I'm a mess! Look at my hair!"

Keno laughed and said, "You look pretty damn good to me, Baby Girl."

"Watch your mouth, Keno!"

"Sorry, Mama-Mama," replied Keno.

Bo-Pete set his flowers on the counter and asked, "Are you feeling okay, Neema?"

"Yes, I'm fine. Just a little tired."

"That's cool."

Each one of her play uncles went and gave her a light kiss on her cheek and told her how much they all loved her. Taz took a step back while his homeboys showed his daughter some love. Sacha grabbed his hand and watched silently as the crew spoke with Tazneema.

After a few minutes, a nurse came into the room and said, "Tazneema needs to take her medication. Afterward, it's going to make her drowsy, so it would be better if you all left for a little while so she could get some rest."

"No problem, ma'am," Taz said as he stepped back next to the bed and gave Tazneema a kiss and said, "We'll be back a little later, Baby Girl."

"Okay, Taz," Tazneema said, and she said good-bye to everyone else inside the room.

As they all filed out of the room, Taz noticed a police officer speaking with a nurse at the nurses' station. *I wondered how long it would be before they would be gettin' at Neema,* he said to himself.

When they had made it to the nurses' station, Taz stopped and said, "Excuse me, officer, but are you here to speak with my daughter, Tazneema Good?"

"Yes, sir, I am. But I've just been told that I won't be able to interview her until later on this afternoon," replied the police officer.

"Yeah, she's just taken her medication. I can answer any questions that you have for her. I was there when everything happened."

"That's a start. Could we go somewhere and talk, sir?"

"Taz. My name is Taz Good."

"Okay, Mr. Good. Can you step over into the waiting room and answer a few questions for me?"

"No problem," Taz said as he followed the police officer.

Once they made it to a row of chairs, they both took a seat and the police officer said, "Tell me what exactly happened, Mr. Good."

Taz started from the beginning, and finished with how he had taunted Clifford. "You see, it's all my fault. If I wouldn't have kept pushing and taunting that fool, my Baby Girl wouldn't be laid up in this damn hospital."

"So, what you're telling me is that neither you nor your daughter are going to press charges against Mr. Nelson?" asked the police officer.

"That's correct. We want to put this incident behind us so we can move on with our lives," lied Taz.

"I understand. Mr. Nelson came down to the station yesterday after the shooting occurred and confessed to everything. From what I've been told, everything you have just told me matches exactly with what he told our detective. While I'm waiting to speak with your daughter, I'll give the lead detective a call and inform him of what you've told me. He may decide not to arrest Mr. Nelson."

"That's straight. If there's anything else that you need from me, I can be reached at my home anytime," Taz said, and gave the police officer the number to his home as well as his cell phone number.

Sacha, who had been listening to the entire interview, knew Taz was lying through his teeth. *You think you're so damn slick, Mr. Good! I'm not letting you commit another murder, mister!* she thought as she watched Taz shake hands with the police officer. After they had gotten into the elevator, Sacha said, "Keno took Mama-Mama home. She said she had a headache, and she was going home to get some rest. She's going to meet us back here later on, baby."

"That's cool. I'm kinda still faded from last night too. That XO don't be playin'."

Sacha smiled and said, "Don't I know it! I'm still feeling it from that time me and Gwen killed that bottle."

They stepped off of the elevator and into the lobby on the first floor, and were walking toward the exit when Sacha asked, "Why did you lie to that policeman, Taz? You know damn well that you have plans on doing something to Cliff."

"Why would you ask me a question that you already know the answer to, counselor? I don't want that clown-ass nigga in jail. He has to pay for this shit! And you know damn well I'm goin' to be the one to make him pay!"

"Even though your daughter is still in love with him?"

"What? Are you outta your mind? Neema's not goin' to fuck with that nigga no more! He shot her!"

Sacha smiled, shook her head from side to side and said, "I saw and heard all of the compassion on her face and in her voice. She's still in love with him, Taz. Why do you think she said what she said? She's still going to be with him, baby."

Taz shook his head violently and said, "No, she won't! 'Cause he won't be around for her to be with him!"

"So, you're going to cause her further anguish by killing the man she loves? How do you think she's going to feel about you after you murder the love of her young life, Taz?"

Taz stopped, stared directly into his fiancée's eyes and said, "To be totally honest with you, Li'l Mama, I don't give a fuck! That nigga is a dead man walkin'!" He then stormed out of the lobby of the hospital.

Sacha was so upset with Taz that she didn't say a word to him as they drove back to his home.

Taz pulled into the circular driveway of his mini-mansion, jumped out of his truck and went inside of his home. He was greeted by his beloved dobermans, Precious and Heaven. His dogs sensed that their master was in a foul mood because they instantly became alert. Each gave a low growl deep in their throats, awaiting the command from Taz to kill something. Taz noticed them, smiled and said, "Relax, girls. Everything is good. Go play, you two." Both Dobermans quickly obeyed their master's command and silently ran off into the large home. Taz went inside of one of his dens and poured himself a drink from his bar.

Sacha followed him into the den, sat across from him on his sectional sofa and said, "I've made an appointment to go see the doctor. Do you want to come with me?"

"When is it?"

"Tuesday at nine A.M."

"Yeah, I'll go. How far along do you think you are?"

She smiled and said, "I don't have a clue. Maybe a month or so."

"That's cool. Look, Li'l Mama. I've got a lot on my mind right now. Not only do I have this shit with Cliff to deal with, but I still got issues with Won to clear up. So I'm goin' to need you to give me some space for a minute."

"Space? What the fuck do you mean by space, Taz?"

He smiled, held his hands up and said, "Hold up, Li'l Mama! Not like that! I mean I don't need you tryin' to make me feel guilty and shit. I can't have you in my way tryin' to fuck up my train of thought and shit. You have to understand that I'm goin' to do me, regardless. You can't stop me from doin' whatever I feel in my heart is the right thing to do. Do you understand what I'm sayin'?"

"Yes. I just don't want you to do something that you might regret later on, baby."

"I know, Li'l Mama, but you're goin' to have to trust me and my decisions."

"I do, and I will, baby."

"Good. Now come here and give me some love," Taz said as he grabbed her and gave her a tender kiss.

After a full minute of kissing each other, Sacha pulled from Taz's embrace and said, "I'm going to head on home so I can get some more of my clothes. Why don't you get some rest before you go back up to the hospital? You look like you need a few more z's."

Taz smiled and said, "Yeah, I could use a li'l rest. But first I gots to make a few calls. Hold up though. What do you mean you got to get some more clothes from your house? What, you movin' in with a nigga or some shit?"

She playfully slapped Taz on his face and said, "You got a problem with that, Mr. Taz?"

With a bright smile on his face, he said, "Hell nah!" They both laughed and shared another kiss.

After Sacha left, Taz went upstairs and took a shower. After he finished, he was putting on a pair of shorts when his cell started ringing. "Hello."

"What's up, Baby Boy?" asked Won.

"What's up, O.G.?"

"I'm in town. Tari's taking me over to Mercy to see Neema. She already told me that she was straight, but I want to see her for myself, you know?"

"Yeah, I feel you. I was about to lay it down for a minute. A nigga's straight drained."

"Go on and get you some rest. I'll come by there in a couple of hours. After we leave the hospital, I'm going to have Tari take me to see a few people. Then I'll be by there. Call everyone and have them at your house around one. We need to talk so y'all can understand everything that's going on."

"All right, I'll holla at you later then," Taz said, and closed his cell phone.

By the time Sacha had finished packing a few bags, she felt as if she was going to pass out. She sat down on her bed, grabbed the telephone and called her best friend, Gwen. When Gwen answered her phone, Sacha said, "What it do, ho? What you doing?"

"Sitting here waiting on Bob to call me back. He promised me he'd call me back before he left."

"Left?"

"Yeah, bitch, he's on his way home. Some guy named Magoo is driving him back to the city."

"Why are they driving all of the way back from New York?"

"Bob told me that it would be safer that way. Obviously something bad went down and they're trying to stay low-key. Hell, bitch, I don't know! You know more about this shit than I do."

"Whatever! After you talk to Bob, give me a call, ho. I'm about to finish packing my stuff, then I'm going back over to Taz's."

"Oh, so you're moving in, huh? 'Bout time, bitch!"

Laughing, Sacha said, "Fuck you, ho!" and hung up the phone. She was happy for her best friend, Gwen. She had endured far too much pain in her life, and she deserved to be happy. Ever since she lost her son and her husband in a terrible car accident, her life was kind of just coasting along. Even though she'd got herself back together by going back to school and getting her degree in physcology, Sacha could tell that her girl still wasn't really happy. Gwen put up a good front though. One could never tell how badly she was actually hurting. But all of her pain seemed to have been eased once she met Taz's homeboy, Bob. Sacha knew every time she saw them together that her best friend had once again found love, and that was a true blessing from God.

But then out of nowhere, tragedy struck again. Bob was shot in his stomach during Taz and the crew's last robbery out in New York. When Gwen found out, she fainted, and Sacha knew in her heart that if Bob didn't pull through, her best friend wasn't going to be able to move on with her life this time around. Thank God that Bob had made it. Now everything can get back to normal. *Normal! Ain't that some shit! Ain't nothing normal about the way Taz, Bob, and the rest of that damn crew is living. This shit has got to stop!* Sacha said to herself as she got back up to finish packing her things.

Keno, dressed in a pair of Ecko sweatpants and matching Ecko T-shirt, came into Taz's home and sat down in the den as he watched Taz pour himself a drink from his bar. Keno's long hair was braided in four French braids going toward the back of his head. Though he was the same height as Taz—five foot eleven, and just as muscular—he gave off an entirely different type of vibe. He was always vibrant and upbeat, where Taz was more quiet and low-key. They had been best friends for what seemed like forever. That's why Keno could tell that Taz had something heavy on his mind. "Damn, nigga! It's barely after twelve and you're drinkin'! What's with that?" he asked him.

"My daughter is layin' in the fuckin' hospital tryin' to heal up from being shot, and you ask me what's up with me havin' a drink? Kill that shit, nigga!" Taz said as he came from behind the bar.

"Come on, my nigga! This is Keno you're talkin' to! I know you better than you know yourself, fool. Now, what the fuck is really good?"

Taz smiled and said, "Fuck you! Nah, on the real, I'm worried about what Won is goin' to get at us about in a li'l bit. I want out, dog. The time is right for us to shake this shit and live the right way for once."

"So, let the nigga know that we want out."

Shaking his head no, Taz said, "It's not that simple, G. We owe that nigga for everything he has done for us. I just can't see me shaking him, especially if he really needs me."

"If that's the case, then why are you trippin'?"

"I told you, I want out."

"But you just said—"

"I know what I just said, nigga! Damn! This shit is confusing enough, dog. I don't need you questioning me over and over."

"Questioning you? Nigga, this shit ain't just about you and your loyalty to that nigga. We are crew, and all decisions are made together. No one in this crew calls the shots, remember?"

"Yeah, I know. How do you feel about this shit then?"

Keno smiled and said, "Nigga, I gots over two hundred million dollars in the bank. How the fuck do you think I feel? It's whatever with me, dog. We can quit and I'll be straight, or we can keep it rollin' too. I really don't give a fuck."

"If you don't give a fuck, then why are you talkin' 'bout the crew and decision-making and shit?"

"'Cause that's how it has always been. The others might not feel the same way as I do. You're goin' to have to bring it to the table, and then we'll all decide together, like we have always done."

"You're right, *G*," Taz said as he went to let the others inside of his home. When he opened the door, he smiled at Bo-Pete, Red and Wild Bill and said, "Right on time, my niggas! We were just talkin' 'bout y'all."

As they entered the house, Red said, "I hope y'all were talkin' some good shit, 'cause I ain't in the mood for no bullshit. Business has to be handled, dog. When are we goin' to get that coward-ass nigga, Cliff?"

Taz didn't answer Red's question until they were all inside of the den. "That nigga is a dead man walkin', G. You already know that. But right now, we have to figure out how and what we're goin' to do with Won."

"What you mean by that, dog? I thought it was already understood. He's outta there, right?" asked Bo-Pete.

"He should be here in a li'l bit. He wants to get at us and explain everything. I feel we should hear him out before we make any decisions. We owe him that much at least. Y'all know what he's done for us. I really don't want to just cross him out of the game like that," Taz said seriously.

"I feel you, G, but he can't expect us to stay in the game just because he wants us to. If we feel the need to get out, we have that right," Wild Bill said.

"You're right, Bill. Is that how you feel, dog? Do you want out?"

"Dog, for real, it's whatever with me. I'm rollin' with y'all either way."

Taz smiled and asked, "What about you, Red?"

"If y'all want to smash Won, then so be it. If y'all want to keep rollin' with him, then so be it. I'm riding with my niggas."

Before Taz could ask Bo-Pete the same question, Bo-Pete said, "I feel exactly the same way, my nigga."

"All right then, this is what I feel we should do. Let's hear him out. Then we'll make our decision. If y'all are feelin' what he's talkin' 'bout, give a nod after he's finished. If we all agree, then we'll roll with it."

"And if we ain't feelin' what he's talkin' 'bout, then what?" asked Keno.

"He dies," Taz said with deadly simplicity.

"Right here?" asked Wild Bill.

"Right fuckin' here!" Red said in a tone just as deadly as Taz's.

Twenty minutes after the crew had made their decision, Won and Tari came over to Taz's home. After they were situated inside of the den, Won said, "It's a pleasure to finally be able to meet each one of you in person. We've been dealing with each other for so long, I feel as if each one of you are members of my family." Won stood close to six foot four inches, with a short salt-and-pepper hair cut. He looked dapper, dressed casually in a pair of black slacks with a black-and-gray sweater on. His warm brown eyes stared at each man in the room for a few seconds before he continued. "Y'all have made a tremendous amount of money over the last past fifteen years. That was my plan from the beginning. You were all to become millionaires. That part of my plan has been accomplished. Now, we're at the last phase of all of this."

"Which is?" Red asked with a little attitude in his voice.

Won smiled and said, "For me to get what I've been wanting for a very long time. But before I go into that, I need to explain a few things. I've been a part of what me and my associates call 'The Network' for the past twenty-five years. The Network consists of ten council members. Each member of the council controls certain areas around the country. What I mean by 'control' is all illegal activities, such as drugs, gambling, prostitution . . . everything. Over these last past fifteen years, I have used my inside connections to weaken seven members of the council. My purpose for doing this was to elevate my position. My goal is to become the top man of the council, and run as well as control the entire Network."

"So that's what you was talkin' 'bout when you said you will soon have the position of power?" asked Taz.

Won smiled and said, "Exactly, Baby Boy! Like I was saying, I have weakened several members of The Network's council without revealing my hand. Every time y'all complete a mission, I gain more and more strength. The reason why I gave y'all all of the money was to keep my promise in making y'all richer beyond your wildest dreams, but also to hurt the other council members' pockets. By hurting them financially, I used the drugs that I kept from every mission to help them maintain their status in the council. You see, I'm not trying to completely axe them out of the council. I just want to be confident that when the time comes for me to make my move, they will feel obligated to stand, by my side."

"A slow power move, huh?" asked Bo-Pete.

"Exactly. There are two members of The Network that I have never been able to get a good line on as far as their business is concerned. Because of this, I had to make sure that I successfully weakened everyone around them. Thanks to y'all, I've done exactly that. Now, it's time for the final two missions to be completed. Pitt, a man out of Northern California is our first target. I will have the details for you within a week or so. All I can say right now is that he's not to be underestimated, 'cause he's no fool. As a matter a fact, I feel he has already figured out that I had something to do with the robberies that have taken place over the years."

"Why is that?" asked Wild Bill.

"Shit went wrong when there weren't supposed to be any problems. I think Pitt made the call and tipped certain people off. Because of that, Bob was shot and shit went haywire, even though the mission was still completed. Anyway, I've finally gotten inside of Pitt's camp, and I'm confident that this mission will go smoothly. Know this, if I didn't think it could go down smoothly, I would never put any of you in harm's way. Like I said, I look at each of you as a member of my family."

"All right, what about the last mission?" asked Keno.

"Cash Flo' is the other member of The Network that I haven't been able to get close to. I know for a fact that he's close to retiring and handing over his position and part of The Network over to Pitt. After we put a nice dent in Pitt's pocket, Cash Flo' is to be terminated."

"So, you're askin' us to kill for you now?" asked Red.

Won shook his head from side to side and said, "No, I just want you to accompany the person who's going to take Cash Flo's life for me."

"And who is that?" asked Taz.

Won held up his hands and said, "I'll get to that in a moment. I understand that things are hectic now, with Neema being shot and Bob out of commission, but we are going to have to be ready to move on Pitt as soon as I get the call. Like I said, it should be within a week or two, tops."

"Dog, we're a six-deep crew. We ain't movin' without Bob," Bo-Pete said seriously.

"Yeah, so it's a no-go if we ain't got our man with us," added Wild Bill.

Won stared at Taz for a minute then said, "I understand. I pretty much figured as much. Magoo and Bob are on their way here as we speak. They should make it into the city some time tomorrow evening. But I know Bob won't be in any shape to handle up. So I've found a replacement for him."

"A replacement? Fuck that shit! We don't need no new nigga in our mix! It's either Bob or nothin'!" Red stated angrily.

Taz held up his hand to calm Red down and said, "Hold up, *G*. Let's hear him out. Who's this replacement, O.G.?

Won smiled and said, "The same person who's going to take out Cash Flo' for me."

"And who the fuck is that?" asked Keno, agitated.

Before Won could say a word, Tari got to her feet and said, "Me!"

Chapter Four

Clifford was so relieved that he felt as if he was going to pass out. He had just been informed by Detective Bean that he was not going to be brought up on charges for shooting Tazneema. No one was pressing charges, so he was going to be able to remain a free man. His heart hurt when he found out that he had lost his child, but at least Tazneema was alive and doing well.

He tried numerous times to speak with her, but Mama-Mama refused to let them talk to each other. Once when he called the hospital he actually heard Tazneema tell Mama-Mama that she wanted to speak with him, and that made him feel real good inside. He could hear the love in her voice, and he was now confident that she still wanted him. He was also confident that if they didn't press any charges against him, it was because Taz had other plans for him. He would have to deal with that whenever the time came. The most important thing to him at that moment was getting in contact with the woman he loved.

He walked into his office, and before he had a chance to sit behind his desk, his secretary buzzed in on the intercom and told him that Mr. Johnson and Mr. Whitney wanted to see him as soon as possible in Mr. Whitney's office. He set his briefcase down and quickly stepped out of his office. When he made it to Mr. Whitney's office, his secretary told him that he could go right in. He took a deep breath and opened the door to Mr. Whitney's office. Once he was inside the office, his heart felt as if it was about to burst, it was beating so hard. Clifford smiled nervously as he stared at Mr. Whitney and Mr. Johnson, the two head partners of the firm, and one of the newest partners, Ms. Sacha Epps.

"Have a seat, Clifford," Mr. Whitney said in a tone that could mean only one thing to Clifford.

I'm outta here, he thought as he did as he was instructed to.

"Clifford, we've received some very disturbing news about you," Mr. Johnson said as he glared at him. "And we want you to know that though you are a very competent attorney, there is no room at this firm for a person who cannot control his emotions."

"I understand, sirs, but if you would let me explain—"

With both of the partners of the firm shaking their heads no, Mr. Whitney continued. "I don't feel that there's an explanation good enough to make us believe that you are still worthy to work for us here at Whitney and Johnson, Clifford. So we have no other choice but to terminate you immediately."

"Please don't make this any more difficult than it already is, Clifford," added Mr. Johnson. "We expect you to have your office cleared out as soon as possible."

"That's it? Just like that I'm out of here? I can't believe this! I don't know what you've been told, sirs, but there are certain factors to this situation that you two need to know about!" Clifford yelled as he glared at Sacha.

Sacha met his glare with one of her own as she said, "Both Mr. Johnson and Mr. Whitney have spoken with a Detective Bean of the Oklahoma City Police Department. They are well informed of your criminal behavior. We also have a copy of the statement you gave Detective Bean, so there isn't anything else to be said. You're very lucky that the Good family chose not to press any charges against you."

"Come on! You know damn well why they didn't press any charges against me. For one, Tazneema would never press charges because she loves me! And, two, your damn thug-ass boyfriend is planning on taking my life! Did you tell the bosses that? You spiteful li'l bitch!"

"Clifford! That is enough! I will not tolerate that kind of language inside my office!" yelled Mr. Whitney. "Now, you are to get your things and be out of this office building immediately! If not, then we will have someone assist you! Am I understood, Mr. Nelson?"

"Man, fuck you and this firm!" Clifford had screamed as he stormed out of Mr. Whitney's office. When he made it back to his office he called for his secretary to come in and told her, "Do me a favor, Kathy. Pack all of my stuff up for me and have it sent down to the front security desk. I'll come back and get it later on."

"Wha—what happened, Mr. Nelson?" she asked.

Clifford smiled sadly and said, "Oh, nothing. I just got canned."

Back inside of Mr. Whitney's office, Mr. Johnson was telling Sacha, "I hope that young lady will not be seeing Clifford any longer. He's obviously a dangerous individual."

"Only time will tell, sir. But I do think Cliff was right. She's still in love with him, so you know how that goes," Sacha said with a slight shrug of her slender shoulders.

"What about Taz? Do you think he was right when he said Taz was planning to hurt him?" asked Mr. Whitney.

"I can assure you, gentlemen, that Taz has no plans to do anything to Cliff. He's very angry at him, but he's no fool. If something was to happen to Cliff, Taz knows that he would be the prime suspect. I've spoken with him repeatedly, and he understands that it's best to try and put this unpleasant incident behind him and his family."

"I hope you're right, Sacha," Mr. Johnson said as he got out of his chair.

I do too, Sacha thought to herself as she followed Mr. Johnson out of Mr. Whitney's office.

Taz was sitting next to Tazneema's bed, trying his best to figure out his daughter's way of thinking. "Can't you understand that that nigga is no fuckin' good, Neema?" he yelled.

"Why can't you understand that I love that man?" Tazneema yelled right back.

Before the yelling match could continue any further, Won said," Look, Baby Boy. Maybe you should let this go for now. There's no need to further frustrate Neema while she's in here recovering."

Tazneema smiled and said, "Thank you, Uncle Won, 'cause he's gettin' on my last nerves. My head hurts enough as it is."

Taz stood and said, "Whatever! But I'm standin' on my word, Neema. Stay the fuck away from that clown!" he yelled as he left the hospital room.

When the door closed behind Taz, Won said, "Don't worry about him, Neema. It'll pass. Just give him some time."

"I don't know, Uncle Won. You know how stubborn he is."

"Yeah, I know, but I also know how stubborn you are too."

She smiled and said, "You better believe it!"

Won bent over and gave her a kiss on both of her cheeks and said, "Get some rest. We'll come back and check on you later on, okay?"

"Okay. Bye, Uncle Won."

"Bye, sweetie," Won said, and turned and left the room. When he caught up with Taz at the elevator bank, he said, "You need to learn how to control your emotions, Baby Boy. I thought I taught you better than that."

"I know, O.G., but when it comes to my Baby Girl, I can't help it. She really wants to be with that nigga! After he fuckin' shot at me! *Me!* Her fuckin' Daddy!"

"Calm down. She's not going to be with that fool. You know I wouldn't let that happen."

"What do you mean by that?"

As they stepped into the elevator, Won said, "I'll take care of that nigga when the time's right. Right now, if he came up missing, you'd be caught the fuck up. We can't afford that, so let's just chill and finish what we gots to finish."

Taz shook his head and said, "Nah. After everything is everything, I'm goin' to be the one that takes out that clown-ass nigga, O.G. Me, not you."

"All right, but only after we're done."

"Whatever! Tell me something. How in the hell did you get Tari involved in all of this shit?"

Won smiled and said, "Tari has been on my team for a very long time. Believe it or not, you two share a similar story. She lost her parents when she was young, so she took to the streets to survive. The same person who introduced us, introduced me to her. I took her out West, cleaned her up and put her back into school. By the time she graduated high school, she told me she wanted to become a nurse, so I sent her to nursing school. From time to time she was called upon to handle certain things for me. And just like you, she's very thorough. Don't underestimate her, Baby Boy. She's a stone-cold killer.

I sent her back to the City and introduced you two because I knew you needed a woman to take your mind off of MiMi from time to time. I also knew that you would never fall in love with her, and I thought she would never fall in love with you, but there I was wrong. That girl would give her life for you if you asked her to."

Taz smiled and said, "Yeah?"

"That's right."

They stepped into the lobby of the hospital, and Taz said, "I have always loved Tee. I just never felt the kind of love like I have for Sacha."

"She knows that, and she respects Sacha tremendously. All she cares about is your well-being. When I asked her, would she help me out for this mission, she said she would, on one condition."

"What was that?"

Won smiled again and said, "As long as this be the last time that I ever asked you to do something dangerous for me again."

"*What?*"

"You heard me. She's doing this so that I can let you live the rest of your life happily."

"So, you're tellin' me that she's doin' this crazy shit for me?"

"You got it, Baby Boy."

"Damn!"

***

Clifford drove around for hours, thinking about what the fuck he was going to do with his life now. He knew for a fact that Mr. Whitney and Mr. Johnson were going to do their best to fuck him over, so getting employed by another firm in the city was definitely going to be out of the question. He couldn't believe that bitch Sacha went out of her way to make sure he lost his job. *That bitch is going to pay—her and her punk-ass nigga!* he thought as he continued to drive aimlessly around the city.

After a few hours of driving around, he found himself rolling through his old stomping grounds. He smiled as he saw some young Crips hanging on the corner of Twenty-third Street and Lottie Avenue. They started throwing up their Hoover Crip gang sign—thumb in between the index and middle finger of their left hand—as he rolled past them. He shocked himself as he instinctively returned the Hoover gang sign back to the youngsters hanging on the corner. Throwing up the Hoover sign made a lot of memories come storming back inside of his head. He remembered how he and Do-Low used to be some of the hardest Crips in Oklahoma City. *Do-Low . . . Damn! That punk-ass nigga Taz killed a lifelong friend!* he thought as he rolled through his old neighborhood. If he hadn't tried to have Do-Low kill Taz, his homeboy would still be alive. Even though Do-Low had been dying slowly of AIDS, he still didn't deserve to be shot dead in the parking lot of some damn club. The hatred Clifford had for Taz was steadily intensifying.

He smiled when he saw someone from his past. He quickly parked his Mercedes, jumped out of the car and said, "What's up, cuz? What's that 107 Hoover Crip like?"

A short, stocky brother dressed in a pair of blue Dickies with a matching blue Dickies shirt on said, "What the fuck! What's up, cuz? What the hell yo' rich ass doing in the 'hood?"

"Shit done got fucked up for me, cuz. You know how it goes. When everything else fails, a nigga still gots the set. What's up with you, H-Hop? How you been?"

"Ain't shit. The same old shit. You know how it is out here, trying to make some ends and shit. Damn, C-Baby! You got the tight Benz and shit. Can't too much be goin' wrong for yo' ass."

"Yeah, my paper is straight for now, but I just got fired from my job."

"I thought you was a big-time lawyer and shit,"

Clifford started laughing and said, "Yeah, kinda. But that's old news. I'm not anymore."

"So, what you gon' do now? I know you ain't tryin' to come back to the block."

"Why not? What, an O.G. ain't welcome back in his 'hood, nigga?"

"Cuz, it's a new day out here. I honestly don't think you'd be able to keep up with these young niggas. Shit, I barely can, and you know I'm still 107's top killa."

Clifford laughed and said, "Is that right? You mean to tell me that these youngstas are out here wildin' like that?"

"You fuckin' right! They tryin' to smoke somebody every fuckin' day! Cuz, I'm out here tryin' my best to stay down for the set, but I got kids to feed so they are my first priority, ya feel me?"

"Yeah, I feel you. Where are you on your way to now?"

"I was about to go holla at the li'l homey to see if cuz has my ends yet. What, you tryin' to meet some of these new niggas from the Groove?"

With a shrug of his shoulders, Clifford replied, "Why not? I don't have shit else to do."

"All right then, come on. Them niggas is gon' trip the fuck out when they see us pull up in that tight-ass Benz," H-Hop said as he started walking toward Clifford's car.

Clifford made the short drive deeper into 107 Hoover Crip's turf, and parked his Mercedes in front of a small group of teenagers dressed in a mixture of orange and blue. As they climbed out of the Benz, H-Hop smiled and said, "What's up, cuz?"

Several of the teenagers responded by yelling out, "Hoover Crip!" or "Ain't nothin' smoother than Hoover over here, cuz!"

H-Hop and Clifford smiled at each other as they walked toward the backyard of the vacant home that they had parked in front of. A few of the teenagers standing out front followed them.

Once they made it to the back, Clifford saw another familiar face. He smiled and said, "Damn, cuz! You still around this bitch?"

A tall, skinny brother with a light-skinned complexion smiled and said, "Look at this shit! It's a fuckin' Hoover legend and shit! What up, C-Baby? What it do, cuz?"

Clifford smiled and said, "My nigga, Astro! You ain't changed at all I see, cuz."

"Yeah, you know how it is. Got a li'l older and shit, but still doin' my thang. What the fuck you doin' around the 'hood? Last time I seen you, you was at Do-Low's funeral."

"Just came through with H-Hop to holla at y'all for a minute. It's been too long, and I wanted to make sure that you young bucks was maintaining this Hoover Groove."

Astro laughed and said, "Is that right? One thang's for sho', big homey. You ain't even gots to worry about how we gets down out here. Every nigga in the city knows how we handle ours."

One of the teenagers who had followed H-Hop and Clifford into the backyard stepped up and said, "Cuz, who the fuck is this old nigga?"

Astro frowned because he knew that Li'l Bomb was a young hothead not to be taken lightly. "Cuz, this is the big homey, C-Baby. He's one of the first Hoovers in the city. When the big homies came out here from Cali, they put him on first to help start the set," Astro said as he fired up a Newport.

"What up, cuz? I'm Li'l Bomb," said the teenager who couldn't have been more than fifteen—sixteen years old, tops.

Clifford extended his hand and said, "What's up, cuz? They call me C-Baby."

After shaking hands, Li'l Bomb asked, "So, you're a *G* from the set, huh?"

"You better believe it, loco!"

"Cuz, just 'cause you're a *G* don't mean shit to me or any of my niggas. We're runnin' the set now, loc. And to be honest with you, cuz, I don't think you gots what it takes to be a 107 Hoover in the twenty-first century!"

A few other young Hoovers had came and stood next to Li'l Bomb as he spoke. Clifford noticed this, and he knew it was his time to either leave or check these youngsters and let them know he was still in fact an original gangster from 107 Hoover Crips. "Let me tell you somethin', li'l nigga. Since when does a killa forget how to kill? Don't get it twisted, cuz. Just 'cause I haven't been around in a minute doesn't mean that I've lost my heart, loc."

Li'l Bomb smiled and simply said, "Prove it."

"What?"

"I said prove it, cuz. If you're still that *G* you claim to be, come and put some work in with me and the homies."

"Li'l nigga, I ain't gots to prove shit to no young-ass niggas like y'all! I've put in mines long before you li'l niggas were even thought of."

"Just like I thought. A has-been-ass Hoover comin' around here talkin' that O.G. shit, but ain't gonna bust a grape on skates. Come on, cuz. Let's let this old nigga chop it up with H-Hop and Astro. We gots some work to put in," Li'l Bomb said as he turned to leave the backyard.

"Hold up, cuz! I like how you seem to have leadership qualities. The set has always needed that. So, this is what I'm goin' to do. Go get the straps and come back and scoop me. But it's goin' to be just you and me, loc. We don't need your li'l fans to roll with us," Clifford said with a sarcastic smile on his face.

"You ain't sayin' shit, cuz! I'll be right back!" Li'l Bomb yelled as he left the backyard to go get some weapons for himself and Clifford to use.

"C-Baby, I don't think you should fuck with that nigga, Li'l Bomb. That nigga is a straight fool wit' it," Astro said as he lit up a blunt of some very strong-smelling weed.

"Fo' real, cuz. That nigga gots bodies all over the fuckin' city," added H-Hop.

"Damn, cuz! What's with you niggas? Ain't shit changed, and I'm gon' show this young nigga that once a Hoover, always a Hoover! These niggas are gon' always give me my props around this bitch, whether I come around here every day or not! I've earned mines."

Even though Clifford was still dressed in a pair of slacks and a long-sleeved buttoned-up shirt, he was ready to go kill some of his enemies with Li'l Bomb. For some strange reason, he wasn't nervous, nor was he worried about the fact that he was about to go commit a murder . . . or possibly murders. He felt just like he used to feel back in the days when he was one of the hardest Hoover Crips in the city. The only difference now was that he wasn't about to go put in work with any of his old crew. They were either all dead or locked up in prison somewhere. H-Hop and Astro were two of the few left from his old wrecking crew.

Cliff took a deep breath and rotated his broad shoulders so that he could loosen himself up a little. His six foot frame was solid, and he was still in pretty good shape for a man his age.

Suddenly, common sense seemed to have slapped him in his face. *What the fuck am I doing? I may have lost my job, but I haven't lost my fuckin' mind! I can't be doing no shit like this!* he thought to himself as he stared at Astro and H-Hop.

Before he could speak his mind, Li'l Bomb came back into the backyard carrying a large duffel bag in his hand. He walked up to him and set the bag in front of him and said, "All right, cuz, choose your shit."

Clifford watched as Li'l Bomb unzipped the bag and pulled out several handguns. There were 9 mm pistols, Tech-9 semiautomatic pistols, as well as an AK-47. *What the fuck am I going to do now?* he asked himself. *Fuck it! I done got myself caught up in this shit now. I can't lose face to this li'l nigga of the Pepsi generation.* He bent toward the bag and chose two of the 9 mm and asked, "All right, who we blastin'?"

Li'l Bomb smiled and said, "Some of those Prince Hall niggas. Who else?"

"I thought since they redid that projects those niggas weren't around no more."

"Nah, cuz. Them mark-ass niggas are still around. You just have to know where to look. And, believe me, cuz, I know right where they be at," Li'l Bomb replied confidently. "Come on, let's go!"

Clifford couldn't believe he was actually falling for some peer pressure from a fucking baby. *This has got to be the craziest shit in the world,* he thought as he followed Li'l Bomb. They climbed inside of a '77 Cutlass Supreme that was obviously stolen, because Li'l Bomb started the ignition with a screwdriver. Once they were on their way, Clifford tried his best to calm his nerves. *Everything is going to be all right. You know how to put in work, nigga. It's just like riding a bike,* he thought as he took a quick glance at the baby driving the car he was inside of. *Fuck it! It's too late now!*

Li'l Bomb parked the Cutlass and said, "Come on, cuz. We're walkin' from here."

"Walkin'? Li'l nigga, you trippin'! Where the fuck them fools at?"

"They're right down the street, cuz. I don't do drive-bys, loc. I like to be up close and personal. I gotta make sure that I gets my man. Now, are you comin' or what?"

"Lead, li'l nigga. I'm right on your bumper, cuz," Clifford said as he followed Li'l Bomb.

Li'l Bomb smiled as he led the way toward their enemies. About halfway down the street from where he had parked the stolen Cutlass, there were about seven teenagers and a few older people dressed in all blue and standing in front of an apartment complex. Li'l Bomb stopped and said, "There they go, cuz. Since you're dressed like a fuckin' goody-goody, this is what we should do. Walk up and ask them niggas, do they have any work. Once they relax a li'l after figuring out you ain't 'one time,' start blastin' they ass. After you put yours in, break back to the car."

"What the fuck are you goin' to be doing while I'm handlin' mines?"

"Watchin'."

"Watching? Cuz, you gots me fucked up if you think I'm puttin' this work in by myself!"

"Chill out, loc. Once you've handled your business, I'm comin' behind you to play the clean-up man. I don't like leavin' witnesses when I put in work, cuz," Li'l Bomb said menacingly.

Damn! This li'l nigga is heartless, Clifford thought to himself. But to Li'l Bomb he said, "Whatever, cuz. Now watch how a *G* does it." He cocked both of his guns and made sure that a live round was inside of the chambers. He then casually walked toward the group of people standing in front of the apartment building.

Once he made it in front of the group, he said, "Man, can I get somethin' for forty?"

Two of the young gang members looked him over for a full minute before one of them asked, "You a police, nigga?"

Shaking his head no, Clifford said, "Nah, man, I'm just tryin' to get some work for me and this freak bitch I got. So, can I get somethin' for forty or what?"

The two young men smiled at one another. "Yeah, I gots you right here, cuz. Where the money at, though?" asked the young man who seemed to be in charge.

Clifford stared at them for a moment then said, "Right here, cuz," as he pulled out his weapons and started firing at them simultaneously. He hit the two youngsters in their upper torsos then he turned his aim toward the others and started shooting at them.

Once both of his guns were empty, he turned and started running as fast as he could back toward the stolen getaway car. He was back inside of the car when he heard Li'l Bomb doing his cleanup. The sound of that AK-47 was loud as ever to Clifford as he waited for Li'l Bomb to finish handling his business. After what felt like forever but in actuality was just a couple of minutes, Li'l Bomb came running back to the car.

He climbed inside of the Cutlass, smiled and said, "Now, that's what I'm talkin' 'bout, cuz!" He started the car and drove off as calm as ever, as if they didn't have a care in the world. Once he had the car out into traffic, he turned toward Clifford and said, "You still a down nigga, O.G. I gots love for you, C-Baby."

Clifford smiled and said, "You better, loc!" They both started laughing as they went back to their 'hood.

Clifford leaned his head back on the seat and let what he had actually done sink in. *I've just committed murder again. I thought this part of my life was over with. I guess not, 'cause now that I've done it again, I'm ready for some more bodies. Taz and his crew are about to feel the wrath of an O.G. Hoover Crip,* he thought to himself with a smile on his face.

on anyone, like that. It's something that I want to try, though." Lyla was telling Taz the
"Come on Lyla, you can't be serious." Taz whispered as he sat up on her bed.
"I don't care what I'm an adult, and I can do whatever I want."
Before she could continue with her tirade, Taz danced the room with a huge smile on her face.

Chapter Five

Taz and Sacha walked into Tazneema's hospital room to see her. Mama-Mama and Tazneema's best friend, Lyla, were laughing about something. "What's so funny?" Taz asked as he stepped up to Mama-Mama and gave her a hug.

"This here crazy li'l white girl was tellin' me and Neema about how she wants to be a stripper! Can you believe her, Taz? A stripper! Her parents done paid all of this money for her to get a good education at OU, and she's talkin' 'bout becoming a stripper!"

Taz laughed and said, "Lyla, I know you're playin', right?"

Lyla, who was a small woman but built nicely, frowned at Taz. Her long, brown hair hung loosely past her shoulders as she sat down and crossed her long, slim legs. She was definitely a pretty young lady. Taz couldn't deny that fact. Lyla smiled and said, "Of course, I'm serious, Taz. It's not like I want to make a career out of it or anything like that. It's something that I want to try, though. It seems exciting to me."

"Come on, Lyla. You can't be serious," Tazneema said as she sat up on her bed.

"I don't see why not. I'm an adult, and I can do whatever I want to," she replied stubbornly.

Before Lyla could continue with her tirade, Tari entered the room with a huge smile on her face. "Guess who's getting ready to be cleared to go home tomorrow?" She gave Mama-Mama, Sacha and Taz a hug.

"Stop playing, Tari! Please tell me you're playing!" Tazneema said anxiously.

"I'm serious. The doctor told me a few minutes ago that he didn't see any reason for you to remain here. As long as you agree to stay off of your feet for a few more weeks, he's going to let you go home in the morning."

"Well, he won't have to worry about that none. She's comin' home with me, and ain't no way I'm gon' let her be on her feet!" Mama-Mama yelled happily.

"I know that's right, Mama-Mama!" Tari said with a smile on her face. She turned toward Taz and said, "We need to talk. It's kind of important."

Taz nodded, turned toward Tazneema and said, "Excuse me for a minute, y'all. I'll be right back."

Sacha smiled and said, "Don't you be trying to steal my man, Tari! I got my eyes on you, girl!"

Tari laughed and said, "He's too damn old for me now, girl. I got my sights set on a teeny bopper!"

They both started laughing as Taz followed Tari out into the lobby. She led him toward some chairs by the elevator bank, sat down and said, "We're moving in the morning. Won got the call he was waiting for last night. He wants us to be at your house in thirty minutes."

"Damn!"

"What's wrong?"

"I haven't had time to get at Sacha yet."

"Get at her about what? She already knows what's what, doesn't she?"

"Yeah . . . kinda."

"What you mean, kinda, Taz?"

"I promised her that I was done with this shit. I never told her about our decision to finish this shit up for Won."

Tari smiled and said, "You're going to be in some big trouble, sir."

"I know. Fuck!"

"Listen. Just tell her that there's something that we have to take care of, and that I'm going with you. She'll never think I'm going to be doing something wild with y'all."

Shaking his head no, he said, "Nah, I'm not goin' to lie to my Li'l Mama. I gots to keep it one hundred with her at all times."

"You sure?"

"Yeah, I'm sure."

Tari stared at Taz, her friend, her ex-lover, and said, "We have to get this hit over with, Taz."

"I know. But tell me something. Why are you so damn worried about Won letting me go?"

"'Cause I love you, stupid! I want you to have the happiness you've been looking for. You deserve it."

"But what about you? You deserve some happiness too."

"As long as you're happy, baby, then so am I."

He stared deeply into Tari's blue eyes and saw the love she had for him in them. *Damn! This girl really does love a nigga. If only I could have loved her the way she wants me to,* he thought.

Tari's long blonde hair was pulled tightly in a ponytail. She was looking extremely good in her nurse's uniform. For a white girl, she was packing some major ass . . . an ass that would make some sistas feel bad. She stood close to six foot barefoot, and was definitely one sexy-ass lady.

"I wish we could have—"

"Stop that shit, Taz. It is what it is. Everything happens for a reason, baby. I know you love me, and I know you're not in love with me. That's life. What matters most to me is that you're safe. Let's get this shit over with so we can move on and live happily ever after," Tari said with a smile on her face.

"You sure?"

"Yep!"

"You know it's gon' be hard workin' with you, right?"

"Don't worry 'bout me. I can handle my own. I'm a big girl, see?" She got out of her seat and slapped herself on her behind.

"Yeah, I see all of that ass you got, but ass has nothin' to do with what we're about to get into," he said seriously.

"Maybe you're right, but you never know what the power of a big ass can do for you."

Taz smiled and said, "You're crazy, girl! Look, let me go get at Sacha then I'll round up the crew so we can all get on point."

"All right. You know Bob made it home last night, huh?"

"Is that right?"

"Yep. Won told me before I left for work this morning."

"Cool. I'll holla at the nigga before we bounce."

"I'll see you in a little bit," she said as she turned and quickly hopped inside one of the elevators before the doors closed.

Taz went back inside of Tazneema's room and told her, "Baby Girl, I want you to make sure that you do everything that Mama-Mama tells you, okay?"

"Since when has she not done everything that I tell her to, boy?" asked Mama-Mama.

"Come on, Mama-Mama. You know what I mean."

Tazneema could tell that Taz had something on his mind and asked, "Is everything all right, Taz? You look kinda funny."

"I'm good. I have to go out of town for a day or so to tie up some loose ends and stuff," he said as he cut his eyes in Sacha's direction.

"Don't worry, Taz. I'll be okay."

"I know, but I want you to know that I don't want you talkin' to that nigga Cliff, Neema."

"Taz," she whined.

"I mean it, Neema. I'm your father, and I expect for you to obey my wishes on this shit."

Before Tazneema could say a word, Lyla yelled, "Her father? How? When? Wait a minute! You're her *what*?"

Everyone inside of the room started laughing, except for Lyla. After the laughter had subsided a little, Tazneema said, "Taz is my daddy, Lyla, not my brother. Everyone thinks he's my big brother, so we let people think what they want."

"But, Tee Tee, why didn't you tell me? I'm your roommate and best friend. I've actually been flirting with your father! Ugggh! That's like so gross!"

"Why, thank you, Lyla!" Taz said with a smile on his face.

"I didn't mean it like that, Taz. I just—"

Taz held up his hand and said, "I know, I know. I was just clownin'. But, look, I gots to go get ready. I'll give y'all a call to see how everything is when I get to where I'm goin', okay?"

"Okay, Taz. I love you."

"I love you too, Baby Girl. Please do as I asked you to."

"I will."

After giving Mama-Mama and Lyla a brief hug, Taz grabbed Sacha's hand and led her out of the room. Before he could say a word, she said, "Take me to my house, Taz. I think I'm going to stay there while you're out of town."

"You're that mad, huh, Li'l Mama?"

"What the fuck do you think?"

"I'm gon' keep it real with you, Li'l Mama. After we finish this mission, there will be one more, and then it's over with."

She laughed in his face and said, "You know what's so crazy about all of this shit, Taz? You actually believe that shit Won is hand-feeding your ass. You're never going to be through with this shit! Won's not going to let you. And you're not even man enough to say no to the big man! I'm telling you, Taz, you really need to think. 'Cause if you don't start using your head, you're going to lose everything you got. And I'm not just talking about me, I'm talking about everything!"

After Taz dropped Sacha off at her home, he drove back to his house and started to pack his bags. After he was finished, he grabbed the phone and called Bob's house.

Gwen answered on the second ring, sounding as happy as ever. "Hello!"

"What's good, Gwen? Where's my nigga at?" Taz asked with a smile on his face.

"He's right here, Taz. Hold on a sec."

Bob accepted the phone from Gwen and said, "What it do, my nigga?"

"Ain't shit. What's with you, dog? You good?"

"Yeah, I'm straight. Still a li'l sore and shit, though."

"Damn, dog! Why you didn't vest up like you was supposed to?" Taz asked seriously.

"I tripped the fuck out, *G*. I mean, I didn't think about it until we were already on our way to do us. By then, I was like, fuck it! Everything is goin' to be everything, so I didn't say shit to y'all."

"That shit is crazy! You know better, dog. Where's that nigga Magoo at? I want to thank him for lookin' out for your crazy ass."

"After he dropped me off, he said he was on his way to go get with Won. He said something about meeting up at your spot. What's up with that, my nigga?"

"We're almost to the finish line, dog. We got two more things to take care of. Then it's a done deal."

"How are y'all goin' to handle up? I won't be able to roll for at least a couple more weeks," Bob said with a hurt sound in his voice.

Bob's cracking voice damn near broke Taz down. "Don't worry about it, dog. We can handle it. Your lucky ass gets to retire a li'l earlier than us," he said, trying to make Bob feel a little better.

"Fuck that shit! We're a six-deep crew! We trained for it always to be that way! And, no matter what, we don't move unless we all move!"

Taz took a deep breath and said, "Look, *G*. We on the clock, and we don't have the time to wait until you can get back on your feet. So, it is what it is right now."

"So that nigga Magoo's taking my place, huh?"

"Fuck, no! You know damn well we don't know that nigga like that."

"Then who is it, Taz? Don't lie to me, my nigga."

Taz took another deep breath and said, "Tari."

Bob burst into laughter and said, "Now, ain't that somethin'! I done got replaced by a bitch! A white bitch at that!"

Bob's comment about Tari pissed Taz off, but instead of getting into it any further with him, Taz said, "Look, we're about to bounce. I just wanted to holla at ya to make sure that you're straight. We'll get over there to see you when we get back."

"Whatever, dog," Bob said sadly, and hung up the phone.

After Taz hung up the phone, he grabbed his bag and went downstairs to the den. He poured himself a drink from the bar and said, "Damn! It seems like all of my peoples are salty at me right now. I can't do any shit good at the moment."

There was a knock at his front door just as he finished draining his glass. He went to let the crew in. Keno, Bo-Peter, Red, Wild Bill and Tari filed inside of his house, and followed him back inside of the den.

"Have you gotten at Bob yet?" asked Wild Bill as he sat down on the sectional sofa.

"Yeah."

Did you tell him?" Red asked with a smile on his face.

"Yeah."

Red started laughing and said, "I know that nigga is pissed the fuck off!"

Taz smiled and said, "That's puttin' it real mild like, dog."

"Aww, poor Bob's mad 'cause I get to play with his li'l friends!" Tari said playfully.

"It don't matter. This shit is almost over any fuckin' way," Keno said as he leaned against Taz's pool table.

Before anyone could respond, Won and Magoo knocked at Taz's front door. After Taz brought them inside of the den, Won said, "All right, peoples, this is how it goes down. Pitt runs the Bay Area out in Cali. His strength in the game comes from the heroin and the ya-yo. After y'all arrive out in Oakland, you will then go check into the Marriot Courtyard, located in downtown Oakland. Your rooms will already be reserved, as usual.

"Downstairs in the underground parking lot will be a blue Navigator parked for y'all. Your weapons will be inside of Taz's room under the bed, with all of the equipment you normally use.

"After y'all strap up, you are to drive to East Oakland. Take Main Street all the way into the

East Side of town. Once you make it to Shaw Boulevard, you are to make a left turn, and on your immediate right, there will be a bail bondsman's office. Bypass it and bust a U-turn down the street.

"Once you have seen that everything is clear, you are to park behind the bondsman's office and go in from the rear. The back door will be unlocked, and the alarm will have already been tripped. Once you're inside, you'll see four safes. Combination are as follows . . ."

Won stopped and waited for Taz as he pulled out a pen and a pad so he could write the numbers down. When he saw that Taz was ready, he continued.

"The combination to the safe on the far left side of the room is 3 to the right, 26 to the left, and 71 to the right. The safe right next to it is 49 to the right, 61 to the left, and 99 to the right. The next one is 52 to the right, 15 to the left, and 66 to the right, and the last safe, which will be placed at the far right of the room, is 33 to the right, 77 to the left, and 84 to the right. Each safe will contain at least twenty or more kilos of cocaine and heroin. If there is any money inside of any of them, it's yours.

"After you've emptied the safes, get back to your rooms and drop everything off. Your return flights are scheduled for early the next morning out of SFO out in San Francisco.

"Though this should be a smooth op, I still want y'all to be on your toes and sharp as ever. That nigga, Pitt is a smart nigga, and he may be trying to anticipate my moves. I doubt it though, but yet and still, I want y'all to be very careful. Any questions?"

"Yeah. How long are we gonna have to wait until we can handle that other nigga you told us about?" asked Keno.

"Once Pitt's spot is hit, I'm sure the shit is going to hit the fan. A lot of accusations will be flying, but with no proof behind them, everything will be good. Cash Flo' will then announce that he plans to back Pitt with his end of The Network. But that won't be enough, because I will have the position I need to challenge him. At that point, Pitt will know that I'm the one been making the power move. Knowing him, he's going to raise hell 'cause he is a ride-type nigga, and a damn fool once he becomes angry. But, like I said, it will be too late for him to do anything. When I get word of the meet that will take place, I'll notify y'all so you can then fly out and take care of Cash Flo'. That way, he will never be able to announce that he's supporting Pitt. I expect the meet to take place within thirty days after you finish this mission."

"Where?" asked Bo-Pete.

"I won't know that until twenty-four hours before the meeting. Most likely it will either be in Waco, Texas, or the West Coast. But I can't be certain of that just yet. Y'all will have to be on standby. Cash Flo's home base is the West, but he's down South around my way too. He's touchable because he's old school. He has a few bodyguards, but they won't be able to handle y'all." Won checked his watch and said, "Y'all have to get going. Your flight leaves in forty minutes out of Will Rogers."

"We're all flying together?" asked Red.

"Yep. There's no need for the normal routine. This is an in-and-out. Hit me up when you get back. If there are any chips, I will split it evenly between y'all and deposit it into your accounts in the islands."

Taz came from behind his bar, stared at Tari and asked her, "You ready for this, Tee?"

She stood up, smiled and said, "Let's go to work!"

Chapter Six

Tazneema, Lyla, Mama-Mama and Won were all sitting inside of Mama-Mama's living room, laughing at Lyla and her antics. Lyla was so determined to become a stripper that she actually came up with a stage name for herself. She told everyone inside the room that she wanted to be called "White Chocolate."

After Tazneema stopped laughing, she asked her, "Why in the heck did you choose a name like that?"

Lyla smiled slyly and said, "Because I'm white, obviously, and I just loves me some chocolate!"

"Oh, my Lord!" Mama-Mama said as she slapped her palm against her forehead.

Won started laughing and said, "All right, ladies, that's about all I can take! I'm outta here! Are you straight, Neema? Do you need anything before I leave?"

"I'm fine, Uncle Won. You know I'm in good hands with Mama-Mama," she said seriously.

"Hey! What about me?" cried Lyla.

"Oh, yeah. And you know White Chocolate here is going to take good care of me."

They laughed some more as Won stood and said, "All right then. I gots me a flight to catch. I'll make sure I get back this way real soon to check on you, Baby Girl. Remember, if you need anything, call me. You still have the numbers?"

She smiled and answered, "Yep!"

"Good," Won said, and gave her a kiss and a light hug. He then stepped over to Mama-Mama, gave her a hug and a kiss also and said, "Do you need anything before I go, Mama-Mama?"

"Go on and catch your plane, Won. We're just fine over here," she happily said.

He smiled at her and said, "Okay, bye, y'all!" As he stepped outside of the house, he couldn't help but wonder if Lyla was serious about becoming a stripper. *She'd make a nice chunk of change,* he thought with a smile on his face.

It was a little after ten P.M. when Taz and the crew made it to their hotel room at the Marriot Courtyard, in downtown Oakland. Taz checked his diamond-studded Cartier wristwatch and said, "All right, y'all, strap up so we can get this shit over with."

Each member of the crew grabbed a silenced 9 mm pistol from the bag that Taz had pulled out from under the bed in his room. After checking and rechecking their weapons, each one of them gave Taz a nod of their head.

"Y'all good?" asked Taz.

"Yep," answered Red.

"Ready," said Keno.

"Strapped," said Wild Bill.

"Locked and loaded," said Bo-Pete.

"Let's do this," Tari said as she jammed her pistol in the small of her back.

They filed out of the room and went straight toward the stairway that led to the underground parking area. Once they made it to the blue Navigator, Keno said, "It amazes the hell out of me every fuckin' time Won does this shit."

"What?" asked Red as he climbed inside the SUV.

"How he has everything already set up when we get to wherever we have a mission."

Tari laughed and said, "You should be used to it by now, Keno."

"I know, but the shit is kinda on the creepy side for real. I be feelin' like that nigga's gon' pop up any minute and tell us that we're not handlin' our business right or some shit."

Taz laughed as he started the ignition, and said, "Man, would you kill that silly-ass shit?"

Everyone inside of the truck got a good laugh at Keno's expense as Taz pulled the Navigator out of the parking lot.

Back in Oklahoma City, Won was talking on his cell phone as he boarded his flight back to Los Angeles. "Yeah, they should already be there by now. By the time I touch down, they should be back at their rooms waiting to get up outta there in the morning. I'll give you a holla after everything is everything. Remember, if you hear from me in any form other than the norm, then you know what needs to be done next," he said to whomever he was speaking with on the other line.

After he closed his cell phone, he found his seat on the airplane and got himself comfortable. *I got your ass, Pitt! Either way this falls, I got your ass!* he thought to himself as he closed his eyes and began to relax.

Taz made a U-turn and headed back toward the bail bondsman's office and said, "Here we go, y'all. Y'all know the drill. Watch your ass at all times. Tari, I want you right next to me at all times."

"Fuck that weak shit, Taz! Let's do this shit! Stop worrying about me. I'm good."

He smiled at her and repeated, "Right by my fuckin' side, Tee! I ain't playin'!"

"Whatever!" she said as they all jumped out of the SUV with their weapons held down at their sides.

Taz led the way to the back entrance, and like always, the door was unlocked just as Won said it would be. He opened the door slowly and entered the back of the office. He saw the safes, and quickly stepped toward the one on the far left of the room. Tari was right next to him as she began to dial the combination to the safe next to the one he was opening.

Keno and Bo-Pete stood by the door and watched their backs as Red and Wild Bill were opening the other two safes. Each of them had large duffel bags for the drugs as they quickly emptied the safes and filled their bags.

Tari finished emptying her safe first and then dragged her bag toward the back door. Keno took the bag from her and carried it back outside to the Navigator. Tari then took his spot as sentry, and waited for the others to finish up.

Taz was next to finish. He slid his bag to Bo-Pete, who grabbed it and took it outside to the truck, while Taz took his place at the door next to Tari.

After Red and Wild Bill had finished emptying the last two safes, they carried their bags past Taz and Tari as they headed toward the truck. Taz and Tari brought up the rear as they followed them out of the office with their guns ready.

Once everyone was inside of the truck, Keno eased out of the parking lot and into the late evening traffic. Mission completed.

By the time Won's flight had arrived at LAX, he received a call on his cell. He smiled as he walked out of the terminal and toward a waiting all-black stretch limousine.

As he stepped inside of the limo, he said to the person who called him, "All right, after they leave, make sure that you hurry up and get everything out of that room. I'm sure Pitt is going to be on the warpath, and he's definitely going to be checking all local hotels and shit. Call me when you're finished." He then closed his phone.

"One down, and Cash Flo, to go!" he said aloud as he reached to his left and grabbed a bottle of XO from the minibar.

***

Mama-Mama was asleep, and Tazneema was bored. She knew that she needed time to heal from her wound, but she missed her man. Clifford was her heart, and she knew that he loved her just as much as she loved him. It was so hard to accept the fact that she had lost her child. She prayed hard that Cliff wouldn't be upset with her. *I have to talk to him,* she thought as she went into her bedroom, grabbed the cordless phone from its base and quickly dialed Clifford's home number. She didn't realize that she was holding her breath until she felt a tightening in her stomach. She exhaled just as Clifford answered the line.

"Hello."

"Hi, baby! How are you?" she asked him.

"Neema?" Clifford asked excitedly.

"Yes, it's me, baby."

"How are you doing? Are you all right? When are you getting out of the hospital? Is the baby all right?"

"If you'd let me get a word in, I'll answer all of your questions! Dang!"

"I'm sorry, Neema. Go right ahead."

"Okay. First off, I'm at Mama-Mama's house. I came home from the hospital earlier today. The doctors said that I'm going to be okay as long as I stay off my feet for a few more weeks."

"As to the baby . . . I lost it, Cliff. The baby could not withstand the stress of the surgery. The bullet traveled further than the doctors had anticipated, and they had to remove it from my back. I have a real ugly scar on my back now, so I guess I won't be getting any of those special back licks of yours anymore."

He smiled and said, "Baby, I can't wait to be able to lick all over that delicious body of yours. I love you, Neema. You know that, right?"

She sighed heavily and said, "Yes, I know. And I love you too, Cliff. But we're going to have to be very careful. Taz wants your head cut off, so we're going to have to keep it on the low-low for a little while, at least until I can talk some sense into him."

"You're never going to be able to talk any sense into Taz, baby. He hates me."

"Trust me, when it comes to me, Taz always lets me have my way. It will be a little harder than usual, but eventually he'll give in and let me do me," she replied confidently.

"Why didn't you tell me he was your father, Neema?"

"Why didn't you tell me that you already knew who he was? You actually used to go with Sacha?"

"Not really. We went out a few times and were starting to get close, but your father came into the picture and everything changed. After that, I was real bitter with the both of them because I thought I really loved Sacha. That is until I met you. Once we got to know one another, my feelings for Sacha evaporated with the quickness. It was all about you, Neema. You have to believe me when I say this, 'cause it's so true. I never lied to you when I told you I was in love with you."

"*Was?*"

"That's not what I mean, baby. I love you so much that it's killing me that I can't hold you in my arms through all of this mess."

She smiled and said, "I love you too, Cliff. There's no need to trip. I'm good. Now, let me go before I wake up Mama-Mama. I'll give you a call some time tomorrow, okay?"

"Okay. Tell me. Does Mama-Mama hate me too?"

"You're not on her favorite persons list right now, but don't worry. She's just as much of a pushover for me as Taz is. She'll come around. I love you, baby!"

"I love you too," Clifford said before he hung up the phone.

After Tazneema put the cordless phone back on its base, she smiled as she climbed on her bed. "Cliff still loves me, and I'm not letting anyone get in the way of our relationship—not even my daddy!" she said aloud as she stared at a picture on her dresser of her and her father.

Chapter Seven

Taz and the rest of the crew arrived back in Oklahoma City a little after two in the afternoon. They went directly to Taz's home so they would be able to check their accounts and check in with Won.

Taz smiled as he walked inside of his home and saw Precious and Heaven as they ran toward him with their tongues happily hanging out of their mouths. He rubbed the both of them under their chins as he walked toward his den. The Dobermans knew better than to follow him to the den, so they sat down right outside of the den and watched as the rest of the crew followed Taz.

Tari stopped, knelt next to the dogs and rubbed their chins tenderly and said, "How's my babies been doing? You miss me?" She played with them briefly then stood and went into the den with the others.

Taz grabbed his laptop from behind his bar and set it on the pool table. Once he opened it, he started punching its keys. When his account came onto the screen, he smiled and said, "I have an extra two hundred gees in my account."

"That means there was what, a li'l over a ticket in those safes?" asked Wild Bill.

"Looks like it. Here, check yours and see if y'all have the same in y'all's accounts," Taz said as he passed the laptop to Wild Bill.

Everyone checked their accounts, and they each had two hundred thousand dollars added into their offshore accounts in the Cayman Islands.

Tari smiled and said, "Well, since I don't have a fancy account over in the Islands, I'll have to get at Won and see what he has set up for me."

"Don't trip, Tee. I'm about to get at him right now," Taz said as he pulled out his cell and called Won.

While Taz was on the phone, Red said, "Call that nigga Bob and see what he's up to."

Keno laughed and said, "That nigga is probably layin' up with his broad, gettin' his freak on."

"How the fuck is that nigga gon' be gettin' his freak on with that damn shit bag on his side?" laughed Bo-Pete.

Taz, who was laughing also said, "Excuse me, O.G. These silly-ass niggas are over here clownin' about that nigga Bob. What it do?"

"Everything is everything out his way. Have y'all checked y'all's accounts yet?" asked Won.

"Yeah, everything is good, all except for Tee. She's wondering where her chips are."

Won started laughing and said, "Tell your li'l snowbunny that I said her ends have been deposited into her credit union account. I know she didn't think I was going to forget about her."

"Nah, she knew you'd have it taken care of. So, now what?"

"Like I told y'all, we wait. When I get work, y'all will be notified. The last leg of this is almost over with, Baby Boy. I suspect Pitt is somewhere having a fucking fit right about now," Won said as he started laughing.

"Do you think he'll try to get at you before we're able to move on that other nigga?"

"Nope. If it was that easy, I would have taken him out of the game years ago. You see, by me being a council member, he has to have some major proof to get approval to move against me. And that's something he doesn't have. So, don't worry about me, Baby Boy. I'm good. Y'all, stay on point. I'll hit y'all when it's time. Out!" Won said, and hung up the phone.

After Taz closed his cell, he told everyone inside of the den what Won had just told him. "So, I guess y'all can go on to the pad and chill out. When everything is everything, he's goin' to get at us."

"What's up for the weekend? Y'all want to hit the club or what?" asked Bo-Pete.

"I'm wit' it," said Red as he got out of his seat.

"Fuck it! Why not?" added Wild Bill.

"I haven't been to a club in years. It might just be fun. Count me in," Tari said with a grin on her face.

"We move as a unit, so you already know I'm in," said Taz.

As everyone started filing out of the den, Tari stopped Taz and said, "What's up with you and Sacha? Are y'all beefing like that?"

"How do you know that we're beefin' at all?"

"You better go on with that silly shit, boy. You know damn well I can tell when you have something heavy on your mind."

"Have you forgotten that my daughter has been shot recently? And the nigga that did it is still breathing? What? That's not heavy enough for you?"

"Stop lying to me, Taz. You know I know better. Call her and let her know we made it back. That lady loves you, boy, and you know you love her just as much." She kissed him lightly on his cheek and added, "Saying I'm sorry really isn't that bad, macho man!"

He smiled at her and said, "Fuck you, white girl!"

She gave a wave of her hand. "I may be a white girl, but there are a whole lot of sistas out there that wish they had an ass like this one!" she said as she slapped herself on her behind.

Taz started laughing and shaking his head as he watched her leave his home. He stood in his doorway and watched as each of his friends climbed inside of their respective vehicles.

Red pulled out of the driveway in his all-black Chevy Tahoe. Bo-Pete followed in his all-black Navigator. Wild Bill was behind him in his all-black Durango. Keno was behind Wild Bill's truck in his all-black Range Rover, and then there was Tari as she climbed into her all-black BMW truck.

What's up with us with all of this black shit? Taz asked himself as if this was the first time he ever realized that the entire crew drove all-black SUV's as their primary vehicles. Even though he had an S-Class 600 Mercedes and a Bentley Azure parked inside of his four-car garage, he also owned an all-black Denali.

Life was good for them all. They had enough money to live the rest of their lives in extreme comfort. Together, the crew was worth more than a billion dollars. *Won lived up to his part of the deal, so it was only right that they finish this shit for him,* thought Taz as he turned and went upstairs to his bedroom.

Sacha stared at the phone as it continued to ring. She saw Taz's number on the caller ID box, and silently thanked God for letting them make it back safely. She knew he'd call her once he had gotten back, but she just wasn't sure if she was ready to talk to him yet. Since her first doctor's appointment for her pregnancy was in the morning, she knew she would have to speak to him. She took a deep breath, picked up the phone and said, "Hello."

"What up, Li'l Mama?"

"Hi, Taz."

"You still mad, huh?"

"What do you think?"

"Do you still want me to go to the doctor with you in the morning?"

"Do you still want to go?"

"Come on, Li'l Mama. What kind of shit are you on? You know ain't nothin' changed with me. This shit is all on you!"

"I know you're not trying to twist this shit on me, Mister Taz! I'm the only one using some common sense in this crazy shit you have me mixed up in!"

"Mixed up in? You're not mixed up in any fuckin' thing! I told you, my business doesn't have anything to do with you. But, no-o-o! You wanted to know everything about what I do. You just had to know what was what. And now that you do, you're trippin'. You see, that's why I didn't want to tell your ass shit in the first fuckin' place!"

"Stop yelling at me, Taz!"

He took a deep breath to try and calm his nerves, and said, "Look, Li'l Mama. You are my now, my tomorrow, my everything, and I love you more than words will ever be able to truly express. But you gots to let this shit go! I'm gon' do me and finish what I've started. Accept it, 'cause it's not goin' to change nothin' if you don't. If you can't accept this, then you can't accept me and who I really am. Now, what time is your appointment again?"

"It's at ten."

"Do you want me to pick you up, or do you want me to just meet you?"

Sounding real professional, she said, "Yes, Taz, you can meet me at my doctor's office. It's located on the South Side, right off of the highway on May Avenue."

His temper rising again, Taz gritted his teeth and asked, "So, that's how it's gon' be, huh?"

"Bye, Taz!" Sacha said and hung up the phone on him.

Taz hung up the phone and quickly dialed another number. When Won answered, Taz said, "Something is really puzzling me, O.G."

"What's that, Baby Boy?"

"Earlier you said that Pitt couldn't do nothin' 'cause there would be too much drama behind it without any proof."

"Yeah. So?"

"If that's the case, then how are you goin' to pull off the next demo with Tari doin' her thang on that nigga Cash Flo'?"

"This is the end game, Baby Boy. Some of the rules are being changed at this part of the game. Don't worry yourself about the particulars. I gots this. All I'm needing from your end is to make sure that Tari will be put in place so she can do what needs to be done."

"All right. Man, with all of this shit on my plate, I'm just tryin' not to miss shit, you know what I sayin'?"

"Yeah, I know. I've just been informed by one of the council members that Pitt is on the fucking warpath. So, I guess he's been notified of his losses out in Oakland. I should be getting a call soon, so I'll keep you posted."

"That's cool."

"All right then. Out!"

"Out!" Taz said. He hung up the phone feeling a little bit better about what was going on. "This shit is crazy," he said to himself as he relaxed back on his bed

Out in Northern California, Pitt, a stocky, brown-skinned man, was sitting at his desk in his plush office right outside the city of Oakland, rubbing his neatly trimmed beard. Though he had a smile on his face, he was currently furious. He couldn't believe that Won had finally made his move against him. He didn't have any proof, but he was positive that Won had his place burglarized. *Won has been putting this thing down for years now. I've always known it, but I've never been able to prove it,* Pitt thought as he sat back and continued to watch the video surveillance tape of his bail bondsman office in East Oakland.

All of a sudden, the screen on Pitt's fifty-five-inch plasma screen went fuzzy. "What the fuck?" he yelled as he raised himself out of his comfortable leather chair. He stepped quickly toward the television and started pushing the buttons on the DVD player. It took close to four, maybe five minutes before the screen resumed back to the footage of the back room of the bondsman's office. "That nigga is good that he had a plug in my shit! How the fuck else would the camera go blank for a few minutes?" he yelled as he went back behind his desk and grabbed the phone.

He lit a freshly rolled Cuban cigar and chomped on it furiously as the phone rang. When the other line was answered, he said, "Cash Flo', we need to meet."

"What's going on now, Pitt? I'm tied up on some very serious negotiations with them dagos out East."

"Fuck that shit! It's Won! Won is the fucker whose been robbing us blind for the last God knows how many fucking years!"

"What the hell are you talking about, Pitt?" asked Cash Flo'.

"Look, I'm on my way down your way. Have some of your people scoop me from LAX in an hour and a half."

"All right, but I hope when you get here you have something solid for us to move on, 'cause if you're wasting my time, Pitt—"

"I know, I know. Kill that shit, Flo'. This is your boy. You know I know the rules to this game. I'll see you in a li'l bit," Pitt said. He hung up the phone and quickly left his office.

As he rode the elevator down to the under-ground parking area of his office building, his thoughts were of Won. *I don't know how you've been pulling this shit off, nigga, but you fucked up by ever fucking with me. Whoever turned against me in my camp is going to be found. Then I'll have the proof I need to smash your ass,* he thought to himself as he pulled out his keys and climbed inside of his 2006 Jaguar, and sped out of the parking area on his way to the airport.

Chapter Eight

The next morning, Taz met Sacha at her doctor's office. He had to smile when he saw her looking so delicious sitting in the waiting room. She was wearing a lavender Baby Phat jogging suit, with a pair of matching Nike tennis shoes on her small feet. Her shoulder-length hair was looking as silky as ever, pulled back tightly in a long ponytail. Her smooth, brown skin was flawless as always, and at that moment Taz knew that he could never let this woman get away from him. After he was seated next to her, he said, "What's up, Li'l Mama?"

"Good morning, Taz," she said in the same businesslike tone she'd used with him the night before.

"Come on, Li'l Mama. Can't we call a truce? I'm not with the simpin' sucka shit. It's just not in me. I love you, though, so I'm willin' to swallow my pride a li'l."

"A little?" she asked with a hint of a smile on her face.

"Yeah, a li'l," he said as he held up his thumb and index fingers inches apart from one another.

Damn, I love this man! she thought to herself. To him she said, "Taz, I really thought I'd be able to deal with how you live, but I can't. You don't know how terrified I am while you're out of town doing that shit. I can't take it! I just can't!"

"I understand, Li'l Mama. That's why I'm about to get out of his shit. I know you don't believe me, but it's almost over. To be totally honest with you, I don't even have another mission to go on. All I have to do is make sure that a person gets where they need to be. After that, everything is a done deal. The party will be over. I know you don't trust Won or believe that he's goin' to stop needing me for things, but I need for you to believe in me. I haven't lied to you since we've met, and I don't intend on starting either. I'm not goin' to lose you over this li'l shit, Li'l Mama. Whatever it takes to prove it to you, I'm willing to do it. I can't take it without you next to me in my bed at night. It just don't feel right."

Sacha smiled as his words weakened her resolve. "Do you give me your word that after you get whomever where they need to be that there will be no more out-of-town trips?"

"My word, Li'l Mama."

"Do you give me your word that you will not under any circumstances do anything illegal for Won ever again?"

"My word."

"Do you love me, Taz?"

"You know I do, baby. With all of my soul."

"Then don't you ever break the promises you've just made to me. Because if you do, I'll never forgive you. Do you understand me, Taz Good? I'll *never* forgive you!"

"I understand, baby. Now, can I have a kiss or somethin'?"

Just as they were about to kiss one another, the receptionist said, "Excuse me, but you two can go in to see Doctor Moses now."

Sacha smiled and said, "Come on, let's go see about our child."

Taz smiled brightly and said, "I'm right behind you, Li'l Mama."

Mama-Mama was up early as usual, cooking Tazneema a big breakfast.

Tazneema was sitting at the dining room table watching her grandmother prepare what looked like a meal for ten instead of two. She smiled and said, "Mama-Mama, why do you always have to cook so much food?"

"'Cause Mama-Mama loves to cook. Whatever's left over, I'll just take it over to the church so the good reverend can eat as much as he wants to."

"Hmph! I think you and the good reverend gots something going on with each other!"

Mama-Mama turned around from the stove, smiled and said, "If we do, you'll never know." They both started laughing as the telephone started ringing.

"I'll get it, Mama-Mama," Tazneema said as she slowly rose from her seat and went into the living room to answer the phone. "Hello."

"Hi, baby! You miss me?" asked Clifford.

Tazneema smiled and said, "You know I do. You shouldn't be calling here, Cliff. What if Mama-Mama answered the phone?"

"I would have asked for someone else, like I had the wrong number. What are you doing today?"

"Nothing but resting. I'm not supposed to be on my feet for at least a few more weeks."

"Man, I wish I could see you."

"Me too. But, look, I have to go. Mama-Mama is in the kitchen making me something to eat. I'll give you a call later on."

"You promise?"

"I promise."

"Tell me you love me."

Tazneema gave a quick peek toward the kitchen and quickly said, "I love you! Bye!" After she hung up the phone, Mama-Mama asked her who was that who had called. "That was Lyla, Mama-Mama," she lied as she walked back into the kitchen.

After the doctor confirmed that Sacha was indeed two months pregnant and in good health, Taz and Sacha left the doctor's office in a very good mood. "Do you want to go get something to eat?" asked Taz.

"Mmmm-hmm. I'm starving," Sacha replied as they stepped outside.

"All right, this is what we'll do. I'll follow you back to your place. Then we'll head on out to Mama-Mama's for some of her good-ass breakfast food."

"How do you know if she's made anything?"

Laughing, he said, "Come on, Li'l Mama. If there's one thing that I know for sure in this world, it's that my mother has been up, since maybe the crack of dawn, cooking something to eat, especially with Neema being over there. By the time Neema gets back on her feet, she's goin' to be so fat that it's goin' to take a hell of a lot of working out to get that weight off of her ass."

They both laughed as Sacha climbed inside of her car. "In that case, let's go then! You know I'm eating for two now!"

After Taz closed her door for her, he smiled and said, "I'm right behind you, Li'l Mama!"

Tazneema had just finished eating when she heard Taz's loud music thumping from his truck. She smiled and said, "Here comes your son, Mama-Mama!"

"I wish that boy would turn that damn music down. He acts like he's deaf or something," Mama-Mama said as she came out of the kitchen wiping her hands on a dishtowel.

Taz and Sacha came inside of the house, hand in hand. Taz smiled when he saw his mother and said, "What's up, Mama-Mama?"

"What's up with you, boy? Why in the hell do you always have that music of yours up so damn loud?"

"You know I live to gets my bump on," Taz said as he turned toward Tazneema, winked his eye at her and said, "What's up with you? You straight?"

Nodding her head yes, Tazneema said, "I'm good. A li'l bored, but good."

"At least you're bored here at Mama-Mama's instead of that stuffy old hospital room," Sacha said as she sat down next to Tazneema on the couch.

"I know. So, what brought you two way out here?"

"Sacha was hungry, and I knew Mama-Mama had something on the stove, so I brought her over here so she could pig out a li'l," Taz said with a smile on his face.

"Girl, get yourself in this kitchen and come make yourself a plate. I gots plenty of food in here for your butt," Mama-Mama said as she turned and went back inside of the kitchen.

After Sacha followed Mama-Mama into the kitchen, Taz asked Tazneema, "How do you feel about Sacha? Do you really like her?"

"Yeah, she's cool. I see you two are getting deep, huh?"

"Yeah. I've asked her to be wifey."

"For real? That's cool, Taz!"

"She pregnant too."

"What? You mean to tell me that after all of these years you're finally about to give me a li'l brother or sister?"

He smiled at his daughter and said, "Looks like it. I just want you to know that, no matter what, you will always be my baby."

"I already know that, Taz."

"And no matter what changes I make in my life, your mother's memory will forever be in my heart. I've finally found someone who I can love and honor, but the love that I have for your mother is forever."

With her eyes watering, Tazneema said, "I know, Daddy. I know."

"*Daddy*? Where did that come from?" he asked with a smile on his face.

"Shoot, you got me getting all emotional and stuff. It kinda just came out. What? You don't like it when I call you Daddy?"

He smiled and said, "It's been so long that it shocked me a li'l bit. You can call me whatever you like, Baby Girl. You know that."

"Since you're in such a good mood, I need to talk to you about something without you going off on the deep end on me, Daddy."

"What's up?"

"I spoke to Cliff last night and this morning. I really need to see him. I love him, and we plan on getting back together when I get back on my feet."

Taz's smile turned to a frown quickly when he heard Tazneema mention Cliff's name. "There is no way in hell that I'm going to allow you to fuck with that nigga, Neema! Do you understand me?

Don't you fuck with me on this shit! That nigga ain't shit, and there is no fuckin' way that I'm going to let you be with that nigga!"

"You can't stop me! I'm a grown-ass woman! How the fuck are you gon' step in and try to play the daddy role now? You passed them duties to Mama-Mama when shit got too rough for you, remember? Now, just because you don't like who I've chosen as my mate, you want to act all 'father knows best,' and shit! Fuck that! I love that man, and I am going to be with him whether you like it or not, *Daddy!*"

Before Taz could respond to Tazneema's outburst, Mama-Mama and Sacha came back into the living room. "What the hell are you two screaming about?" yelled Mama-Mama.

"Your son here thinks he can run my life and tell me who I can and can't see!" screamed Tazneema.

"Nah! Your damn granddaughter has gotten too damn fast for her li'l ass! She thinks I'm goin' to let her be with that nigga, Cliff. I'm tellin' you, Mama-Mama, you need to talk some sense into this girl before I beat some into her ass!"

"Watch your mouth in my house, Taz! Now, Neema, you know we don't particularly care for that man. He done wrong in my home and almost took you away from us."

"But, Mama-Mama, it was Taz's fault! If he would have left Cliff alone, he would have never pulled that trigger!"

"So, it's my fault that the nigga shot you, Neema? Is that how you truly see it, Baby Girl?" Taz asked calmly with a hurt expression on his face.

Tazneema stared at her father, and though she knew the words she was about to speak would hurt him, at that point and time she didn't give a damn. She loved her man, and she was going to stand behind him no matter what. "You damn skippy! I don't hate you for it, so you shouldn't hate my man. You have your future wife with you, and y'all have a baby on the way. I'm happy for the both of you, so why can't you be happy for what me and Cliff plan to share with each other?"

"Baby? Wife? What the hell is she talking about, Taz?" asked Mama-Mama.

"Sacha's pregnant, and I've asked her to marry me, Mama-Mama," Taz said quickly. He took a deep breath and told Tazneema, "You can go against the grain if you want to, but just remember, once you step over that line, you're goin' to have to live with that for the rest of your life. I left you in the loving care of my mother because I knew I couldn't give you the balance you would need in this crazy-ass world. Sometimes I regret the decisions I've made, and sometimes I know that leaving you with Mama-Mama was the best decision I've ever made. I love you, Neema. You're my only child. Please, don't go against me."

Tazneema was shocked . . . shocked because she had never heard her father speak to her in this manner. Her anger overrode all rationality though. She was in love, and she had the right to be with whomever she wanted. And she wanted Cliff. It was as simple as that. "I love you too, Daddy. But I also love my man. Whether you accept it or not, I'm going to keep loving Cliff."

Taz's voice turned stone-cold as he asked, "Are you sure you want to go against the grain, Tazneema?"

"I'm standing behind my man, Taz," she replied just as coldly."

Taz nodded and said, "So be it. When he dies a slow death, I hope you won't hate me."

"If he does die, I will hate you for the rest of my life, Taz."

"So be it."

"You two, stop this nonsense right this minute! Taz, you are not going to do anything to that man! Do you hear me?" yelled Mama Mama.

"Yeah, I hear you, Mama-Mama. But you and I both know that when my mind is made up, no one is goin' to change it. I'm in no way tryin' to be disrespectful, but that nigga has to die by my hand."

Taz then turned his attention back toward his daughter and said, "I have given you all of the love and financial support any child could hope for. I know my not being around all of the time has hurt you, but it was for your own protection. You don't know me, Neema. You don't know what I'm really capable of. I've always sworn that I would never let you see that part of me. But you have now forced my hand, and because of that, you are about to see a part of your flesh and blood that you're going to wish you had never seen. So, warn your man. Let him know that the coldest nigga in Oklahoma City is comin' after his ass." He grabbed Sacha's hand and said, "Come on, let's bounce, Li'l Mama."

As they walked out of Mama-Mama's house, Tazneema cried in her grandmother's lap. "Why? Why can't he let me be happy with Cliff, Mama-Mama?"

"He's your father, baby. All he wants to do is protect you from the evils of this world."

"But Cliff isn't evil, Mama-Mama! He's a good man!" she cried.

"Not in your daddy's eyes, baby. I know my son better than anyone in this world. When he lost your mother, he was on the verge of going crazy. To this very day, I don't know exactly what brought him back to me. I'm thankful to God that he's still here and has done so well for himself. I'm no fool, and I know that he got all of that fancy stuff from doing something illegal. He has taken care of the both of us for a very long time now. I have to respect him for that. You have to respect him for it also. If he doesn't want you to be with that man, then you should listen to your father and not be with him."

Tazneema tried to speak, but Mama-Mama stopped her with a raised hand and continued. "Wait, child, and hear me out first. I understand that you are all grown up and all, but that man hurt you because he tried to kill your father. He tried to take my only child away from me. If he had succeeded in doing that, I would have killed him myself. Do you hear me, baby? I would have committed murder behind the death of my only child. So, how do you think Taz feels about that man shooting *his* only child? Put yourself in his place. How would you feel?"

"I understand his anger, Mama-Mama. When I was lying up in that hospital bed, I was mad at Cliff too. I never thought I'd want to see him again, let alone be with him. But after thinking about it, I realized that I still love him. It's as simple as that. I love him, Mama-Mama. I love my daddy too. I know how cold Taz is. I've heard the stories about how he was a killer, and how everyone around the city fears him. He doesn't know I know, but I know. Even though I respect what he has done for me, he has no right to try and dictate how I live my life. None whatsoever! I love him, that fact is true, but I'm not scared of him, Mama-Mama. If he can kill, so can I."

Chapter Nine

Pitt was picked up at Los Angeles International Airport by a chauffeured limousine. It took the driver less than twenty minutes to arrive in front of a gigantic office building in downtown L.A. Once the driver opened the door, Pitt slid easily out of the limousine and marched inside of the building. He rode the elevator to the twenty-first floor of the building. The door to the elevator was barely open as he squeezed his stocky frame through it. He stepped quickly toward the receptionist, who was staring at him as if he had lost his mind.

"May I help you, sir?" asked the receptionist.

"I'm here to see Cash—I mean Mr. Harris. My name is Pitt."

"Is Mr. Harris expecting you, sir?"

"Call him and find out!" Pitt said arrogantly as he pulled out one of his hand-rolled Cuban cigars.

The receptionist rolled her eyes slightly as she pressed the intercom button and said, "Excuse me, Mr. Harris. There's a Mr. Pitt out here to see you."

"Send him in," Mr. Harris replied over the intercom.

When the receptionist raised her head to speak with Pitt, he had already stepped past her and was on his way inside of Mr. Harris' office. *Prick!* she said to herself as she went back to her work.

Pitt stepped inside of the office and said, "What's up, Cash Flo'?"

"You already know what's up. What do you have to tell me that's so damn important, Pitt? You know I've been caught up with those dagos in the East. On top of that, them bitch-ass Colombians are trippin' too. They are actually trying to up the price on The Network 'cause they feel we're not getting enough work from them. Can you believe that shit? We've been getting anywhere from thirty to thirty-five hundred kilos a month from them, and they say that's not enough! I'm telling you, Pitt, that's one of the reasons I'm about ready to get out of this shit. Anyway, what's the deal with you?"

Pitt smiled at the small man sitting behind the large cherry wood desk and said, "It's that nigga Won. I told you a long time ago that it was that fool. Won has been the nigga responsible for all of those mysterious-ass burglaries and licks the rest of the council have been taking."

"Do you have any proof, Pitt? Because without any solid evidence, we won't be able to move on this. You know that, right?"

"Yeah, I know. I don't have any yet, but I will soon. You see, that nigga has finally fucked with the wrong council member. I knew sooner or later he would try to get at me, but you see my clique is too tight. No one has the heart to cross the Pitt."

Cash Flo' smiled and said, "I thought you told me that you just got hit for a nice chunk."

"I did. Yeah, someone finally got enough nuts to cross me, but that's a good thing. I've set up a meet for my entire crew out in Oaktown. At this meeting, I will find out exactly who it was that crossed me, and in turn, they will tell me the person who put them up to it. Once I get that information, I'm sending a heavy hit squad at that nigga Won."

"Whoa! Hold up a second, bad boy! How do you know that it will be Won that your people give up? What if he had someone else get at them? Then what are you going to do?" Cash Flo' asked.

"If Won was involved, I will get his name sooner or later, Flo'. All I want to know is, do I have your support on this shit?"

Cash Flo' leaned back in his comfortable leather chair and thought about what Pitt had just asked him. He stroked his salt-and-pepper beard slowly as he stared at his longtime friend and business partner. They went back as far as the late seventies, when Pitt was a teenager out in Northern California.

Pitt was known as hotheaded sometimes, but only when he felt that he was dead to the right. His position over the years had grown inside of The Network only because Cash Flo' felt he was worthy of the promotions. *If I give him my support on this and he's wrong, there's going to be a war within The Network,* Cash Flo' thought. Then he said, "I'm going to give you my support, Pitt, but only if you're right on this shit. If you're wrong and you go falsely accusing Won, you know what kind of position that will put you in. I won't back you if you're wrong, but if you are indeed correct about Won, then you will have everything you need to deal with the situation accordingly."

"Always got to protect ya neck, huh?"

Cash Flo' smiled and said, "Always."

"Cool. I ain't got a problem with that. I'll get at you when I have that nigga's name," Pitt said as he raised up out of his seat and left the office.

Cash Flo' sat back in his chair and gave some more thought to this situation. *What the fuck would Won have to gain from doing all of this shit? He's already a fucking millionaire a few times over,* he thought to himself. Then, as if a brick hit him, the answer came to him. "Power! If this shit is true, Won's on a fucking power trip!" he said aloud as he grabbed the phone on his desk and started dialing.

By the time Taz and Sacha made it to his house, he was so upset, he could hardly think straight. He went downstairs to his indoor gym and started working out furiously. He did some curls with some lightweight dumbbells to loosen up. Afterward, he went to the curl bar and started repping some heavy weight. After an hour of this, his entire body was dripping wet with sweat, so he went upstairs and jumped into the shower.

While he was showering, he was trying his best to think of a way to get Sacha to tell him where Clifford lived. He knew she wasn't going to tell him, but he had to try to get that information out of her.

While Taz was working out, Sacha chose to stay out of his way. She took the Dobermans outside and let them run around Taz's gigantic backyard. She threw a tennis ball as far as she could and smiled as both Precious and Heaven ran to go fight for the ball. Whichever dog got to the ball first would run and bring it back to her. She did this with them for over an hour before she finally started feeling a little fatigued.

She brought the dogs back inside of the house and went upstairs to take a shower. When she walked inside the bedroom, she smiled as she watched Taz get dressed. Her smile turned into a frown quickly when she focused and saw exactly what Taz was putting on. He had on a pair of black Dickies pants and a black sweatshirt. As he tied up the laces to his black leather Timberlands, she said, "So, you're about to go hunting, I see."

"Don't fuck with me on this, Li'l Mama. I'm not tryin' to hear you right now."

"What about the promises you made to me, Taz? Have you forgotten about them already?"

"Let me see if I'm correct. I gave you my word that I would not be going out of town to do anything for Won after I finish up what I have to do with my peoples. I also recall me saying that I give you my word that after I'm done, I won't let Won get at me with any more missions or anything illegal. I plan on standing on every promise that I made to you, Li'l Mama. But I did not say anything about not dealing with that nigga Cliff. So, you can't put that shit in this now."

"Dammit, Taz! You know damn well what I'm talking about! Why can't you leave that man alone? Can't you see that your daughter really cares for him? You're going to ruin the relationship you have with your only child because of some macho bullshit! That's ridiculous, Taz! Let them be. If Neema wants to be happy with him, then give her that opportunity."

Taz stood, clapped his hands a few times and said, "Very good, counselor! That was a very convincing speech. But you see, this shit has nothin' to do with being macho. Baby, you know that I know I am the man. I know that nigga ain't really worth my time for real. But, you see, he hurt mines, and when someone hurts mines, I hurt them. It's that simple. As for Neema, she went against the grain. So, basically, it's fuck her too. I love her, and I always will. If she doesn't say another word to me for the rest of my life, that's on her. I'm doin' what I feel has to be done, period! End . . . of . . . discussion, Li'l Mama!"

"Ooh! You make me so damn sick with this craziness!" Sacha screamed, and went into the bathroom and took her shower.

Taz smiled sadly as he left the bedroom. He went down into the den and called Keno. After Keno answered the phone, Taz said, "I'm about to go huntin', G. You want to roll wit' me?"

"For that nigga Cliff?"

"You got it."

"I'm on my way over right now!" Keno yelled excitedly.

"Nah, I'm on my way to scoop you," Taz said before he hung up the phone. He grabbed the keys to his truck and said, "Now, where in the hell do you live, nigga? 'Cause death is about to knock on your front door!"

Chapter Ten

It had been two days since Pitt met with Cash Flo' out in Los Angeles. Pitt was as happy as can be as he walked into the conference room he had rented at the Marriot Hotel in downtown Oakland. Every last member of his team was inside the room. He spoke to everyone as he went to the head of the long conference table. Now was the time to find out exactly who it was that crossed him. "What's up, everyone? Y'all good?" he greeted.

Everyone inside of the room gave a positive response to him as they got themselves comfortable in their seats.

"Good. Now, I know y'all are wondering why I called this emergency meeting, so I'll get straight to the matter at hand. Someone in this room has crossed me, and I'm here today to find out exactly who that person is. There are approximately thirty-six people in this room, not counting myself. And no one is leaving until I find out who gave up the information on the bail bondsman spot. It is now ten minutes after three. At three thirty, my men, Leo and Tru here, will start executing each one of you until someone confesses their wrongs committed against me."

There were several murmurs around the conference room as the members of Pitt's crew stared at Leo and Tru, who had both pulled out silenced 9 mm.

Pitt continued. "Now, I want to give you my word that once the guilty party confesses, he or she will not be harmed. All I want to know is who the person is that made contact with them, and got them to cross that line. Other than being dismissed from this crew, nothing will be done to them." He then raised his right hand and said, "I swear to God! You see, this matter has to be dealt with immediately, because it endangers not only our daily operations, but our safety as well." He stopped talking, sat back in his chair and lit up one of his Cuban cigars. He gave a quick glance toward the clock mounted on the right wall of the conference room and said, "Fifteen more minutes, and the executions will begin."

A tall gentleman dressed casually in a pair of Dockers and a short-sleeved Polo button-up shirt stood and said, "Come on, Pitt. This shit is crazy. Ain't no way you're going to be able to blast everyone in this room and get away with it. This shit is ridiculous!"

"Munk, have you ever known me to give faulty threats?"

"Nah, but—"

"I have this room rented for the rest of the day. We will be long gone by the time Leo and Tru finish handling their business. I really didn't expect to have to go through with this shit, but I see the person who's crossed me really doesn't give a fuck about y'all either. 'Cause if that person did, they would have come forward by now . . . that is . . . unless that person is you, Munk."

Shaking his head furiously, Munk said, "You know I'd never cross you, Pitt. It wasn't me. I swear!"

"Have a seat, Munk, and shut the fuck up then!" Pitt glanced toward the clock again and said, "Twelve more minutes."

After about three more minutes of silence, a petite woman stood up and said, "It was me, Pitt."

Pitt frowned and asked, "Why, Brenda? We've been together for years. I've always made sure that you were eating well from this table. Why would you do me like that?"

Brenda gave a slight shrug of her petite shoulders and simply said, "Greed, Pitt. He offered me a million dollars to give up the bail bondsman spot. He also promised me that no one would be hurt. I figured I'd score me a quick ticket, and all would be well. I knew your losses would be made up eventually, 'cause a nigga like you ain't gon' fall off over some shit like a few kilos of heroin. So, I said fuck it, and gave up the info. True, you've made sure that I have always eaten well, but I don't have a meal ticket stacked in the vault."

"But you do now, huh?" Pitt asked sarcastically.

"Yeah, I do now," Brenda said with her head bowed in shame.

"All right then. Who was it that approached you? I need to know his name and how to get in contact with him."

"The name he gave me was Gee. I have a cell number right here in my purse," Brenda said as she opened her purse and pulled out a white slip of paper with a telephone number written on it. She passed it to Tru, who had come and stood right next to her. He then went to the front of the conference table and gave it to Pitt.

Pitt sighed heavily, because it hurt him deeply to know that Brenda was the person who had crossed him. She had been with him for a very long time, and he thought she would always remain loyal. *Damn! This some fucked up shit!* he thought. Then he asked her, "Did this Gee mention anyone else?"

"Nope. All he was worried about was the location of the spot, and security and shit like that. He was on some sneaky shit, but his primary concern was the drugs."

"Is there anything else you're not telling me, Brenda?"

"That's everything, Pitt. I swear to God."

"Come here," Pitt said as he waved his hand for her to come to him.

Brenda walked to the front of the conference table and stood in front of Pitt. "I know saying I'm sorry is worthless right about now, Pitt, but I am. I let my damn greed get the best of me, and I'm truly sorry for that."

Pitt grabbed Tru's silenced 9 mm and said, "You know I have to take you, right?"

"Bu—but you said that I wouldn't be harmed! You swore to God and gave all of us your word, Pitt!" screamed Brenda.

"I'm a criminal just like everyone else in this room, baby. You know my word ain't shit," Pitt said to her before he shot her right between her eyes. Her lifeless body dropped to the floor instantly.

Pitt gave Tru his gun back and said, "Clean up this mess. I'll have some janitors of mine come and get the body in a little bit. Now, as for the rest of y'all, I want y'all to know that you were never in any danger. I knew that the person who was responsible for this shit would come forward before the deadline expired."

"Bullshit, Pitt! You're one cold nigga!" someone yelled from the back of the conference room.

Pitt smiled a deadly smile and said, "You better fucking believe it! You cross me, and you die! It's that fucking simple. This meeting is now adjourned. Get back to getting that fucking money!"

Back in Oklahoma City, Clifford was talking to his homeboys, H-Hop, Astro, and Li'l Bomb.

"So, you got heavy beef with them niggas, big homey?" asked Li'l Bomb.

"Yeah, cuz. That nigga Taz is real salty at a nigga 'cause his daughter's in love with me," replied Clifford.

"Do you think he's goin' to try and take it to the next level, cuz?" asked Astro

"That fool ain't no joke, cuz. I didn't want to tell y'all, but I ain't really got no choice. Taz is the same nigga who killed Do-Low."

"*What?*" all three of the Hoover Crips yelled in unison.

"So, this nigga Taz is the nigga Do-Low tried to jack at the club that night, loc?" asked H-Hop.

"Yeah."

"Cuz, that nigga gots to go!" Li'l Bomb said angrily.

"I'll take care of that nigga, cuz. I'm going to need y'all to help a nigga out with his crew though. Those fools got major chips, so I know they're strapped like out of this world," Clifford said seriously.

"Cuz, we're strapped out of this fuckin' world! Fuck them niggas! How you want to do this?" asked Li'l Bomb.

"They normally go out to the club on the weekends. They don't be slippin', so we gots to make sure that when we move, we move correctly. Let me check into a few things, and I'll get back at y'all."

"All right, C-Baby. You do that, cuz. When the time is right, we gon' smoke all of them fools! For my nigga, Do-Low! Hoover in peace!" H-Hop said seriously.

Clifford smiled and said, "Fo' sho, loco!"

Taz was frustrated. It had been two days, and he still wasn't able to get a line on where Clifford's home was. He even went to his old job and tried to see if he could get the information from one of Clifford's former coworkers, and he still came up short.

When Sacha heard that Taz was at her job asking questions about Clifford, she became infuriated. She called Taz and told him to meet her at her house for lunch. Taz, knowing that she was about to rip him a new asshole, reluctantly agreed.

As soon as she entered her house, she went straight off on him. "How fucking dare you come up to my place of employment and try to find out where Cliff lives! What's the fuck wrong with you, Taz? Don't you realize that if anything happens to him now, you're going to be the number one fucking suspect? Are you trying to beat the fucking door down to the pen? What the fuck were you thinking about?" she screamed.

Taz sat down onto her sofa and said, "I guess I wasn't really thinkin' at all, Li'l Mama."

"Taz, baby, you have to let this go. You're letting this completely consume you, and it's eating up your fucking brain cells! I'm not trying to lose you to nobody's jail, baby. Please, let this go."

He shook his head no, and said, "I slipped, Li'l Mama. It won't happen again. I promise. Now, calm down before you make yourself sick or somethin'. That nigga has to die. It's as simple as that."

"I can't fucking believe this shit! You're going to let this man put you behind bars for the rest of your fucking life, and for what? Just because your daughter loves him? You are the dumbest fucking millionaire I have ever met in my fucking life! Get the fuck out of my house, Taz Good!"

"Come on, Li'l Mama! Stop trippin'! Damn!"

"I mean it, Taz! Get the fuck out!" she screamed as she pointed toward her front door.

Taz got to his feet and walked out of Sacha's home feeling like a rookie in the game. *Damn! How did I slip like that?* he asked himself as he climbed inside of this truck.

When Taz made it back to his place, he called Tari and asked her if she was still going out to the club with them.

"Ain't nothing changed, baby. I told y'all I was with it," she said as she closed the door to the nurses' station at her job.

"All right, I was just checkin' to make sure that you was still rollin'. We'll most likely all meet here around ten-thirty. We don't normally hit the club until eleven or eleven-thirty."

"That's cool. Should I wear something sexy, or something comfortable?"

Taz started laughing and said, "It don't matter, Tee. You know how we get down. Some of us will be fly, and some of us will be on some *G* shit. I was thinking about sportin' my new pieces tonight though."

"Yeah? What you got now, 'Mr. Baby Birdman'?"

"Birdman? You got me twisted, Tee. I ain't no Li'l Wayne. I'm that nigga, Taz! You know I got the tightest shit around this clown-ass town."

"Whatever! What have you gone and bought now, boy?"

"Last month when me and Sacha were in L.A., she bought me this tight-ass canary-yellow diamond bracelet and ring. So, I took it a step further and had my grill man out in H-Town hook me up a canary-yellow diamond grill to match."

"Top and bottom?"

"Yep! That shit is way tight too. Watch. You'll see later on," he said happily.

"So, what are you wearing tonight? I know it's going to be something real fly since you're going to be flossing all of those yellow rocks."

"Nah. You know I rarely get my floss on like that. I leave that shit to Keno. I'm rockin' a pair of brown Rocawear jeans, with my butter-colored Timbs, and a white tee."

"I swear, I don't understand how you got all of that money and you dress as if you're still out hustling on the block."

"It is what it is, Tee. What? I should be suited and booted every fuckin' day? You know I don't get down like that."

"Yeah, I know. And I also know that you have Armani, Gucci, and every other top-name designer inside of your closet too. Why don't you wear one of those sexy-ass tailormade suits of yours?"

"'Cause that shit is for funerals, weddings and other special events. Not for no fuckin' club in the city. Look, I'll see you later. I got some calls to make and shit."

"Wait! Did you and Sacha smooth things out with each other?"

"Yes . . . and no."

"What did you do now, boy?"

"I'll tell you about it later on, Tee. I gots to go."

"All right, bye." She hung up the phone and went back to work.

Keno, Bo-Pete, Red and Wild Bill arrived at Taz's house a little after 10:00 P.M. They were all dressed casually, in jeans and shirts. They either had Timberland boots on, or a pair of Nike by Jordan or Kobe Bryant. With all of their expensive jewelry on, they looked like a group of rappers.

Taz smiled as everyone complimented him on his new canary-yellow diamond grill.

"Damn, nigga! When you bust those pieces?" Keno asked as he walked to the bar to pour himself a drink.

"A few months ago," answered Taz.

"How many carats you got in your mouth now, nigga?" asked Red.

Taz shrugged and said, "About one twenty, I think. I'm not really sure. I called my grill man out in H-Town and had him hook this up for me."

"You always gots to outshine a nigga, huh?" asked Keno.

"Nigga, ain't no way I can outshine you! You're the number one stuntin' nigga in the city!"

Keno smiled and said, "I know, huh!"

Everyone laughed at his silly ass.

"Dog, what's up with Katrina? I haven't heard you talkin' 'bout her in a minute," asked Taz,

"We're good, G. As a matter a fact, she's goin' to be at the club later on. We've been chillin' and shit. She has really shocked me."

"How's that?"

"She's not the normal around-the-way broad. She actually goes to school and is trying to get her degree in literature. She wants to be a school teacher."

"Yeah, that's straight. So, you think she's wifey material?"

"It's possible, my nigga. It's possible."

"What's up with you, Red? Have you hit her homegirl yet?"

"Yeah, I tossed her a few times. She's good too. I told her not to sweat me though, so she's been givin' a nigga plenty of room. I know she'll be in the spot tonight, so most likely she's goin' to be bouncin' up outta there with me."

"I guess that leaves you two. What's crackin' in y'all's sex life?"

Bo-Pete just smiled as he stood sipping his drink.

"Dog, I ain't goin' out like you chumps. I'm a fuckin' millionaire, and I ain't tryin' to get tied down by no broad. I can fuck who I want, when I want, and that's just how I fuckin' like it," Wild Bill said with a smile on his face.

They all started laughing at Wild Bill as he stood and went to the bar and had Keno pour him a drink.

Even though Wild Bill was the smallest member of the crew, he was still considered one of the most dangerous. Taz didn't know if it was because Wild Bill had a complex about his height or what. He was a stone-cold killer. He stood under five foot six inches, and wore a pair of gold-rimmed glasses. He was damn near blind, but when it came to handling his business, he had never let any of them down.

Taz smiled as he looked at his homeboys. He loved each one of them as if they were his blood brothers. *These are niggas that I would die for,* he thought to himself as he sipped on his glass of XO.

Taz heard his front door open and smiled, because he thought Sacha had calmed down and come over to the house. His smile quickly left his face when he saw that it wasn't Sacha who had just entered his home. It was Tari.

Tari noticed the look on his face, smiled and said, "I guess I'm not who you were expecting, huh?"

Taz ignored her and said, "What's good, Tee? Damn! You're lookin' like you tryin' to catch somethin' tonight!"

"Nah, I'm just trying to make some of them sistas hate a li'l bit," she said with a sexy smile on her face.

Tari was wearing a pair of low-cut Apple Bottom jeans, and a cut-off T-shirt that showed off her belly ring. Across the front of her shirt were words in bold lettering that read, "I GOT ASS TOO!" Her long blonde hair was hanging loosely past her shoulders. She was looking extremely sexy, and every man inside the room knew it. *Long legs, sexy blue eyes and a body like a sista, that white girl was right!*

"Well, since everybody's here, y'all already know what time it is," Taz said with a smile on his face.

"Already?" Bo-Pete said, and downed the rest of his drink.

Then in unison, the rest of the group said, "It's time to go clubbin'!"

Chapter Eleven

Clifford, Astro, H-Hop and Li'l Bomb sat parked across the street from Club Cancun's parking lot, waiting to see if Taz and his crew had chosen to come out and have a little fun. *If indeed they did, they would have a big surprise waiting for them after the club let out,* Clifford thought as he watched as the club hoppers started filling up the parking lot.

"What makes you so sure that they're comin' up here tonight, cuz?" asked Astro.

Clifford shrugged his shoulders and said, "It's just a feeling I got, loc. They might not though. I figure it's maybe sixty-forty in favor of them showing up though."

"I hope they do, cuz, 'cause on 107 Hoover Crip, I want that nigga who took the big homey, Do-Low!" Li'l Bomb said seriously from the backseat of the stolen Nissan Maxima they were sitting inside of.

Clifford smiled and said, "If they show, you're going to get your chance, li'l homey. So, let's just wait and see, cuz."

"Didn't you say they all pushed all-black whips?" asked H-Hop.

"Yeah."

"Well, that gots to be them right there, loc," H-Hop said as he pointed toward the small fleet of all-black SUV's pulling into the parking lot of Club Cancun.

Clifford smiled and said, "Yeah, you're definitely going to get your shot at them niggas tonight, cuz!"

Li'l Bomb smiled and pumped a live round into the chamber of his AK-47 and said, "Good!"

Taz and Tari rode together in his truck, while Red rode with Bo-Pete and Wild Bill in Bo-Pete's Navigator. Keno didn't want to ride with Taz because he knew Taz would most likely want to leave the club before he did, so he chose to drive his Range Rover solo.

After they had parked their vehicles side by side in the parking lot, everyone exited their trucks and started walking toward the club's entrance. Since they had a ritual of how they entered the club, Bo-Pete and Wild Bill entered the club first. Three to four minutes later, Red and Keno entered the club. Five minutes after that, Taz led Tari inside. Normally, Bob would have been paired with Red, but since he was laid up, Keno was his replacement, because Taz was going to make sure that Tari was by his side at all times.

Once Taz and Tari entered the club, Taz saw that Red and Keno were posted up on the far left side of the club, while Bo-Pete and Wild Bill were posted up on the far right side. He gave them all a slight nod and stepped toward the bar with two fingers held up, signaling Winky, the bartender to give him his usual drink, a double shot of XO.

Winky passed Taz a brandy snifter with his drink, smiled and asked, "Anything for the lovely lady, Taz?"

Taz turned toward Tari, and she said, "Yeah, give me a Hpnotiq."

Taz smiled and said, "Now, what the fuck you know 'bout a Hpnotiq?"

"Taz, you may think I'm some kind of hermit because I don't do the club scene that often, but I do have friends, and occasionally we go out and have drinks and stuff."

He laughed and said, "My bad, Tee!"

"Fuck you, boy!" she said, and started laughing also.

Taz noticed that Keno had found Katrina, and smiled. "Looks like Keno's girl is here."

"Which one is she?" Tari asked, and sipped her drink.

"The thick one right there with the microbraids in her hair. The girl standing next to her is her homegirl, Paquita. She's the one Red's been gettin' at."

"The light-skinned one with all of that damn weave in her hair?"

Taz laughed and said, "Yeah."

"Damn! She didn't give that horse a break, did she? She knows she's wrong for that shit!"

"Be good, Tee. Red seems to like her."

"She is kind of cute though. Her body is bangin' too. But she could lose like ten to twelve inches of that damn weave!"

They both started laughing as they watched Keno and Red talking to their lady friends.

Keno smiled at Katrina and said, "So, what's poppin', *mami*?"

Katrina returned the smile and said, "Nothin', *papi*. What's up with you?"

"The same old shit."

"What's up, Red? What? You can't speak tonight?" asked Paquita.

Red smiled and said, "Hah! It ain't like that, ma. What it do? You good?"

Paquita smiled and answered, "I am now."

"I know that's right! Y'all want somethin' to drink?"

"Yeah. I'll have me a glass of Henny," said Paquita.

"Get me an Absolut Peach," said Katrina.

As Red went to go get their drinks, Katrina asked Keno, "So, am I leaving with you tonight, *papi*?"

"It depends."

"Depends on what?" she asked with a pout on her pretty face.

"If you're goin' to be as freaky as I want you to be later on!"

She punched him lightly on his arm and said, "You know you need to quit, with your nasty self!"

He laughed and said, "You know I'm clownin', *mami*. Of course, you're bouncin' with me. I need some sexual healing, and I know you're goin' to look out for your boy."

She smiled seductively and said, "You got that right, *papi!*"

"Ooh, y'all so damn nasty! Y'all need to quit that shit!" Paquita said just as Red returned with their drinks.

"Girl, you the one who needs to quit, 'cause you know damn well you gon' leave with Red and get your freak on too!"

Red gave them their drinks, smiled and said, "I don't know what y'all have been over here talkin' about, but I sure hope you're right, Katrina!"

They all started laughing as they sipped their drinks and enjoyed their evening.

Bo-Pete and Wild Bill were busy on the other side of the club, trying to impress two lovely ladies.

The rest of the evening went by rather quickly to Taz. He was surprised that he was having so much fun with Tari. They danced for a few songs, and continued to laugh and make jokes with one another about any and everything. Taz never realized that Tari was such a clown. She was talking about almost every other female inside of the club, from what they were wearing to the bad weave jobs they had in their hair. That shit was hilarious to him.

What took the cake was when a guy with a Jheri curl came up to Tari and asked to buy her a drink. Tari smirked and said, "I already have one, dear," trying to sound extra white and shit. But when Jheri Curl persisted and asked her, did she want to dance with him, she said with plenty of attitude in her voice, "Look, I don't feel like dancing, okay?"

"Damn, baby! I'm just trying to be entertaining!" said Jheri Curl.

Tari burst into laughter and said, "Man, will you get the fuck away from me!"

Jheri Curl was about to say something he was definitely going to regret, but Taz saved him just in time by saying, "She's my peoples, dog. Why don't you go on and let her make it, huh?"

Jheri Curl stared at Taz briefly then said, "Whatever, dog. She ain't all that anyway."

As Jheri Curl was walking away, Tari had to hit him off with one last jab. "I may not be all that, but at least I'm not dripping no damn jheri curl juice all over the fuckin' club either, you fuckin' clown!"

"Come on with that shit, Tee!" Taz said as he tried his best to control his laughter. Seeing that she was a little heated, he said, "Let's shake this spot and go get somethin' to eat. I'm a li'l hungry. What about you?"

"Yeah, I've had enough of this club to last me a minute. What about the others?"

"Let's go get at them and see what's on their plates," Taz said as he led her toward Bo-Pete and Wild Bill. When they made it to where they were, Taz said, "We're about to shake the spot and go get our grub on. What's up with y'all?"

"Ain't nothin' really crackin' in here for me. I'm gon' bounce too," replied Wild Bill.

"Yeah, I'm a li'l tired. Might as well call it a night," said Bo-Pete.

"All right, let's go get at Keno and Red real quick then."

Keno was kissing Katrina on her neck, when Taz walked over to him. Keno smiled and said, "I know that look, nigga. You're about to shake the spot, huh?"

"Yeah. I've had all my fun. We're out. Y'all good or what?"

Keno stared at Red, who gave a shrug of his broad shoulders and said, "Yeah, we're good. We got some shit to take care of after the club is over anyway."

Keno smiled brightly and added, "That's right. We gots shit to take care of."

They all laughed and stared at Katrina and Paquita.

Katrina blushed, slapped Keno on his face lightly, and said, "Stop that shit, Keno!"

Paquita, with no shame at all, said, "You damn right, you got something to take care of tonight, and you better take good care of it too!"

Taz shook his head from side to side and said, "Y'all are made for each other, for real! Watch yourselves," he said as he grabbed Tari's hand and walked toward the club's exit.

As she watched them leave the club, Katrina frowned and said, "I thought Taz was all in love with old girl. What's her name, Sacha?"

Keno laughed and said, "Don't worry about that shit, *mami*. My nigga is always gon' be all right. Now, come here!" he said playfully as he grabbed her by her hand.

Tari had her arm around Taz's waist as they followed Wild Bill and Bo-Pete out of the club. They stopped and inhaled some of the fresh air once they were outside.

Just as they were about to walk toward Taz's truck, Tari suddenly reached under Taz's shirt, pulled out his 9 mm, pushed Taz to the side and screamed, "Watch your ass, Taz!" She then began unloading his weapon at the four guys in dark clothing who were charging them with what looked like assault rifles in their hands.

After Tari started shooting, Bo-Pete and Wild Bill reacted instantly. They pulled out their weapons and started shooting at the men in the dark clothing too.

Realizing that they had lost their advantage, H-Hop, Astro, Clifford and Li'l Bomb began retreating. Even though they had heavier firepower, they were being shot at from one too many angles. Therefore, they weren't able to get a good shot off at their targets.

Taz, who had regrouped quickly after Tari pushed him to the side, knelt on one knee and watched as she, Bo-Pete and Wild Bill handled their business. *Ain't this a bitch!* he thought as he watched the niggas who tried to blast them run and jump inside of a black Nissan Maxima. As they sped out of the parking lot across the street from the club, Tari, Bo-Pete and Wild Bill ran into the middle of the street and stood side by side, and continued to unload their weapons at the Maxima.

Once the car was out of their sight, Bo-Pete came back and checked on Taz. "You straight, *G*?"

Taz got to his feet and said, "Yeah, I'm good. Go inside of the club and get Keno and Red."

Bo-Pete went to go do as Taz had told him, while Tari and Wild Bill came to Taz's side.

"What the fuck was that shit, dog?" asked Wild Bill.

"I don't have a fuckin' clue, my nigga."

"You still got beef like that out here in these streets, Taz?" asked Tari as she was breathing heavily.

Shaking his head no, Taz said, "Nah, you know I don't fuck with niggas out here no more."

"Then what the fuck was those clowns doing? Playing? Baby, I think you have some beef and don't even know it. That little fucker with the orange bandanna around his face was aiming that fucking assault rifle right at your head when I spotted his ass."

"Orange bandanna? Ain't that Hoover colors, Wild Bill?"

"Yeah, dog. But we don't fuck with no gang niggas."

"What the fuck!"

Keno, Red and Bo-Pete came outside of the club with their weapons in their hands.

"What the fuck happened out here?" asked Keno.

"Some niggas tried to dump me. Tari saved by ass, G. Look, let's shake this spot. You know 'the ones' will be here in a minute. I'll get at y'all in the morning so we can look at this shit clearly."

"All right," they replied in unison, and they all went toward the vehicles they came to the club in.

After Tari and Taz were inside of his truck, she said, "I think it'll be safer if we went back to your house and I make us something to eat."

Taz smiled and said, "Ya think?"

Chapter Twelve

Even though Tari handled the situation at the club like a pure veteran, she was still a little shaken by the time they made it back to Taz's home. She went straight into the den and poured herself a stiff shot of XO from the bar. After she downed her drink, she quickly poured herself another one and sat down on the couch. "What the fuck was that all about, Taz?" she asked as she sipped her second drink.

"I don't even know, Tee. We'll try to figure this shit out tomorrow. Right now, I'm taking my ass to bed and get me some sleep," he said as he yawned.

"I thought we were going to eat something."

"I ain't got the energy to wait for you to put somethin' together. I'm out. You can lay it down in here, or you can use the guest room if you want."

Tari smiled and asked, "Why can't I come and sleep with you? You scared of me now that you're all in love?"

Taz returned her smile and said, "You know if we sleep in the same bed what's goin' to pop off, Tee."

"So? I won't tell if you won't."

"I'm engaged, Tee."

"Engaged, yeah, but you're not married."

He took a deep breath, turned toward the door of the den and said, "Come on, you."

Tari smiled as she followed him up the stairs and into his bedroom. She continued to smile as he started to undress. Once he had his clothes off, he got under the bed covers and said, "This is never goin' to happen again, Tee. Do you hear me?"

After taking off her jeans and sliding out of her transparent thong, she said, "In that case, let's make this a night to remember." She slid onto the bed and pulled back the covers from Taz's chiseled body and began to slowly lick him from his head to his feet.

Chills ran all over his body as he tensed when Tari sucked each one of his toes. *Damn, I miss this type of shit!* he thought to himself with his eyes closed tightly.

When Tari finished with his feet, she worked her way up to his crotch area and began sucking his testicles. His dick was so hard that he felt as if he was about to cum any moment.

She left his balls alone for the moment and started sucking his rock-hard dick greedily. The slurping sounds she was making while giving him one of the best blow jobs he had ever had in his life seemed to drive him over the edge.

He grabbed her by her long blonde hair and held her tightly as he came inside of her mouth. After she swallowed every last drop of his cum, she smiled and said, "M-m-m-m-m!"

He shook his head from side to side as he pulled her up toward his face, and they began to kiss passionately.

After Taz felt he had regained his strength, he turned her over and said, "Now, you li'l freak, it's my turn!" He started at her breasts and nibbled on each one of her rock-hard nipples until she moaned with pleasure. He smiled as he licked his way lower. When he made it to her sex, she was so wet and sticky, he felt as if he had just stuck his tongue into some warm milk.

Tari's clit was so hard that it looked like a mini-missile. Taz sucked and nibbled on it, causing Tari to scream out with pleasure. "Oh-h-h-h, Taz! Don't stop! Please, Daddy! Don't you fucking stop!" She screamed as loud as she could as she gyrated her hips and ground her pussy in his face.

When she came, she felt as if every fiber of her body was on fire. "Damn, Taz! I'm cumming! I'm cumming! I'm cumming, baby!"

Her body went limp under his tongue assault. He didn't give her a chance to recoup. He slid on top of her and entered her piping-hot pussy quickly.

She gave a gasp as she felt all of his manhood deep inside of her love box. "Damn, that feels so-o-o good, Daddy! Give it to me, baby! Give it to me!" she screamed as he worked her over real good for close to twenty minutes.

By the time Taz reached his second orgasm, his entire body was covered with sweat. Tari had already come several times while he was pounding away in her sex.

It's time for the finale, he thought as he quickly flipped her over onto her knees and entered her from behind. Her fat ass was raised high in the air as he rammed himself deep inside of her.

"Here it goes, Tee! Here it goes!" he screamed as he let go a monstrous nut inside of her pussy. After the last tingling sensations had subsided, he slid out of her and fell onto the bed completely spent. "Damn, that was good!"

"Do you miss this pussy, Taz? Do you miss it as much as I've missed this dick?" Tari asked lazily with her eyes half closed.

"Mmmm-hmmm," Taz replied as he closed his eyes and drifted off to sleep.

The next morning, Taz was awakened by his phone ringing. He opened his eyes and groggily answered it. "What up?"

"Good morning, Taz," said Sacha.

Upon hearing his fiancée's voice his head cleared instantly. "What up, Li'l Mama? You all right?"

"I should be asking you that question. I heard about last night, Taz."

"What? From who?"

"Gwen called me this morning and told me that Bob told her that Wild Bill called him this morning and told him what happened at the club last night. What's going on, baby? I thought you said that you didn't have that kind of beef in the city."

"I thought I didn't, but obviously I was wrong. Don't worry about it though. I'll take care of this shit, Li'l Mama."

"Don't worry about it? How can I not worry about it, Taz?"

He smiled and said, "I thought you was mad at me."

"I am. That hasn't changed, mister. But just because I'm mad at you doesn't change the fact that you are my man, my fiancé, the man I plan on spending the rest of my life with. I love you, Mr. Good, and don't you ever forget that."

Her statement gave Taz a tremendous attack of the guilts as he stared at Tari sleeping soundly right next to him in his bed. He climbed out of bed and went downstairs with the phone to his ear as he listened to Sacha talk. "Yeah, I love you too, Li'l Mama. I don't need you all stressed out behind this shit though. I'll deal with it, I promise. My seed needs to be stress-free while he's growing inside of you."

"Your seed needs you to be here when he or she comes out of this womb too, mister."

He laughed and said, "I know. Look, what you got planned for the day?"

"After I get dressed, I'm going over to Bob's house and have breakfast with him and Gwen. You wanna come?"

"Nah, I'm about to get with Keno and 'em so we can try and figure out what the fuck is crackin' with them fools that tried to blast me."

"So, you know who they are?"

"Not exactly, but I do have an idea. Give me a holla after you finished gettin' your eat on. And tell that nigga Bob I said to relax and don't be over there trippin'. We got this shit."

"Is it true that Tari saved you last night?"

Taz smiled and said, "Yeah, she spotted the fools first, pulled my strap from my back, pushed me to the side and started servin' them fools."

"Damn! That sounds like something that happens in the movies!"

"I know, huh? All right then, Li'l Mama, let me go so I can get dressed."

"Okay, baby. I'll call you in a couple of hours. I love you, Taz."

"I love you too, Li'l Mama. Bye," he said, and hung up the phone.

"Do you feel as guilty as I do?" Tari asked, standing behind Taz in the kitchen.

Taz jumped and yelled, "Damnit, Tee! Don't be creepin' up behind me like that! You scared the shit outta me!"

Tari laughed and said, "I'm sorry, scaredy cat! Damn!" She stepped toward the refrigerator and asked, "What do you want for breakfast?"

This shit is crazy! Here we are, standing in my kitchen, butt-ass naked like nothing was wrong with this picture, thought Taz. "Whatever you feel like puttin' together is cool. I'm 'bout to go take a shower and call up Keno."

"All right. You don't want to talk about last night, I assume."

He turned and faced Tari and said, "We did what we did because we will always be close like that. You know I still love you, Tee, and I will never stop loving you."

"But that was the last time, right?"

He smiled at her and said, "Yeah, that was it, baby."

Tari smiled and simply said, "Okay. I'll have something ready for us to eat by the time you finish with your shower." She then opened the refrigerator and bent over as she grabbed some food out of it.

Taz stared at her fat ass and shook his head as he left the kitchen. *Damn, she's fine as fuck!* he thought as if that was the first time he had ever seen her behind. He was still shaking his head as he walked up the stairs to his bedroom.

Clifford was sitting up in his bed talking to Tazneema, when someone called him on his cell phone. "Hold on for a minute, Neema. I need to answer my cell real quick."

"Just call me back after you're finished with your call, baby."

"Are you sure? I thought you didn't want me calling over there while Mama-Mama was around."

"I'll explain all of that when you call me back. Go on now," Tazneema said and hung up the phone.

He had a smile on his face as he hung up the phone and grabbed his cell phone. After flipping it open, he said, "Hello."

"What up, C-Baby?" asked H-Hop. "What you doin', cuz?"

"Just sitting here chillin'. What's up with you, loco?"

"Cuz, I was layin' here thinkin' 'bout them niggas last night. It ain't gon' be as easy as I thought it was gon' be to get at them niggas."

"I told you, cuz, them fools ain't to be taken lightly."

"But who was that bitch that was with them? If it wasn't for her, we had they ass!"

"I don't even know, loco. It damn sure wasn't Sacha. She looked like a fuckin' white girl, huh?"

"Yeah, she did. But ain't no snow bunny gon' be dumpin' like that. That bitch almost got us, cuz!"

Clifford laughed and said, "I know, loc. Don't trip. Let's lay back in the cut for minute. That nigga is bound to slip sooner or later."

"I don't know, cuz. That nigga's crew is solid. I think we might have to take that nigga hard. Do you know where that fool stay?"

"Nah, but I can find out. Give me a minute and I'll get back at ya. Tell that nigga Li'l Bomb I said to be patient. We'll get 'em, loc."

H-Hop laughed and said, "All right, cuz. I'll holla."

After Clifford hung up the phone he called Tazneema back at Mama-Mama's house. "Now, what's up with Mama-Mama letting me call the house now?"

"Well, you're still not on her favorite persons list, but she's accepted the fact that I love you, and no matter what, I'm going to be with you. So she's keeping her feelings to herself."

Clifford smiled after hearing that and said, "Hopefully she'll let me show her that I am a good person."

"Don't worry about it. Everything will be all right in time, baby. So, what are you getting into today?"

"Nothing much. I was getting ready to redo my resume so I can try to find me some employment."

"I'm so sorry that you lost your job behind this mess, baby. I wish I would have known that Sacha was going to get you fired. I would have stopped her."

"Don't worry about that. I'll be all right. How are you feeling?"

"Actually, I feel pretty good. I'm so tired of being cooped up in this house. I wish I could do something, but Mama-Mama ain't having none of that. The only time I can get some fresh air is when she lets me go outside to watch her work in her garden, or out back when she dumps some food scraps to the hogs in the hog pen."

"Don't worry, you'll be able to get out and about real soon. I can't wait either, because I'm so-o-o horny!"

Tazneema laughed and said, "Me too! You're going to be in trouble when I get a hold of that body of yours, baby."

"I love you, Tazneema Good."

"I love you too, Cliff. Don't you ever forget that."

"I won't."

By the time Taz and Tari finished eating, Keno, Bo-Pete, Red and Wild Bill had made it over to Taz's home. They were sitting in the den, thinking about the same thing—*What caused them to have a beef with the Hoover Crips?*

"Fuck it! Let's go get at them punk-ass niggas! They ain't nothin' but a bunch of wannabe L.A.-ass niggas!" yelled Wild Bill.

"Yeah, but some of those guys are brutal, Wild Bill," said Tari.

"Eight out of ten brutal men are straight cowards, Tee. They move with force when their numbers are deep. Them niggas ain't built for war for real," Keno said seriously.

"All right, check this shit out. Put some feelers out and see what we can come up with. Keno, you and Red get at Katrina and Paquita and see what they can find out for us. I don't like the fact that we're walkin' around this bitch in the blind. The sooner we find out what's what, the sooner we'll be able to deal with this shit," said Taz.

"What the fuck is it to find out? Them niggas got at us! Let's get right back at they ass!" screamed Bo-Pete.

"What you wanna do, Bo? Just go and blast them niggas up?" asked Red.

"You fuckin' right! If we don't make a move, all they're goin' to do is keep on gettin' at us until they eventually get lucky and pop one of us. I'm tellin' you, dog, we should take the offense and move on them niggas as soon as possible."

"You're right, Bo-Pete. Do them niggas still be over there on Lottie?" asked Taz.

"I guess. How the fuck would I know? But it don't fuckin' matter. Let's go huntin' and see what we can find."

"All right then, we'll move tonight. But today we're goin' to roll through the city and see exactly what we can find out. Cool?" asked Taz.

"I'm with it," said Bo-Pete.

"Me too," said Red.

"Ride or die, baby," replied Wild Bill.

"It is what it is," added Keno.

"Don't think you're leaving me out of this mess!" said Tari.

Shaking his head no, Taz said, "You gots to stay ready for Won's mission, Tee. We can't put that in jeopardy behind this bullshit. You done handled your business, so let us take care of these wannabe drive-by-ass niggas."

"Drive-by? Them clowns had assault rifles, Taz! They ain't playing, and they shouldn't be taken lightly. Go ahead and handle them, but do not for one second underestimate them. If you have to do them, then make sure that they're done," she said in a deadly tone.

Taz smiled at her and said, "Got'cha!"

Chapter Thirteen

Tazneema was horny, and she just couldn't take being away from Clifford any longer. So, after Mama-Mama went to bed for the night, she threw on a pair of sweatpants and a T-shirt, grabbed her purse, and sneaked out of the house. Since her car was still over Mama-Mama's house, it was easy for her to make her temporary escape. She climbed inside of her car and put the gearshift into neutral and pushed her Camry out of the driveway. Once she had her car out into the street, she jumped inside and started the ignition. She smiled as she pulled from in front of her grandmother's home. She pulled out her cell phone and dialed Clifford's number, praying that he was at home. When he answered his phone, she said, "Get ready for me, baby. I should be there in about twenty minutes or so."

"Stop playing with me, Neema! Are you serious?" he asked excitedly.

"Yep. I snuck out of the house. I won't be able to stay long 'cause you know Mama-Mama gets up before the crack of dawn. A couple of hours, tops, is all that we'll have."

Clifford smiled and said, "That's a lot of time, baby. Hurry up!"

Tazneema laughed and said, "I'm hurrying!"

As soon as the sun had set, Taz and the crew went hunting. Earlier they had found three different streets where the Hoover Crips were known to hang out, so Taz decided to get at all three locations. He and Keno were inside of Taz's Denali, while Bo-Pete, Red and Wild Bill were inside of Bo-Pete's Navigator. Their destination was the corner of Twenty-third Street and Lottie Avenue. There was a paint and body shop that the Hoovers were known to hang at.

As they drove by the auto body shop, Taz saw a couple of gang members standing in front of the shop, smoking and drinking some Olde English malt liquor. He smiled as they drove down to the next block and made a U-turn with Bo-Pete right behind them. When Taz pulled in front of the gang members, he rolled down the passenger's side window and Keno said, "Hey, homies, y'all want to play with the big dogs?"

"What you say, cuz?" asked one of the young Hoover Crips.

"If you wanna play with the big dogs, you gots to know how to get your man!" said Keno as he pointed his 9 mm at them and shot each one of the Crips twice in their midsections.

Taz pulled away from the curb and made a right turn back onto Twenty-third Street as if everything was completely normal.

Their next stop was a half a mile on Twenty-third Street and MLK. This time when Taz saw the Hoovers standing in a small group, he didn't pass by them by. He stopped right in front of them and jumped out of his truck, followed closely by Keno. They didn't say a word as they started shooting every one of the gang members in their sights. The Crips that were lucky enough not to be hit by Taz and Keno on sight really weren't that lucky, because they ran right into more bullets from Bo-Pete, Red and Wild Bill.

Just as suddenly as the shooting began, it ended. Death was all around the corner of Twenty-third Street and MLK as Taz and the crew sped away onto their third and final destination.

Clifford and Tazneema were lying next to one another, bathed in their own sweat and completely out of breath. After Tazneema had made it over to Clifford's house, they made love until they felt as if they were going to pass out.

Clifford turned onto his side and asked, "Are you all right, baby? I lost control of myself. I hope I didn't hurt you."

She smiled and said, "I'm fine, baby. I have to admit that I kinda forgot about my injuries. I'm sore as hell. I think my shoulders going to be killing me in the morning."

"We shouldn't have done this, Neema. I need you back in tip-top shape. I'm sorry, baby."

"Would you be quiet with all of that? I'm a big girl, Cliff. I'll be all right. Now, let me go take a shower so I can get back to Mama-Mama's before she wakes up and realizes that I'm gone," she said as she climbed out of the bed.

Clifford smiled as he watched her sexy body sway back and forth as she walked into the bathroom. He relaxed back on his pillow, completely drained. *That girl is something else!* he thought to himself as he closed his eyes.

Ten minutes later, Tazneema came out of the bathroom wrapped in one of Clifford's towels. She smiled when she saw that he had fallen asleep. Just as she had finished getting dressed, the telephone rang.

Clifford reached for the phone on the night-stand without ever opening his eyes and said, "Hello."

"Them niggas is gettin' at us, cuz!" screamed H-Hop.

"Wha—what are you talking about, Hop?" Clifford asked groggily.

"Cuz, them fools just finished blastin' up two homies on Twenty-third and Lottie! And then they served about seven of the homies on the corner of Twenty-third and Martin Luther King! After that, they caught six more of the homies slippin' on Thirty-sixth at one of the homeboy's bud spots. I'm tellin' you, loc, them niggas are on a fuckin' warpath!"

"How the fuck did they know to get at us? Them fools shouldn't have a clue about who put that work in!"

"Cuz, all I'm tellin' you is that the homies are mad as fuck! We got about twelve homies shot the fuck up!"

"Did anyone get smoked?" Clifford asked as he climbed out of his bed.

"Yeah, the first two homies that got hit on Lottie are dead. Them fools dropped them right on the spot. I'm tellin' you, loc, we gots to hurry up and get at them niggas! They ain't playin', cuz!"

"Calm down, cuz! Where are you now?

"I'm at the pad. When I heard about all of that fuckin' bustin', I got the fuck outta dodge," H-Hop stated wisely.

"I'm about to get dressed and come scoop you, loc. Give me about twenty minutes."

"All right, cuz," H-Hop said, and hung up.

After Clifford hung up the phone, he didn't notice the funny expression on Tazneema's face. He jumped out of his bed and threw on a pair of jeans and a T-shirt. As he was tying his tennis shoes, Tazneema asked him, "Is there something wrong, baby?"

"Huh? No . . . uh . . . kind of, Neema. A few of my friends have been hurt tonight. I really need to go check on them."

"You're in a gang, Cliff?"

"Huh? Baby, that's a long story, but to answer your question, not really is the best I can tell at this time. Gang-banging is a part of my past, though. I guess it will always be a part of me. I worked real damn hard to stay away from that part of my life, but here lately it seems like something or some unknown force is trying to pull me back to 'cripping.'"

Shaking her head, Tazneema said, "No one can make you do something that you don't want to do, Cliff. It's solely on you, baby. If your heart's not in it, please don't destroy yourself by wasting your time with that craziness."

He smiled as he stepped into her embrace and said, "Don't worry, baby. I won't. I'm just going over to show some support to my people and their families. Go on back to Mama-Mama's, and I'll give you a call in the morning."

After sharing an intense kiss, Tazneema smiled and said, "I'll be back over here tomorrow night at the same time, 'kay?"

He returned her smile and said, "Good!"

After leaving the bloody scene on Thirty-sixth Street, Taz called Bo-Pete on his cell and told him, "Dog, let's split up. We'll get at y'all in the morning. If you have any problems before you make it to the pad, get at me. If I don't hear from either of y'all, then I'll know everything is everything."

"That's straight," Bo-Pete replied before he closed his cell phone.

Keno smiled and said, "That should show them punk-ass niggas that we are not to be fucked with."

"Yeah, it should, G, but I got a funny feelin' this shit has just gotten started," Taz said seriously.

"What makes you say that, dog? They ain't gon' want to fuck with no niggas they know ain't playin' with they ass."

"If that's the case, then why in the fuck did they get at us in the first place? I'm tellin' you, homie, somethin' just ain't right about all of this shit. I can't put my finger on it, but somethin' just ain't right."

"Everything will be everything, my nigga. Watch. You'll see. Now, drop me off at the pad so I can go scoop Katrina and tap that ass a li'l bit," Keno said, and they both started laughing.

Chapter Fourteen

The next morning, every news channel and newspaper in the Oklahoma City area was focused on the slayings of the night before. Local preachers were seen on television yelling about this sudden gang violence and how it has to stop before the black community is completely destroyed.

Taz watched the news as he sipped on some orange juice. He was waiting for the crew to arrive for their daily workout. Even though they had slacked up lately, he felt that it was time for them to get back to their normal routine. This sudden beef with the Hoovers was really bothering him. He wanted to make sure that they were at the top of their game for this unexpected and unwanted drama. He wasn't trying to go to anyone of his homeboys' funeral, and he damn sure wasn't trying to go to his own.

Sacha called him just before the crew arrived, and started rambling on about the same thing he was watching on television. "Isn't it sad the way these youngsters are out there killing each other, baby?" she asked.

"It is what it is, Li'l Mama. I'm not really concerned with that shit right now. I gots enough on my plate as it is," Taz answered irritably.

"What's wrong with you this morning? Why is your attitude all funky?"

"I just told you, I got a lot on my plate. Why are you trippin'? Look, let me go. The homies just pulled up, and we're about to work out. After I finish with that, I have to go check on some of the IHOPs and some of my rental houses."

"Okay, give me a call when you have some time," she said then hung up the phone.

Since Taz was doing so well financially, he hardly paid much attention to any of the small food chains that he owned in Oklahoma City. He basically let his attorneys and managers take care of everything. He took pride in the fact that between himself, Keno, and the rest of the crew, they all owned a nice percentage of rental property in the Oklahoma City area—over one hundred homes apiece to be exact. Each member of the crew cleared close to two hundred thousand dollars yearly off their rental properties, so money was not an issue with any of them. Unfortunately, the Hoover Crips were.

Once the crew had made it down to Taz's built-in gym and began to warm up and stretch, Taz said, "I'm tellin' y'all, we're goin' to have to watch ourselves now that we've made our move against them niggas."

"Dog, fuck them fools! They ain't gon' try no stupid shit," replied Bo-Pete as he stretched next to Red.

"Yeah, after the demonstration we gave them niggas, they're probably somewhere licking their wounds," Wild Bill said as he bench-pressed some light weight to loosen up his arms.

"Dog, we can't be underestimating these young niggas. Don't forget that they got at us first. Just because we gave them a li'l somethin' doesn't mean that they won't try to get back. All I'm sayin' is to stay on your toes when you're out and about. It's been a long time since we had any beef in town. I ain't tryin' to lose none of y'all. Feel me?"

"Yeah, we feel you, nigga. Now shut the fuck up so we can get our workout on!" Keno said, and everyone started laughing.

Taz smiled and said, "Fuck you, clown!"

They then started their intense workout for the day.

"I'm tellin' you, loc, we gots to get at them niggas!" yelled Li'l Bomb.

"I know, my nigga. That's why I'm trying to find out where that nigga Taz rests his head. A while back I got his tag number, so I gave it to a partner of mine who works for the Highway Patrol. I'm waiting on him to get back at me now. If he can give me that nigga's hookup, we'll be able to get at him at his pad. So relax, cuz. We're going to get them," Clifford said confidently.

"Relax? Cuz, them niggas smoked my nigga, Li'l Lights! If I wouldn't have went back into that shop, I would've been right out there with Li'l Light and C-Rag! They could have got me too! I'm tellin' you, cuz, I ain't really with this waitin' shit!"

"So, what are you going to do? Just ride around the town to see if you can get lucky and catch one of them niggas? I know you're hurting, loco. We all are. You're just going to have to remain calm until we can get something solid to move on."

"Fuck this shit, cuz! I'm outta here! Hit me when y'all know somethin', H-Hop," Li'l Bomb said as he left H-Hop's apartment.

"This is the fucked up part of the game, my nigga. You remember how it goes. Now we have to sit back and bury some more Hoovers. And that shit ain't even cool, cuz," said H-Hop as he lit a cigarette.

"Yeah, I remember, loc. How could I ever forget some shit like that? Believe me, I can't wait until we get them niggas, cuz. I want them dead more than anybody else," Clifford said seriously.

After Taz and the crew had finished their workout, they all went upstairs to Taz's kitchen and raided the refrigerator.

Red pulled some steaks from the freezer and threw them into the microwave to defrost them. "Y'all tryin' to eat some steaks or what?" he asked as he stepped back toward the refrigerator.

"Yeah, hook me up one of those bad boys," Keno said as he sipped on a bottle of Evian water.

"Yeah, me too," added Wild Bill.

"Nah, I'm good. I'm goin' to see if Sacha is down to do lunch. I'm not tryin' to be around you clowns all damn day," Taz said with a smile on his face as he grabbed the phone and gave Sacha a call. When she answered the phone, he asked, "Are you busy, Li'l Mama?"

"Not really. I just finished a meeting with my paralegal. What's up?"

"Do you want to have lunch with me today, or are you still salty with me, boo?"

She laughed and said, "It seems as if I'm always going to be mad with you, Mister Taz. I'm kind of getting used to it. I'd love to have lunch with my boo. What do you have in mind?"

"Let's go get something to eat at the new spot in Bricktown. I think it's called The Daiquiri Zone. I heard they got the bomb hot wings. I know you can't do no drinkin', but Tari told me that their daiquiris are pretty good too."

"That sounds like a winner to me, baby. I might not be able to drink any alcohol, but I can still have me a virgin daiquiri. Do you want me to meet you there, or are you going to come and pick up?"

"Yeah, I'll come scoop you in about thirty minutes. I just finished working out, so let me jump in the shower real quick and I'll be on my way."

"All right, baby, I'll be waiting."

Taz ran upstairs and took a quick shower. After he was finished, he put on a pair of loose-fitting Azure jeans and a fresh white tee. He then grabbed his new Jordan's and slipped them onto his feet. After hitting himself with a few spurts of his D&G for Men cologne, he grabbed his 9 mm pistol and slipped it into the small of his back. He turned and went to his dresser and grabbed his diamond Cartier wristwatch and his long 220-gram platinum chain with a diamond-encrusted Jesus piece and put it around his neck. Last but not least, he put his platinum and diamond grill inside of his mouth. He smiled a sparkling smile and said, "Lookin' like a million bucks, baby!"

By the time Taz came back down stairs, his homeboys were busy munching on their steaks that Red had prepared for them. When Keno saw that Taz was all spiffy he said, "Damn, nigga! You just goin' to get somethin' to eat! Why you get so clean on a nigga?"

Taz laughed and said, "Fool, I'm eating with wifey. She likes it when a nigga is lookin' and smellin' good. Stop hatin', clown!"

"Fuck you, nigga!"

"Look though. After I finish eating, I'm goin' to go check on some of my rental houses on the South Side. What y'all got up for the day?"

"I'm goin' to go kick it with that nigga Bob," Red said from the other side of the kitchen counter.

"I think I'm gon' hit the mall up and do me a li'l shoppin'. It's been a minute. I need me a few new outfits," replied Keno.

"I'm tired as a muthafucka. I'm goin' to the pad and lay it down," said Bo-Pete.

"Me too," added Wild Bill.

"All right then, lock up the spot when y'all bounce, and make sure you messy niggas clean up y'alls mess. I'm outta here."

"Dog, have you heard anything from that nigga, Won yet?" asked Keno as he wiped A-l Steak Sauce from his lips.

"Nah, I ain't heard shit from that fool. He'll holla when it's time though. You better believe that."

"Yeah, I know."

"All right then, my niggas, I'm out," Taz said as he turned and left the kitchen.

By the time he arrived in front of the office building that housed the offices of Whitney & Johnson, Sacha was standing outside looking gorgeous yet businesslike in a brown pantssuit. Her shapely figure could be seen, even though her pants were somewhat loose-fitting. She had her long, jet-black hair tied up in a bun. Taz smiled as he pulled in front of her and quickly jumped out of his car and opened the door for his fiancée. She smiled as she climbed inside of the car.

After he had gotten back inside of the Bentley, Sacha asked, "What made you bring the Bentley out today, baby?"

He shrugged his shoulders and said, "I don't know. I was in the mood to roll around with my Li'l Mama in a li'l luxury, I guess." Truthfully, the real reason he chose to drive one of his other vehicles was that he didn't want to take the chance of being seen by any of them Hoover niggas in his truck. He was not about to let anything happen to Sacha. Not if he could help it.

They arrived at The Daiquiri Zone and enjoyed a lunch of hot wings and French fries. Sacha's appetite shocked Taz as he watched her totally devour a plateful of hot wings. "Damn, Li'l Mama! You kinda hungry, huh?"

After wiping hot sauce from her lips, she smiled and said, "You know I'm eating for two, baby."

He laughed and said, "Yeah, I know!" He sipped his strawberry daiquiri. *I normally don't drink sweet fruity type drinks, but this one tasted pretty good,* he thought to himself as he stared at his fiancée.

Sacha noticed him staring and asked, "What?"

He smiled and said, "I want you, Li'l Mama. Do you have to go back to work? Or can you take the rest of the day off?"

She smiled seductively and said, "I've already taken the rest of the day off, baby. I was thinking the same thing as soon as I got off the phone with you."

"Then hurry up and finish off the rest of those wings, so we can go to your spot and work up another appetite!"

Chapter Fifteen

Keno and Katrina were relaxing on Keno's bed, engaging in a little pillow talk. Katrina had just finished sexing the hell out of Keno, and he was as content as ever. She smiled lazily, stretched and said, "I asked around about what's been up with them Hoover dudes, like you asked me to, baby."

"Yeah? Did you find out anything?" Keno asked as he reached and grabbed a Black and Mild cigar off of his nightstand.

"Do you know a guy by the name of C-Baby? He's an original 107 Hoover. He was one of the first ones that started Hoover in the city back in the days. Them L.A. Hoovers liked him and put him in charge of organizing the rest of the guys in the city."

"Is that right? Nah, I don't know no nigga like that. Why? What's up with him?"

"I don't know, but there has to be a connection somehow. Remember that guy that Taz shot in front of the club a few months back?"

"Yeah."

"He was from Hoover."

"What? You bullshittin'!" he asked excitedly.

"Uh-uh, I'm serious. As a matter a fact, he was real tight with C-Baby back in the days."

"So you think this C-Baby nigga has the beef with us?"

"I'm just saying, your boy did kill his homeboy. That has to be it. Why else would the Hoovers be trying to get at Taz? Y'all ain't on no gang-bangin' shit."

"Real talk, baby, that's good lookin'," Keno said as he grabbed the phone and quickly dialed Taz's home number. When Taz answered the phone Keno repeated everything Katrina had just told him and said, "That's got to be the reason, my nigga. You took that fool, C-Baby's dog. And since he's supposed to be an O.G. over there, he has to get back at ya."

Shaking her head no, Katrina said, "Uh-uh, it's not C-Baby whose getting at y'all. He don't even come around no more. He's some big-time lawyer now downtown at Whitney & Johnson law firm. He has the rest of them Hoovers all fired up to look at y'all 'cause he don't get down like that no more. At least that's what I heard."

Taz heard what Katrina had just told Keno and asked, "What did she just say, dog?"

"She said that that nigga C-Baby ain't the one who actually put in the work 'cause he's some big-time lawyer now."

"How the fuck can an O.G. Hoover Crip become an attorney?" Taz wondered aloud.

"Maybe the nigga found Jesus and changed his ways or some shit. How the fuck would I know?"

"She did say that that clown worked at Whitney & Johnson, huh?"

"Yeah. Why?"

"Think about it, nigga. Sacha's a partner at that firm, remember?"

"That's right! I forgot about that shit, dog! This shit is hittin' too fuckin' close to home, Taz. What the fuck is up?"

"I don't know, my nigga, but I'm about to find out. I'll get at ya in a li'l bit. Tell your girl that I said good lookin'."

"Fa' sho," Keno said, and hung up. He then turned to Katrina and said, "You done good, baby, and just for that, I'm gon' break you off some more of this good dick."

She smiled and said, "M-m-m! Is there anything else you want me to find out for you, baby?"

"Not right now, mommy, but you can find your way back on top of this!" he said as he held his erect penis in his hand.

***

Back at Taz's house, he was wracking his brains trying to figure out how the pieces to this puzzle fit. All of a sudden it came to him. "Nah! Hell nah! I know that nigga didn't!" he screamed as he grabbed the phone and called Sacha on her cell phone. When she answered, he asked her, "Where are you, Li'l Mama?"

"I'm on my way home. I just left Bob and Gwen at Bob's house. What's up, baby"?"

"Tell me somethin', Li'l Mama. How well did you know that nigga, Cliff when y'all were goin' out and shit?"

"What do you mean?"

"Did he tell you anything about his past?"

Sacha thought about Taz's question for a minute while she drove, and then she said, "Now that you mention it, not really. Why? What's goin' on, Taz?"

"Baby, you're not goin' to believe this shit, but I got a funny feelin' that the nigga Cliff is the reason them Crip niggas tried to get at me at the club the other night."

"*What?*"

Taz quickly explained to her what Katrina had told Keno. Afterward he said, "But how could that nigga have been caught up with the Hoovers, and then become an attorney and shit?"

Sacha pulled into her driveway, cut off her car and said, "That's easy, baby. As long as he was never convicted of a felony, there would be nothing in his way to stop him from becoming an attorney."

"Well, I'll be damn! And to think I was actually thinkin' 'bout lettin' that clown-ass nigga make it!"

"What are you talking about, Taz?"

"Don't you see it, Li'l Mama? That nigga Cliff is C-Baby! He had that nigga I smoked in front of the club try to rob us. But, on the real, he wasn't just goin' to rob us; he was supposed to smoke me! He wanted to get me out of the way so he could get to you!"

"Come on, baby. That's a little far-fetched, don't you think?"

"Think about it. Cliff's friend from back in the day tries to rob us, and I smoke his ass. Months later, some Hoover niggas try to dump on me at the same fuckin' club. I don't believe in coincidences, Li'l Mama. It all makes fuckin' sense. That nigga tried to have me smoked! He knew that he had to get me out of the way to be able to get at you!" Taz yelled excitedly.

"Calm down, baby. All you have is circumstantial evidence. You still don't have any solid proof against him."

He smiled and said, "There goes that lawyer in you talkin', Li'l Mama. I have all of the proof I fuckin' need. That nigga's a dead man now for real!"

Sacha climbed out of her car, walked inside of her home and said, "Baby, what about Tazneema?"

"What about Tazneema? What about *me*? That fool has tried to take me out—not once, but twice! You want proof, Li'l Mama? All right, I'll give you some fuckin' proof. What's that nigga's telephone number?"

"Why?"

"I'm gon' call him and ask for C-Baby. If he doesn't acknowledge that he's in fact C-Baby, I give you my word, on MiMi's grave, that I'll leave this shit alone and never bring it up again."

"Deal! But what are you going to say if he does or doesn't acknowledge you?"

"I'll just hang up the phone. My number's unlisted, and it won't show on his caller ID."

Sacha smiled and said, "Okay, his number is 427-7023."

Taz clicked over and quickly dialed the number that she had just given him, and then clicked back over to Sacha while the phone rang. The telephone rang three times before it was answered. When Cliff picked up the line, Taz made his voice sound deeper than normal and said, "Can I speak to C-Baby?"

Clifford hesitated momentarily, and then said, "This is him. Who's this?"

Taz hung up the phone in his face and yelled, "I told you! I fuckin' told you, Li'l Mama! That nigga is fuckin' dead!"

Sacha sat down at her dining room table and said, "Shit!"

After Clifford hung up the phone he said, "Fuck! That was Taz! That nigga has figured out my ties with the homies! He's going to try to get at me for real now!" He picked up the phone and called H-Hop. When H-Hop answered the phone, Clifford said, "Cuz, my peoples wasn't able to get a line on that nigga's pad from his tag number. It came back to his mother's house out in Spencer. We have to get them niggas, loc. I think he's about to try and make a move on me."

"What makes you say that, cuz?" asked H-Hop.

Clifford told him about the call he had just received, and said, "That nigga didn't know me by C-Baby, cuz. He has done his homework, loc, and figured shit out."

"How you wanna play this shit, cuz?"

"Whichever way we play this shit, we gots to play to win, 'cause that nigga's going to come at us real hard."

Chapter Sixteen

Pitt was sitting inside of his office with a content smile on his face. He was about to get at whomever this Gee person was, and after that, he was confident that he would be able to get all of the proof he needed to hang Won's ass. There was a knock at his door and he yelled, "Come on in!"

A short white woman entered his office, followed by Leo and Tru. She smiled at Pitt and asked, "How are you doing, Pitt?"

"Just fine, Vixen, just fine. Did you bring everything you're going to need for this one?"

With a nod of her head, she said, "Yes, I have everything right here. All you have to do is keep this guy on the line for at least thirty seconds, and I'll get a direct line on him. I'll only be able to hold onto him for thirty to thirty-five seconds though. So it's important that you apprehend him as soon as you can, or we'll have to go through this all over again."

"Don't worry, I won't miss. Leo and Tru here are going to make sure that they get him on the first try," Pitt said confidently as he smiled at his two heavy hitters.

Leo was a Samoan who stood a little over six foot, and was very muscular. He kept his long hair pulled back into a tight ponytail. Just by looking into his eyes one could tell that he was not to be fucked with. Pitt liked to refer to Leo as his "personal torpedo" because when Leo hit, he hit hard and fast and caused a tremendous amount of damage.

Though Tru was older than Leo, he was equally as dangerous. He stood at six foot two inches, and was small compared to his partner. His body language made people feel as if he was harmless, but that was not true at all. Tru had executed more men than anyone else in Pitt's camp. And most of his victims died by his hands. Pitt thought that was strange at first, but he quickly understood that Tru got some kind of crazy rush when he killed a man or woman with his bare hands. Pitt really didn't give a damn how the work was completed, just as long as the job was done effectively.

Pitt sat back in his leather chair and said, "All right, Vee, do you."

Vixen smiled and pulled out a small laptop computer. After she turned it on, she started typing what looked like a thousand words a minute. Her fingers were a blur to one's vision as she typed at a superspeed. After about six or seven minutes of this, she finally stopped and said, "I'm ready, Pitt. What is the telephone number?"

Pitt grabbed the white slip of paper that Brenda gave him and read the number off it. When he was finished, he said, "Tru, you and Leo head on downstairs to the truck. I'll call y'all and give you directions on where to go get this nigga as soon as Vixen gives me his hookup. Make sure that he remains breathing, Leo. He's no good to me dead."

Leo smiled and said, "Don't trip, Pitt. I got you."

After Leo and Tru left the office, Vixen tapped some more keys on her laptop and said, "All right, this is how this works. I have plugged my laptop to your phone here, and all you have to do is call this guy and keep him on the phone for at least thirty seconds like I said. Once you hang up, I'll have a line on all of his movements as long as he has his cell phone on his person."

"I'm telling you, Vee, this is some crazy shit. This shit is like that TV show, 24 on Fox. Do you ever watch that shit?"

Vixen smiled and shook her head no.

Pitt started laughing and said, "You know what? You're my 'Chloe'!"

ou're what?" she asked with a smile on her
ce.

"Chloe. You know, the computer geek broad
who saves Jack's ass all of the time. She's the
best at that shit. As a matter a fact, I think she
did some shit like this before for Jack."

Vixen laughed then said, "Okay, Pitt. Are you
ready or what?"

He lit one of his hand-rolled Cuban cigars and
said, "Yep, I'm ready if you are."

"Make the call," she said as she focused on her
laptop.

Pitt dialed the number to the cell phone of the
mysterious man named Gee. The cell was answered on the third ring. "Hello?"

"Yo, let me speak to Gee," Pitt said in a deep
tone of voice.

"Who's this?"

"Is this Gee?" Pitt asked as he took a quick
peek at his platinum watch by Jacob the Jeweler.

"Yeah, this is Gee. Now, who the fuck am I
talkin' to?"

"Check this out, clown. My name is Pitt, and I
want to know who put you onto my girl Brenda.
If you give me this information, I'd highly ap-
preciate it."

Gee started laughing and said, "Yeah, I bet you
would, dog. But check this out. Fuck you, nigga!

You've wasted your fuckin' time gettin' at me, partna!"

"I'm sorry you feel that way," Pitt said as he watched as Vixen gave him thumbs-up, indicating that she had what she needed. He smiled and told Gee, "I guess I'll be seeing you then, my man."

"Whatever, Mr. Big Man!" Gee said as he started laughing and hung up the phone in Pitt's ear.

After Pitt hung up the phone, he stared at Vixen as she tapped furiously on her laptop. After she finished, she turned the screen toward him and said, "Right now he's over in Fairfield, out by Travis Air Force Base. He's not moving, so I assume he's at his home right now. Go on and tell your boys to head out toward Fairfield. I'll have his exact address within the next five minutes."

"You mean you can tell me exactly where he lives at?" asked a shock Pitt.

Vixen nodded. "Sure can. You'd be surprised how much I can do with this bad boy right here," she said as she lovingly rubbed the side of her laptop.

Pitt started laughing and yelled, "You *are* my Chloe!" He then called Leo and Tru and told them to head out to Fairfield, which was maybe twenty minutes outside of Oakland. "Gee, you're

about to get the surprise of your fucking life!"
he said as he smiled and inhaled deeply on his
Cuban cigar.

Won had become slightly concerned. *Cash Flo'
and Pitt should have called for a meet by now,* he
thought as he walked around his luxurious home.
He stepped out onto his sun deck overlooking
the Pacific and smiled. For as long as he could
remember, he had lived the good life. His hunger
for power was what kept him motivated to have
more. Once he obtained complete control over
The Network, there would be no stopping him. It
would be as if he owned a nice chunk of the world.
"Come on, Cash Flo', don't change up on me now,
you old bastard!" he said aloud as he turned and
went back inside of his home.

Back in Oakland, Pitt was on the telephone
talking to Leo on his cell phone. "The address is
2671 North Williams Avenue. Vixen just told me
that he's still at that address right now. How far
are y'all from Fairfield now?"

"We've just made it in. We'll be at his place
within the next ten minutes," Leo said, and gave
the address to Tru.

"All right, call me after y'all got that nigga," Pitt said, and hung up the phone. "All right, Chloe, how much do I owe you for your services this time?"

Vixen smiled and said, "The usual, Pitt. But shouldn't you wait until your boys have grabbed your man?"

"Nah, they'll handle everything. You can go on and have some fun. As a matter a fact, I'm throwing in an extra thousand for your superb work," he said as he passed her an envelope with eleven thousand dollars inside of it.

Vixen accepted the money from him and began to disconnect her equipment from Pitt's telephone line. After she had all of her stuff together, she said, "You know where to find me if you need me, Pitt."

"That I do, babe. Take care of yourself," he said as he watched her leave his office. Just as he reclined in his chair his cell phone rang. "Hello."

"What's going on with you, old boy?" asked Cash Flo'.

"Everything is just fine up here in Northern Cali, baby. What's up with you down there in the South?"

"I'm sitting here wondering why haven't I heard anything from you. But since you sound so fucking happy, I guess it's safe to assume that everything is going the way you want it to."

h, you can say that. I'm waiting on a call
ab.... speak to confirm that I got that nigga who
paid my people to cross me. Once I have him, it
won't be long before I give you a call so you can
green light that nigga Won."

"I'll be waiting," Cash Flo' said, and hung up
the phone.

Just as Pitt closed his cell phone, the phone
on his desk started ringing. He glanced at the
number on the caller ID and smiled as he picked
up the receiver and said, "Tell me that you got
his ass."

Leo smiled and said, "Yeah, we got him. Tru
just put him inside of the truck."

"All right, you know where to take him. I'll
meet y'all there."

"Cool," Leo calmly replied.

After speaking with Leo, Pitt jumped out of
his chair and grabbed his suit jacket. He had a
huge smile on his face as he left his office. He
went down to the underground parking area
and jumped into his Jaguar, and sped out of the
parking lot.

It took him under ten minutes to make it to
East Oakland. He pulled into the driveway of a
house that looked as if it had seen better days.
The windows were boarded up, and the grass
looked as if it had been scorched for years.

Pitt's Jaguar looked totally out of place in this neighborhood as he climbed out of it and walked toward the front door of the broken-down home. He pulled out his keys, unlocked the front door and quickly stepped inside.

Though the house was a boarded-up wreck on the outside, the inside was a completely different story. Inside of the living room sat a fifty-five-inch plasma screen television equipped with a DVD player. To the far right of the living room was a comfortable-looking sectional sofa. It wasn't all that plush, but it was definitely comfortable. Pitt sat down on the sofa and pulled out his cell phone and called Leo. "Where y'all at?" he asked when Leo answered his cell.

"We're turning onto the street now. I see your car in the driveway right now," replied Leo.

"Good," Pitt said and closed his cell. He went to the front door and watched as Leo pulled into the driveway and parked his truck behind his Jag. Since the sun had already set, it was dark enough for no one to really pay any attention to Leo and Tru as they walked Gee inside of the boarded-up home in handcuffs.

Once they had him inside of the house, Pitt smiled and said, "Hi, Gee. My name is Pitt. I'm the guy you got real fly with earlier. I want you to know that what you're about to go through will be very very painful—that is if you choose not to cooperate with us. If you do cooperate, then your death will be swift. Either way, you are going to die today. So, the choice is yours on how you go out. Do you understand what I'm saying, Gee?"

Gee, a tall, dark-skinned man, smiled and showed a mouthful of bright white teeth and said, "Since I'm dying regardless, I think I'd rather go out the hard way." He shrugged his shoulders and continued, "I'm kinda funny like that. I've never been with taking the easy way out, ya know what I'm sayin'?"

Pitt smiled and said, "I can accept that. But you are going to tell me what I need to know."

"That remains to be seen, Mr. Big Man!" Gee replied arrogantly.

Pitt sighed heavily and then told Leo and Tru, "All right, you two, get to work." He then went and sat back down on the sofa and watched as his men began to viciously torture Gee.

Chapter Seventeen

"I'm tellin' you, Tee, I should have been taken that punk-ass clown out the game! That nigga is actually tryin' to get at me! That fool really doesn't know who he's fuckin' with!" yelled Taz.

"Obviously he does, Taz. If he didn't, he would not have tried to get at you in the first place," Tari replied logically.

"I bet you that that punk-ass nigga wasn't even at the club that night. It was probably some of his li'l homeboys. He don't have no heart like that."

"How do you know that, Taz? There were four of them that night. One of them could have been him. You were on the ground, remember?"

Taz smiled and said, "Fuck you, Tee!"

Tari laughed and said, "I didn't mean it like that, silly. I meant that he could have been there, you know."

"Yeah, but I doubt it. But, look, I gots to have that nigga, and I mean like yesterday. Until I do, I'm makin' sure that the homies stay out of the way."

"Just remember to use your head, Taz. Don't let your emotions control you on this shit."

"I won't."

"I spoke with Won the other day."

"Yeah? What's up with him?"

"I don't know. He sounded sort of strange to me. I don't think things are going the way he planned them to. If that's the case, then he's in a real funky mood."

"I wouldn't know shit about that one. I've never been around him when shit ain't goin' his way."

Tari laughed and said, "Well, I have, and believe me, it's not a pretty sight."

"Oh, well! He'll get it together. You just make sure that you're ready when he does."

"I stay ready, Taz," she said seriously.

"Good. Now, let me roll. I got some shit to check on."

"Be careful out there, Taz."

"I will. Bye!" After hanging up with her, he called Sacha and asked, "Are you ready, baby? It's Friday night, and I'm tryin' to have a pleasurable evening with my Li'l Mama."

"Umm . . . Taz, baby, I kinda invited Bob and Gwen to join us for dinner," Sacha said hesitantly.

Taz laughed and said, "You *kinda* invited them, huh? How can you kinda invite someone out with us, Li'l Mama?"

"You know what I mean! Stop that, baby! They've been cooped up inside of Bob's house since he got back from New York. I thought it would be fun for them if they came and had dinner with us. Are you mad at me, baby?" she asked sweetly.

"Don't even try it, Li'l Mama! That sweet shit ain't gon' make everything all good. On the real though, nah, I ain't mad at ya. I haven't seen my nigga since he made it back anyway. With all of this drama goin' on, I've been too caught up. I'm on my way over, so please be ready when I get there. I'm not tryin' to be sittin' there for forever waitin' on you to finish gettin' dressed."

"I'm not even going to respond to that comment, mister! Bye!"

Taz smiled as he hung up the phone, grabbed his keys and went into his four-car garage. He jumped into his Bentley and hit the garage door opener. As he was pulling out of the garage he saw Bo-Pete's Navigator pulling into his circular driveway. He stopped, climbed out of his car and walked toward Bo-Pete's truck. "What up, my niggas?" he asked Bo-Pete and Wild Bill once he made it to the driver's side of the Navigator.

"Ain't shit. Bored as hell, really. We just came over here to see what you had poppin' for the night," said Bo-Pete.

"I'm on my way to go have dinner with Sacha, Gwen and Bob. What? Y'all tryin' to tag along?"

"Fuck nah! We might as well hit the club and have some drinks," Wild Bill said from the passenger's seat.

"Might as well. We ain't got shit else to do," replied Bo-Pete.

"Dog, why don't y'all get with Red and Keno if y'all gon' hit the club up? You know shit is too hot right now. I don't want them Hoover niggas to have any action at gettin' at any of us."

"First off, fuck them fools, G! And, second, Keno and Red are doing the same thing you and Bob are doing. They're spending time with their broads. Don't worry about us, G. We'll be straight. Believe me, when we walk out that bitch, we'll have the straps in our hands cocked and locked!" Bo-Pete said confidently.

"All right, but make sure that you hit me after y'all leave the club."

Wild Bill started laughing and said, "Look at this nigga, all worried and shit! Don't sweat it, my nigga. We gots this."

Taz laughed and said, "Fuck you two niggas! I'm out!" He turned and walked back to his car.

Just like Taz figured, when he made it over to Sacha's house she was still in the process of getting dressed. "Damn, Li'l Mama! Why you always got to do me like this? I told you I didn't feel like waiting forever for you to get ready."

Sacha smiled as she applied the last of her makeup. She came out of the bathroom and said, "You can't rush a woman when she's getting dressed, Taz. That's not polite."

"Polite? Whoever said I was a polite nigga? You better bring your ass on before you get left!"

"O-o-o-h! I like it when you're all tough and demanding with me!" she said as she grabbed her Chanel purse.

Taz smiled and had to admit that his fiancée was looking real damn good. She was wearing the hell out of a sexy black-and-gray dress by Prada, with matching gray pumps. Her hair was hanging loosely past her bare shoulders just the way he liked it. Her cleavage was looking edible to him. "We need to gon' and bounce before I end up changin' our plans for the evening," he said as he stared at the long split that went straight up the middle of her dress.

She smiled and said, "I'll take that as a compliment. Come on, silly. I'm ready."

Clifford was on the phone talking to Taznee-ma, when he got a call from H-Hop on his cell phone. "Hold on, baby," he told her, and then answered his other phone. "What up, cuz?"

"Since we haven't had any luck finding them niggas, me and Li'l Bomb are about to go post up at that club and see if them niggas pop up again. You tryin' to roll, cuz?" asked H-Hop.

"I don't think they'll show, but fuck it, cuz! I ain't got nothing else to get into for the night. I'll be over there in about twenty minutes. It's early, so I know those fools won't be there yet—that is if they come out."

"All right, cuz, see you in a li'l bit."

Clifford grabbed the phone as he set his cell phone on the table, and told Tazneema, "Looks like I'm on my way out, baby."

"Where are you going?" Tazneema asked jealously.

He laughed and said, "I'm about to go have a few drinks with some lawyers I know from another firm. You know, network a little. I am trying to get another job, remember?"

"Oh. I thought you had a hot date all of a sudden. You know I was about to tell Mama-Mama I gots to go stop my man from being naughty!"

They both laughed at her joke. "You don't ever have to worry about anything like that, Neema. I'm yours and yours only for as long as you want me."

"Then that means you're mine forever, Cliff."

He laughed and said, "So be it, baby. Give me a call on my cell a little later if you want. You can come on over, and we can cuddle for a little while."

"Cuddle? If I sneak out of this house, I'm not coming way over to your house just to cuddle. I'm coming to get me some, boy!"

He laughed and said, "You are crazy, girl! I love you!"

"I love you more. I'll give you a call later. Bye!" she said and hung up.

Clifford went into his bedroom and put on a pair of black jeans and a blue sweatshirt, and grabbed his car keys. He was off to see if he could get lucky enough to kill Taz tonight.

Bo-Pete and Wild Bill were standing outside of the club, checking out their surroundings. Bo-Pete tried to remember every single car parked close to and across the street from them. He wasn't about to let those Crips get a lucky shot at him and Wild Bill.

After they felt comfortable, they put their 9 mm in the small of their backs and entered the club. It felt good to know that they could always enter the club with their weapons. They had it like that. There were no metal detectors for any members of their crew. *That shit was for suckas*, thought Bo-Pete as he stepped to the bar and ordered a glass of Hennessy for himself and Wild Bill.

Taz and Sacha met Gwen and Bob at the Outback Steakhouse. While they were enjoying their meal, Taz had a feeling that something was just not right. For some reason, he just couldn't relax. *Bob seems to be back to his old self,* he thought as he watched his homeboy clown with his girl Gwen.

"I'm tellin' you, baby, as soon as they take this bag off, I'm gon' break you off somethin' real proper for the way you been handlin' a nigga," Bob told Gwen with a smile on his face.

"Humph! You need to! I'm sick and tired of having to do all of the damn work, with your nasty ass!" Gwen said as she smiled lovingly toward her man.

Ever since Bob had made it back from New York, their relationship seemed to have intensified. Gwen was so scared that she was going to lose him, she clung to him tighter than ever now.

Even though Bob was on some "tough man time," he had been just as scared of losing Gwen.

He didn't fear the thought of dying. What scared him most was the thought of not being able to be with his soul mate for the rest of his life. He was in love for the first time in his crazy life, and it felt real good.

They laughed and joked for the rest of the evening. After dinner was over, they decided to head over to Bob and Gwen's place for some more drinks. As Taz followed Bob out to his home, he still couldn't shake that funny feeling he'd been having evening. He grabbed his cell and called Keno. When Keno answered his cell phone Taz asked, "What's up, dog? Y'all straight?"

"Yeah, we're good. What's up with you?"

"Chillin'. We just finished eating, and we're on our way over to Bob's spot to chill out for a Li'l while longer. You heard from Bo-Pete and Wild Bill?"

"Nah."

"They told me that they were goin' to the club and hang for a minute."

"Is that right? Well, you know them niggas are most likely gettin' their drink on and clownin' with some hoes or some shit."

"Yeah, I know. All right then, my nigga, I'll get at you in the morning."

Keno didn't like the sound of Taz's voice, so he asked, "What's wrong, dog?"

That nigga knows me like a book, Taz thought. "What you mean?" he asked.

"Come on, nigga. You know I be knowin' when somethin' ain't sittin' right with you. What's up?"

Taz sighed and said, "I don't know, dog. I've been havin' this funny feeling all night, like I'm missin' somethin', or that I should be somewhere I'm not."

"Keep your eyes open at all times, dog, and everything will be all good. We're in some stressful times right now. You just mind fuckin' yourself, that's all. Everything's goin' to be everything."

"Yeah, I know. I'll holla," Taz said and closed his cell phone.

As he pulled into Bob's driveway, Sacha said, "Are you really okay, baby?"

Taz shrugged his shoulders and said, "I guess. Come on, let's go on inside and chill with these two clowns."

Sacha laughed and said, "You got that right! I swear they're made for each other. I'm so happy for Gwen. She really deserves to be happy."

"Yeah, I'm happy for my nigga too. I never thought he would have been capable of crackin' a broad of Gwen's caliber. I guess it's true what they say."

"What's that?"

"Love is a muthafucka!" They both started laughing as they walked inside of Bob's ranch-style home.

Clifford, Li'l Bomb, Astro and H-Hop were sitting across the street from Club Cancun, staring at Bo-Pete's Navigator. "Do you think that's one of them niggas' shit?" asked Li'l Bomb as he racked a live round into the chamber of his AK-47 assault rifle.

"It could be, but I don't see any of them other niggas' trucks. I told you, they don't roll unless they're six deep," Clifford said as he let his eyes roam all over the parking lot of the club.

"They might feel that they've handled their business enough to make us lay it down. But you never know. They might be cocky enough to slip, cuz," said H-Hop from the back seat of the stolen SUV they were sitting in.

"Why don't you go on inside and see if you can spot them real quick. Ain't no need for us to be sittin' out here all night for nothin', loc," Astro said.

"All right, I be right back," Clifford said as he climbed out the truck. He jogged across the street and walked inside of the club. He stopped right before he made it to the downstairs entrance. He saw Bo-Pete and Wild Bill talking to a couple of females. He quickly scanned the rest of the club to see if he could spot Taz and others, and once he was positive that they weren't there, he turned and went back outside to the truck with his homeboys. When he got back inside of the SUV, he said, "Them niggas are slippin' tonight, cuz. There are only two of them in there. That nigga Bo-Pete and that li'l nigga they call Wild Bill."

"All right, now we wait. You never know. The rest of them niggas might just show up. If not, then we'll serve them two punk-ass niggas, cuz. That'll let that fool Taz know that we ain't playin'!" Astro said seriously.

"I'm with that shit, cuz. I'm gettin' my man tonight. That's on 107 Hoover Crip!" yelled Li'l Bomb.

Back inside of the club, Bo-Pete and Wild Bill were bored. "Dog, we should have went on and hung out with the homies. I'm sick of these fake-ass hoes up in this spot. Ain't none of them wifey material for real," Bo-Pete said as he set his glass of Hennessy on the bar.

"Nigga, I ain't tryin' to find no fuckin' wifey any fuckin' way. All I'm tryin' to do is get me some ass from one of these hoes tonight. You're right though. Ain't nothin' up in this spot worth getting at tonight," replied Wild Bill.

"Let's go shoot some pool up at the Plum Tree. There might be a few hoes up there we can get at."

"I'm with you, my nigga." Will Bill downed the rest of his drink and set it down on the bar next to Bo-Pete's empty glass.

They stepped away from the bar and started walking toward the exit of the club. As soon as they made it to the door, they paused and pulled out their weapons. They then stepped outside of the club side by side, and let their eyes roam quickly all over the parking lot. Neither of them saw anything out of the norm, so they started walking toward Bo-Pete's truck.

The first shot almost hit Wild Bill as he ducked and yelled, "Watch it, Bo! They're on your right!"

Bo-Pete turned to his right and started firing his weapon at the three guys running toward him and Wild Bill. Wild Bill was right by Bo-Pete's side, firing his pistol at the Crips attacking them.

Neither the Crips nor Wild Bill nor Bo-Pete were backing down from one another. It was basically a modern-day shootout at the OK Coral, the only difference being that they were in the parking lot of Club Cancun. The Crips kept charging

Bo-Pete and Wild Bill, and Wild Bill and Bo-Pete kept calmly walking toward the Crips with their weapons spitting fire. The night was lit up with sparks as the gunshots rang out.

They were about six feet from each other when Wild Bill saw Bo-Pete fall to the ground. Wild Bill knew that Bo-Pete had been hit, but he couldn't stop to help him. He knew the only way either of them was going to survive was if he got his man. He aimed carefully and picked off Astro. He hit Astro twice in his chest and quickly aimed his gun again, this time toward Clifford. He missed Clifford by inches. Even though he missed, his last two shots did what he had hoped they would. Clifford turned and started running back toward the truck, and so did Li'l Bomb, because his AK-47 had jammed and he didn't want to take the risk of trying to un-jam it and get himself hit.

While they retreated to their SUV, Wild Bill ran back to Bo-Pete, scooped his gun out of his hand and ran toward the truck the Crips were climbing inside of. He let off three shots at the truck before he felt himself spin and fall to the ground. He rolled over onto his side and fired some more at the fleeing SUV. He slowly got to his feet and staggered over to where Astro was lying in the street and shot him twice in his face. He then stumbled toward where Bo-Pete was lying. He screamed as he knelt next to his home-boy. He held Bo-Pete's lifeless body in his arms as he continued to scream. *"No-o-o-o-o!"*

Chapter Eighteen

Keno was walking to his kitchen when the telephone started ringing. "Who the fuck is this callin' me this fuckin' late?" he said aloud as he grabbed the cordless phone from its base on top of the kitchen counter. "Hello!"

"Dog! Them niggas got Bo-Pete! They got Bo-Pete!" screamed Wild Bill.

"*What?* Where y'all at?"

"I'm in a fuckin' ambulance right now! They're taking me to Baptist! I got hit in my shoulder, but Bo-Pete didn't make it, dog. He's gone! He's fuckin' gone!"

"Look, calm down, Baby Boy. Just calm down. We'll see you at the hospital, *G.* Go on and let them fix you up my, nigga. We'll be there in a few minutes."

The only response he got from Wild Bill was, "He's gone, dog! Bo's gone!"

Keno hung up the phone and quickly called Taz's cell. After he told Taz what Wild Bill had just told him, Taz said, "I'll meet y'all at the hospital." Taz closed his cell phone and told Bob, "Them niggas got Wild Bill and took Bo-Pete, dog!"

"*What?* Come on, my nigga! Please tell me you're playin'!" cried Bob.

"I wish I was, *G.* I gots to go. I'll give you a call when I know more."

"*What?* Nigga, I'm rollin' with you!"

"Nah, stay here and get your rest, dog. I'll get at ya when everything is everything."

With tears sliding slowly down his face, Bob said, "Fuck you! You can't stop me from goin' to the fuckin' hospital! I said! I'm! Rollin'! With! You!"

With tears of his own falling freely, Taz shook his head and said, "Come on, dog, let's bounce then."

Gwen and Sacha both knew better than to say anything. The shit was about to hit the fan, and there was absolutely nothing either one of them could do to stop it.

By the time Taz and Bob made it to Baptist Hospital on the northwest side of town, Red and Keno were sitting in the waiting area of the emergency room.

Red was visibly shaken. His eyes were blood-shot from crying so hard, and the look on his face told all that looked his way that he was in a murderous mood.

Keno sat in his seat with his hands covering his face, trying his best to control his emotions.

When Taz saw the both of them, his heart felt as if it had stopped. He actually couldn't breathe as he sat down next to Keno.

Keno felt his presence, looked up at his home-boy and said, "They got him, dog. He was dead before he made it here. Those punk-ass niggas hit him twice—once in the neck and once in his chest with somethin' real heavy, my nigga. The cat in the ambulance told me they tried every-thing they could, but his wounds were just too severe."

"Where's Wild Bill?" asked Taz.

"He's in surgery right now. They said he's goin' to be all right. He caught a shell in his shoulder."

"Did you get a chance to holla at him again?"

Shaking his head no, Keno said, "Not since I've been here. When he called me, he told me that them Hoover niggas got at him and Bo-Pete, and that Bo was gone. That's all I know right now, my nigga. They killed one of ours, *G*! You know what that means, don't you?"

Taz stared hard at his lifelong friend and said, "Yeah, I know what it means. Are you ready to do this?"

Keno stared at Taz for a moment, and then said, "Yeah, I'm ready. None of this really matters no more to me, dog. We started this shit together, and we gots to end it together. Fuck the world, my nigga! Fuck the muthafuckin' world!"

Taz shook his head no and said, "Nah, fuck them Hoover niggas! Fuck every last Hoover! And that's exactly what we're about to do." He turned toward Red and said, "I've always hoped and prayed that it would never come to this, but we made a pact years ago. If somethin' like this ever happened to one of us, we would ride until the beef was settled. The only way we can settle this beef is to remove every last one of them coward-ass niggas. You know that, right?"

Red stared hard at Taz as if he had lost his mind and said, "Nigga, you don't have to explain shit to me. Let's get this shit started!"

Taz held up his hand, signaling Red to wait a minute as he turned toward Bob. "Dog, you'd be in the way more than anything if you tried to ride with us on this shit. You gots to stand down, dog."

"Fuck that! I made the same pact as the rest of you niggas! This shit bag ain't shit to me,

Taz! Don't do this, dog! I gots to roll too!" Bob screamed.

"No, you don't!" screamed Gwen. "All you have to do is bring your ass home with me and let them take care of whatever they have to take care of!" she yelled, tears streaming down her face.

Bob was shocked because he hadn't seen her or Sacha enter the waiting room. He stepped over to where she was standing, grabbed her hand and said, "Gwen, I love you more than you'll ever imagine. Please believe me, because it's so damn true. But nothin' and nobody can stop me from gettin' the niggas who killed Bo-Pete. If I have to die, then so be it. I gots to do what I gots to do."

Before Gwen could respond, Taz stepped behind Bob and began to choke him out. He put Bob in a full-nelson chokehold until he was unconscious. He then gently sat him down in one of the chairs in the waiting room and said, "That was the only way, Gwen. He was goin' to go with us no matter what you said to him."

"I know, Taz, and thank you. Thank you so much!"

Taz turned and told Red, "Grab Bob and take him and Gwen back to his spot. Make sure when you get there that you take all of his weapons. Leave one with Gwen. He's still gon' need some-n' to protect them, just in case them fools find out where he stays." Taz turned back toward Gwen and said, "No matter what, make sure that he doesn't know that you have a weapon in that house. Make him think that we took everything out of there. We're also taking the keys to his truck, your car, and his other vehicles. If y'all need anything, call Sacha and she'll make sure that y'all are straight."

Gwen didn't say anything. She just gave Taz a nod of her head, indicating that she understood what he had just told her.

Taz turned toward Sacha finally and said, "I'm sorry, Li'l Mama. I'm so sorry." Before she could say a word, he told Keno, "Come on, dog. We gots work to do."

Sacha sat down and cried as she watched Taz and Keno leave the hospital. When Gwen tried to help her to her feet, she shook her off and put her face into her hands and cried even harder, and screamed.

Taz was walking down the hallway when he heard his fiancée scream. "Damn! This is so fucked up!" he said as he stopped and faced the door of the emergency room.

"I know, my nigga, but we gots to do what we gots to do," Keno said seriously.

"I know," Taz said as he led the way outside to the parking lot.

Clifford was sitting inside of his car talking to H-Hop. "Cuz, they got Astro! What the fuck are we going to do now?"

"We gon' stay down, cuz, and finish this shit we started. This shit done got real personal, loc. You know Astro was my li'l cousin. Them niggas gots to die! Every last one of them fools ain't gon' be breathing this time next month! And that's on 107 Hoover Crip!" yelled H-Hop.

"It's too damn hot right now, cuz. We're going to have to kick back for a minute."

"Fuck that shit, loc! We about to ride! Fuck the ones and anyone else who tries to get in our fuckin' way! So either you're with us or against us, cuz!"

"I'm with you, you know that. My life is on the line just like everyone else's. Don't waste your breath getting at me like I'm some busta-ass nigga. I'm still 'bout my work."

"All right then, I'll get at you in the morning, loco. The word will be out by then that we got one of them niggas, so you know it's gon' be on."

"Yeah, the word is also gon' be out that they got one of us too. We're going to have to tread lightly at first, loc. I'm telling you, that nigga Taz is about to go crazy on our ass."

"Yeah? Well, there's about to be two crazy muthafuckas goin' at it, cuz. They took my people, loc, and for that they have to die! It's as simple as that," H-Hop said as he climbed out of Clifford's CLS 500 Mercedes Benz.

Taz, Keno and Red had stayed up the rest of the night preparing for what they were about to do. They were downstairs in Taz's gym, checking and rechecking their weapons. Taz owned a heavy arsenal, complete with everything from pistols to assault rifles. Semiautomatic guns to fully automatic ones. Bulletproof vests and enough ammunition to supply a small army.

After they loaded all of the weapons they planned on using, Red said, "It would be best if we waited for the sun to set. That way we'll be able to move a li'l easier."

"Yeah, you're right. Plus, I'm tired as hell," Keno said as he yawned and stretched.

"All right, y'all niggas gon' and bounce. We'll meet back here around six." Taz then called Gwen and asked her, "How's he doin'?"

"He's still asleep, Taz. How are you?"

"Hurtin', Gwen. I still can't believe my nigga is gone."

"I understand. Believe me, I do understand. But, Taz, you have to realize that by retaliating there is only going to be more and more bloodshed. Sooner or later you'll have to feel this pain again, because another one of your friends will get hurt. Then what? You go off on another rampage? That doesn't make any sense. Y'all have too much going on for yourselves to take the risks y'all are about to take. What happens if something happens to you, Taz? Aren't you the least bit concerned for Sacha and the baby? I don't want to lecture you or anything like that, I just want to make sure that you're fully aware of what you're putting at risk. It's not just all about Taz right now. You have your mom, your daughter, your fiancée, as well as your unborn child to think about. You could stop this madness if you chose to. You do know that, don't you?"

"Can I? What about that nigga Cliff? He's the one taking this war to us, Gwen. If it wasn't for that clown, Bo-Pete would still be alive! So, to answer your question, yeah, I know I can stop this shit if I chose to. But that's not the decision I'm making. That nigga has shot my child and lived to talk about it. He's shot at me and lived to talk about it. Now he's responsible for killin' one of my closest friends, and he's *still* fuckin' breathin'! That is unacceptable, and nothin' and no one will stop me from hurting him and every last one of his niggas. I love Sacha and my unborn seed more than anything in this world. But I can't and I won't be deterred from handling this shit the way it's supposed to be handled. You make sure that you keep Bob under wraps for us, 'cause when that nigga gets up, he's gon' be on one for real!"

"Don't worry, I'll handle his ass. Thank you again for keeping him away from this mess. I'd die if I lost another love of my life. I just wouldn't be able to recover from that."

"Yeah, I know. I'm gon' keep it real with you, Gwen. If Bob was in good enough condition to ride with us, I wouldn't have done what I did. Like he said, we all made the same pact years ago. We're goin' to honor that, no matter what. Hopefully we'll be able to put an end to all of this and be able to move on with our lives. Whatever happens has to happen though. And it is goin' to happen as soon as that sun sets. Tell my Li'l Mama I said, no matter what happens, I will always love her."

"I will, Taz. Bye."

"Bye," he said, and went into his bedroom and collapsed onto his bed. While lying flat on his back, he stared at the ceiling as tears slid down his face and said, "We gon' get 'em, Bo-Pete. We gon' get every last one of them bitch-ass niggas, or die tryin', dog! Real talk!"

Chapter Nineteen

Pitt couldn't fucking believe his eyes. No matter what Leo and Tru did to their captive, Gee, he took it with a scream and a big-ass smile. Though he was in tremendous pain, Gee refused to give Pitt the information he desired.

"Listen, you fucker! Why are you making this so damn hard on yourself? You're going to die anyway!" screamed a very frustrated Pitt.

After catching his breath from Leo and Tru's torture, Gee smiled, spit out a mouthful of blood and said, "Watching you sit there and squirm gives me strength, Mr. Big Man. I'm gon' take whatever your boys got to give. You ain't gettin' shit outta me. I'm goin' to my grave, yeah, that's true. But I'm goin' to die with the satisfaction that you never got what you wanted outta me."

Leo slapped the shit out of Gee and started back with his torturing. He stuck an ice pick straight through the top of Gee's right kneecap. Leo smiled as he watched Gee scream over and over. Gee screamed but he never broke down. That infuriated Leo. He then untied Gee's hands and pushed him to the floor. With Gee's feet still tied Leo wasn't worried about him going anywhere, especially with an ice pick stuck in his knee.

"I got somethin' for your ass, nigga," Leo said seriously as he pulled the ice pick out of Gee's kneecap and put it into his back pocket. He pulled Gee's pants down around his ankles and told Tru, "Go into the kitchen and grab me one of those pot scrubbers. If this don't break this nigga, then nothin' will."

As Tru went inside the kitchen to get the pot scrubber, Pitt asked, "What are you going to do now, Leo?"

"You'll see," Leo said as he grabbed a bottle of vodka out a bag that he had set on the floor when they first came inside of the house. Tru came back into the room and gave Leo the pot scrubber. Leo smiled and said, "Let's see how you handle a li'l ass-play. Tru, spread that nigga's ass cheeks for me."

"What? Man, I ain't fuckin' wit' dat nigga's ass!" yelled True.

Pitt smiled and ordered Tru, "Do it, nigga. Earn your fucking money."

"Give me some fuckin' gloves or somethin'! I ain't about to be touchin' that nigga's ass! Fuck your money! I don't get down like that, Pitt."

Pitt laughed and said, "I thought you liked to use your damn hands on your victims."

"Fuck you, Pitt!"

They all started laughing as Leo passed a pair of leather gloves to Tru and said, "Here you go, you old soft-ass nigga."

Tru accepted the gloves and said, "Ain't nothin' soft 'bout me, youngsta, and you damn well know it." Tru then slid on the gloves and knelt down next to Gee and did as Leo told him to. After Tru had spread Gee's ass cheeks wide open, Leo sat next to him on the floor and began to rub the metal pot scrubber up and down the inside of Gee's ass.

Gee screamed louder than he had since he'd been held captive. The excruciating pain that he was absorbing was incredible. He prayed that they would end it for him soon, but he knew in his heart that they were going to keep on until he broke down. He was loyal to Won and he would die before he broke down. Won warned him when he accepted the million dollars for handling his business that it could get dangerous for him. So this was what Won had warned him about. *I guess I'm going to die, but I'm not breaking my promise to Won for nothing,* Gee told himself just as Leo poured the entire bottle of vodka down Gee's raw asshole. Gee screamed as the liquid burned his tortured body. His body could no longer take any more abuse, and went limp as he slipped into a state of shock.

"Ain't this a bitch! What the fuck are we going to do now?" screamed Pitt.

Leo shrugged his shoulders and said, "Man, he's one tough muthafucka, Pitt. We're going to just have to keep working his ass. Sooner or later he will break."

Pitt shook his head and said, "He has to, Leo. He has to."

Just as the sun was setting, there was a knock at Taz's front door. Taz, who had just finished getting dressed in all-black army fatigues, finished tying the laces to his black leather Timberlands, grabbed his bulletproof vest and walked downstairs to see who was knocking at his door. He smiled sadly when he saw that it was Sacha. He opened the door and said, "What up, Li'l Mama? Where's your key?"

Sacha entered his home and said, "I must have left it at the house, because I can't seem to find it." She focused on what Taz had on and said,

"Please tell me that there is something that I can say that will stop you from going out there and doing something crazy tonight, baby."

"Bo-Pete's dead, Sacha. Do you hear me? He's dead! There is no way in this fuckin' world I'm gon' let them niggas get away with killin' my nigga! No fuckin' way!"

"What if they kill you? What if you get caught and go to jail for the rest of your life? What am I going to do then? What is the baby going to do without a father? Think, Taz! Don't do this to yourself! Don't do this to us!" she screamed.

Taz listened to his fiancée's pleas, and it hurt him deeply, but he refused to let her affect his decision. His mind was made up. It was as simple as that. "I ain't gon' die, Li'l Mama, and I ain't goin' in nobody's cage. I will die before I let some shit like that go down. If it's meant for me to go be with MiMi, then so be it. The cowards that did this to my man have to die! Every last one of them!"

Sacha grabbed a hold of her stomach with her right hand and said, "I need to sit down. You're stressing the hell out of me, Taz."

He followed her inside of the den and watched as she sat down on the couch. She stared at him and asked, "So, you're going to completely disregard me and the baby?"

Before he could answer her question, there was a knock at his front door. He turned and went and let Keno and Red inside of the house.

When they returned to the den, Sacha saw that both Keno and Red were dressed exactly as Taz, in all black. Taz sighed as he grabbed a black duffel bag with the weapons they were about to use inside of it. Red went downstairs and came back with the assault rifles, as well as silencers for their pistols.

As Taz screwed a silencer onto his 9 mm, he said, "You should go on home, Li'l Mama. I don't know how late I'll be tonight."

Shaking her head no, she said, "I'm not going anywhere. I'll be here when you get back . . . that is if you make it back."

Taz stepped to her, kissed her on her forehead and said, "I'll be back, Li'l Mama. That's a promise." He turned toward Red and Keno and said, "Let's do this."

Just as they made it to the front door, Taz stopped suddenly as if he had forgotten something. He turned and yelled, "Heaven, Precious! Come!" Both of the Dobermans that were lying down in the living room came running toward their master. They stopped and stood at Taz's feet and awaited for their next command. Taz smiled and said, "Come!" and they followed him, Red, and Keno out of the house.

Once they were all inside of an all-black Suburban, Taz watched as his dogs climbed inside of the truck and sat down in the third back seat. He smiled and said, "They might come in handy tonight. Where did you get this truck, Red? It looks brand-new."

Red turned the ignition and started the Suburban, and said, "A friend of mine at the Chevy dealership owed me a favor. He heard about Bo-Pete, so he looked out. When we're through, I'll give him a call and he'll report it stolen."

Taz nodded and said, "Good thinkin'."

Precious and Heaven were sitting in the back of the SUV, relaxing as if they knew that they were about to on the kill. Keno smiled at the dogs and said, "Damn, dog! Look at them! It's like they know we're about to go huntin'."

Taz smiled and said, "They do. Let's go."

Clifford was sitting on his bed sweating bullets. *Taz and the rest of his crew are going to come at me hard now. I have to get the fuck out of this house. I know Sacha told them where I live by now,* he thought to himself as he got up and started packing some clothes inside of a gym bag. Just as he finished packing, the telephone rang. "Hello."

"Hi, baby. Whatcha doing?" asked Tazneema.

"I've just finished packing, baby. I was about to call you to let you know that I have to go to Dallas for an interview. I'll be gone for a few days," he lied.

"Interview? Dallas? Why are you trying to get a job way out in Texas, Cliff?"

"Because it seems like they're the only ones willing to pay me what I'm worth. To tell you the truth, I'm tired of the city anyway. It's time for a change."

"But what about me? You're just going to up and leave me?"

"Come on now, you know better than that. Once you're back on your feet, you can come and stay with me."

"What about school? I still have to finish, Cliff."

"That's true. Look, OU isn't that far from Dallas. You could still finish school and come be with me on the weekends. And if it gets too hectic, I can always come up to Norman and spend some time with you during the week. I love you, Neema, and nothing is going to stop me from being with you. But I have to get back to work."

"I understand. I just wish that there was someone here that would pay you what you're worth."

"Me too, babe . . . me too. I'll give you a call as soon as I make it to a hotel, okay."

"Okay. I'm going to do a little shopping tomorrow, so I'll call you on your cell while I'm out."

"Out? Mama-Mama's actually letting you go out?"

Tazneema smiled and said, "Yeah. She told me that since I've been sneaking out of the house every other night, I might as well go on out and get ready to go back to school."

"She knew?"

"Yep! And she didn't even say anything about it. That's just how Mama-Mama is. That's why I love her so much," she said with a lot of pride in her voice.

"That's cool. Okay, baby, let me hit the road. I love you!"

"I love you too, Cliff," Tazneema said and hung up the phone.

Clifford grabbed his bag and quickly left his home. For a minute there he actually thought Tazneema had called to stall him for her father. *Shit, I'm fucking paranoid for real!* he thought as he got inside of his car and pulled out of his driveway.

Taz, Red and Keno were driving slowly around 107 Hoover Crips' turf, looking for anyone who even resembled a gang member. Taz saw two

Crips walking down the street and said, "There goes the first two. This is how I want to play this. We need to find out where that fool Cliff rests his head, 'cause once we start puttin' this shit down, he's goin' to get spooked and shake the spot. None of this will matter if we don't get the nigga who started it all."

"I feel you. So, what's up?" asked Keno.

"You'll see," Taz said as he turned toward the backseat of the truck and said, "Heaven, Precious." Both dogs raised their heads, jumped over the seats and climbed out of the truck as Keno held the door open for them.

Taz stepped out of the SUV also and said, "Get 'em, girls!" Heaven and Precious took off running in the direction that their master was pointing.

The two young Crips weren't paying any attention to the two deadly Doberman Pinschers as they ran their way. By the time they noticed the dogs, it was too late. Precious attacked the first Crip's leg viciously, and Heaven did the same to the next Crip. They were screaming at the top of their lungs as Taz slowly walked up to them.

"Stand down, Heaven! Stand down, Precious!" Taz commanded. Both of the dogs stopped their attack and watched the two youngsters as they laid flat on their backs, crying uncontrollably. Taz smiled and said, "I'm gon' ask y'all one time, and one time only. Where does your big homeboy, C-Baby, live?"

"Ahhh, cuz, we don't know! That nigga just started comin' around a few months ago!" whined one of the Crips.

"That's on the real, loc! We don't know where that nigga live at!" the other Crip replied.

"You know what? I believe y'all. But y'all are goin' to have to give me somethin', or I'm gon' have to do y'all."

"Come on, cuz. We ain't got no beef with you," said the Crip who had spoken first.

"You see, that's where you're wrong. I got beef with *all* 107 Hoovers. I know y'all know about my homeboy that got smoked last night. So either give me somethin' I can use, or I'm gon' lay y'all down. Or better yet, I'll let my girls here finish y'all off."

"Cuz, all of this shit is because of Li'l Bomb! He wanted y'all dead because y'all did Do-Low!"

"Nah, loc, it was H-Hop too! He wanted to get y'all because of that nigga, C-Baby!" yelled the second Crip.

"All right, where can I find H-Hop and this Li'l Bomb nigga?"

"H-Hop stays out on the North Side in the Highland Glen Apartments, apartment 1697, way in the back. You'll know if he's at home because his orange Cutlass will be parked right in front of his apartment building."

"Li'l Bomb should be over on Lottie at the auto body shop right now. That's where he hangs out and serves his bud, loc."

Taz smiled and said, "All right then, that's good lookin'. Now, I'll make this fast so y'all won't feel too much pain," he said as he pulled out his silenced 9 mm.

"B—b—but you said that you wasn't gon' do us, cuz!" yelled the first Crip.

"Ye-yeah, you said we had to give you somethin', loc, and you wasn't gon' smoke us!" cried the other Crip.

Taz shook his head and said, "Y'all are Hoovers, so y'all gots to go." He then shot both of the Crips right between their eyes. He turned and jogged back to the SUV, followed by his dogs.

Once he was inside of the truck and Red had pulled off, he said, "Head over to twenty-third and Lottie. Park in front of that auto body shop that's across the street from that old steakhouse."

"Gotcha!" Red said, and they headed toward their next destination.

Li'l Bomb was leaning against an old rusty Ford when his eyes grew wide as saucers. He couldn't believe what he was seeing. Two Doberman Pinschers were attacking any and everyone inside of the shop. "What the fuck?" he yelled as he pulled out his nine and tried to get a clear shot at one of the dogs.

All in all, there were seven Hoover Crips in the back of the auto body shop. Every last one of them was running around for their lives as the vicious dogs attacked.

Taz, Red and Keno smiled as they stood on the side of the building and watched Precious and Heaven get busy. Taz frowned when he saw Li'l Bomb pull out his gun and cock a live round into its chamber. He stepped around from the side of the building and started unloading his nine toward Li'l Bomb. Li'l Bomb caught two bullets in his right leg and one in his left arm and he fell to the ground.

Taz yelled for Precious and Heaven to stand down. Both of the dogs stopped their attacks and watched as Red and Keno commenced to shooting every gang member inside of the room. Taz stepped over to Li'l Bomb and asked, "Where does that nigga C-Baby live, li'l nigga?"

Li'l Bomb spit toward Taz's face and yelled, "Fuck you, cuz! I'm Li'l Bomb! I ain't no fuckin' snitch! This is Hoover Crip 'til I die, cuz!"

Taz didn't say another word as he shot Li'l Bomb three times in his face. The young gang member died instantly. Taz turned and saw a female, who couldn't have been more than seventeen years old, cowering behind a beat-up old Chevy. He stepped over to her quickly and asked, "Are any of these li'l niggas related to you?"

The teenager shook her head violently and said, "N—n—no, s—s—sir!"

"All right, this is what I want you to do. Get the hell outta here, and if anyone asks if you were here or anything about what happened here tonight, you bet' not tell them anything about what you saw, because if you do, then I'm goin' to have to come find you. And even though hurting women and children ain't my thang, you would have forced my hand. Do you understand what I'm tellin' you?"

The terrified teenager stared at Taz and said, "Ye-yes, s-sir, I understand."

"Good. Now get outta here!" Taz smiled as he watched the scared teenager run out of the auto body shop without a backwards glance. He turned toward Red and Keno and said, "Let's go get that nigga they call H-Hop."

After Clifford had checked into the Westin Hotel in downtown Oklahoma City, he called H-

Hop to see if everything was all right around the way. As soon as H-Hop answered the phone, he said, "Cuz, them niggas is tryin' to take the whole fuckin' set out! They done blasted about ten or twelve of the homies already!"

"*What?* When did this happen?" Clifford asked as he sat down on the bed in his hotel room, trying to absorb the news that H-Hop just gave him.

"About twenty minutes ago, cuz. I don't know about you, but I'm up out this bitch, loc. Them niggas are on the war ride for real! I'm about to get outta dodge for a minute," H-Hop said.

Though it wasn't a laughing matter, Clifford laughed and said, "I thought you was about to get your ride on. What happened to that slick shit you was talking, cuz? I told you them niggas ain't playing."

"Yeah, I'm feelin' you now, cuz, 'cause I'm outta here!"

"Where are you going to go?"

"I gots a bitch that stays out in Midwest City. I'm gon' lay it down at her pad until this shit dies down a bit. You know the ones are goin' to be all over the fuckin' place. I ain't got time to be get-tin' caught up with them. You know I'm still on paper."

"Yeah, I feel you. What's up with Li'l Bomb? Have you heard from him yet?"

"Nah, but from what I heard, he might just be dead too, cuz. Them niggas went to the auto body shop where that li'l nigga is always at and tore shit up. One of the homies said something about some killa dogs or some shit too."

"Killer dogs? Where the fuck did that come from?"

"Ain't no tellin'. You know how niggas get to stretchin' shit, loc. I ain't waitin' around to find out if it's true or not, though. I'm outta here. Hit me on my celly if you find out anything. We still gon' get them niggas, cuz. It's just goin' to take a li'l longer than I expected."

"All right then, I'll get at you," Clifford said, hung up the phone and relaxed back on the bed. *Damn! Taz is on the warpath. Astro's dead, and Li'l Bomb is probably dead too. This shit has gotten way out of hand,* he thought as he tried his best to calm his nerves.

Timing and a lot of luck was on H-Hop's side. He pulled out of his apartment complex about three minutes before Taz, Red and Keno pulled up to his apartment building. When Taz didn't see H-Hop's car parked in front of his building, he decided enough was enough, at least for the time being.

"Let's take it in, my niggas. That nigga H-Hop gets a pass tonight. We can't keep rollin' around in this 'Burban."

"Yeah, the message has been sent. Them fools know we ain't playin' with they ass no more," Red said as he turned the truck around to leave the apartment complex.

"What are we gon' do now, dog?" asked Keno.

Taz sighed heavily and said, "We goin' to put the homey to rest and let the heat cool down in the city. After that, we're goin' to turn it right back up until we get H-Hop and that nigga Cliff. They have to die before I'll even consider stoppin' this shit."

"You gots that right, my nigga," said Red.

"Listen, after you dump this truck, you need to take the straps we used tonight and get rid of them too. Ain't no need for us keepin' some hot heat. Can you handle it, or do you need some help?"

"I got it, dog."

"Have you heard anything from Wild Bill?"

"Yeah, he's straight. He said they stitched him up and his arm's in a sling. He's good though," said Keno. "But you know that li'l nigga is gon' be on one as soon as he feels up to it."

"Yeah, I know. I can't believe that he's gone, dog. Bo-Pete is fuckin' gone! This shit is too fucked up!" said Taz as he rested his head on the headrest of his seat.

"Yeah, I never thought we'd ever have beef like that out here. It's been so damn long that we had to get at anybody in the city that I just didn't think some shit like this could ever happen, dog," Keno said as he lit himself a Black and Mild cigar.

"They say everything happens for a reason, G," said Red.

"I wish someone would explain to me the reason why we gots to bury Bo-Pete. 'Cause for the life of me, my niggas, I just can't understand this shit," Taz said as he closed his eyes for the remainder of the ride back to his home.

Chapter Twenty

As soon as Taz walked into his home, Sacha ran into his arms and gave him a tight hug. He scooped her into his arms and carried her upstairs to his bedroom. No words were exchanged as they both undressed and made passionate love for the next few hours.

Just before Taz fell asleep, Red called him and told him that he disposed of the truck as well as the weapons they'd used earlier.

"All right, dog, get at me in the morning so we can start gettin' Bo-Pete ready."

"All right, my nigga. Oh, you better call that nigga Bob. He's pissed! I mean *P-i-s-s-e-d* at your ass!" Red said and laughed.

Taz smiled and said, "All right, I'll call his ass now. Out!"

"Out!"

Taz smiled at Sacha as she snored lightly next to him. He climbed out of the bed, grabbed the cordless phone and took it downstairs with him.

When he made it to his living room, he sat down on his sofa and called Bob.

Bob answered on the first ring and said, "Nigga, you ain't shit! How the fuck could you do me like that, Taz? That shit was fucked up, dog! You think I'm a coward or some shit, nigga? Huh? Is that it, Taz? You think 'cause I fucked up in L.A. and in New York that I'm on some soft shit, *G*?"

"Calm the fuck down, nigga! Damn! You know damn well I know you're not a coward. I just didn't want you in the fuckin' way. You still fucked up, dog, can't you see that? I'm not lettin' Wild Bill get down with us either, not until he's a hundred percent to the good. So you might as well sit back with your broad and relax, 'cause ain't nothin' goin' down until you're ready, my nigga."

"You know what? Fuck you! Nigga, you can't tell a grown-ass man what the fuck he can and can't do! You think you took all of my straps? You think you took the keys to all of my rides? Fool, I got somethin' for your ass. There are some things about the Bob that you don't know, nigga! Them niggas took my nigga, so I'm takin' some of them! It's as simple as that!" Bob yelled angrily.

"Look, dog, we done put it down for the night. The city is too fuckin' hot for you to go out there right now. All you'll fuckin' do is end up gettin' caught the fuck up. Stand down for at least the rest of the night, my nigga."

"Fuck you, Taz!" Bob screamed and hung up the phone in Taz's ear.

Taz shook his head from side to side as he went back upstairs to his bedroom. *Everything happens for a reason,* he thought to himself as he climbed back in bed with his fiancée.

Gwen had tears falling down her face as she watched Bob put on his black Army fatigues. She knew that nothing she could say was going to stop him from doing what he felt he had to do. She took a deep breath and calmly said, "Bob, can you wait for a minute?"

"Wait for what? I told you, them niggas have to be dealt with, baby, and I'm about to deal with they ass!"

"I understand that, Bob, I really do. I just need you to wait for a minute, because if you're going to go out there and handle your business, then I'm going with you."

Her words stopped him from getting dressed. He turned toward her and asked, "What the fuck did you just say?"

"You heard me. I said I'm going with you. I lost William because I wasn't with him, and there hasn't been a day that has passed by that I haven't wished I was inside of that car with him and my baby. If you have to do this, Bob, then I'm doing it with you. That way if something goes wrong, at least I'll know I was by your side the entire time. And, believe me, there is nothing you can do or say to stop me. I'm going with you!" she stated coldly.

Bob smiled and said, "Are you sure you can stomach what I'm about to put down, baby?"

"I guess I'm about to find out."

"I gots me a straight gangsta bitch on my team, huh?"

Gwen shook her head no and said, "I'm a psychologist, Bob. I'm nowhere near a gangsta. I've made this decision simply because there is no other way for me to be able to deal with this logically. I'm in love with my man, and I'm willing to die before I let him leave me."

He gave her a nod of his head and said, "All right then, baby, let's go."

Tazneema was watching the news with Mama-Mama, listening to all of the killings that had taken place in the last few hours. "Dang! What's going on in this city?"

"Them damn heathens are out there actin' a damn fool," Mama-Mama said from the other side of the room. "That shit don't make no damn sense, killin' each other like that. And for what? A damn gang? Lord, please help these children!"

As Tazneema listened to her grandmother, for some strange reason her father came to her mind. "Have you talked to my daddy, Mama-Mama?"

Mama-Mama smiled and asked, "Your Daddy? Who is that, girl?" She laughed and continued, "I can't remember the last time I've heard you refer to Taz as your Daddy." She slapped herself on her forehead and said, "Wait a minute! Yes, I can! Just before your boyfriend shot you, you called Taz *Daddy*."

"Would you stop that, Mama-Mama, and answer my question?"

"You know how that boy is, girl. If he don't call me, I don't bother him none. Why? What's wrong with you? You're missing your 'Daddy'?" Mama-Mama teased.

Tazneema shrugged her slender shoulders slightly and said, "I'm just wondering why he hasn't called or come by, that's all."

"Well, why don't you give him a call then?"

"I will. I'll call him in the morning. Right now I'm about to go to bed. I'm a little tired."

"Humph! You bet' not be sneaking out of this house tonight. I know that much. You ain't completely healed yet, girl, and there is too much killin' goin' on out in them streets for you to be wandering around the town for some man."

Tazneema laughed and said, "I'm not going anywhere tonight, Mama-Mama. Relax!"

Mama-Mama didn't respond. Instead she just smiled, because she knew Tazneema wouldn't be sneaking out of the house because she took the keys to her car and had them safely tucked in her bosom.

Bob and Gwen rolled all over the East Side of the city looking for Hoover Crips, but all they saw were police cruisers. On almost every other block there was a police car either parked or patrolling the area. "Damn! Taz wasn't bullshittin'! The town is like super fuckin' hot."

"Does that mean we can go back home now, baby?" Gwen asked nervously.

He smiled at his girl and said, "I guess so, scaredy cat. You gave a nigga a pretty good front back at the house, but I knew your ass was scared as fuck."

"I never said anything about not being scared, Bob. I just refused to stay at home and watch you go out and act a damn fool without me by your side," she said with a smile. She turned onto the Broadway Extension, headed back toward Bob's home and feeling relieved.

The next morning, Sacha woke Taz and said, "Baby, get up! The police are at the front door!" she said urgently.

Taz opened his eyes and said, "All right, Li'l Mama, I'm up! Don't panic. Everything is all good." He climbed out of his bed and put on a pair of his pajama pants, slipped his feet into his Nike slippers and went downstairs to see what Oklahoma City's Finest wanted with him this early in the morning. When he opened the front door, he frowned and asked, "Yes, may I help you?"

"Good morning, Mr. Good. May we have a moment of your time please?" asked Detective Bean as he flashed Taz his badge to confirm what Taz already knew—the po-po was in the house.

Taz stepped aside and said, "Come on in." They followed Taz into his living room. He smiled when he saw the look of awe in both of the detectives' faces as they looked around his luxurious home.

"Now, how may I help you two officers this morning?" Taz asked as he sat down on the sofa.

"Detectives," said Detective Bean. "We've had several reports that you and some of your associates have staged a personal war against the Hoover Crips here in the city."

"What? Do I look like a gang-banger, Detective? I think someone is playing with you all. Why would I have a problem with some Crips?"

"Maybe because they shot your close friend, Billy Trent, in his shoulder the other night outside of Club Cancun," said Detective Bean.

"Or better yet, because they also shot and killed your other close friend, Reggie McClelland," said the other detective.

"Come on, Mr. Good. We didn't come way out here to waste our time with you. Please, don't insult our intelligence," said Detective Bean.

"Both of my friends were shot the other night at the club, but what makes you think that those Hoover Crip guys had something to do with it?"

"Would you let us do the questioning, Mr. Good?"

Taz smiled and said, "Go right ahead."

Before either of the detectives could ask another question, they were interrupted by Sacha. She came into the living room dressed casually in a pair of Capri pants with a matching top. She smiled and said, "Excuse me, detectives, but I'm Mr. Good's attorney. If you have any questions for him, I'd prefer for you to go through me."

Detective Bean smiled and asked her, "And your name is?"

"My name is Sacha Epps. I'm a partner at Whitney and Johnson."

Detective Bean turned toward Taz and asked, "Is it routine for you to have your legal representation at your home this early in the morning, Mr. Good?"

Before Taz could answer his question, Sacha said, "I'm also Mr. Good's fiancée. Now, may we get to the bottom of this early-morning intrusion?"

"Sure. We have reason to believe that Mr. Good and some of his associates have retaliated on the Hoover Crips for the shooting death of Reggie McClelland and the shooting of Billy Trent. There have been ten homicides committed since that particular shooting outside of Club Cancun. We don't feel that it was a coincidence that every last person murdered was a Hoover Crip."

"So, you have reason to believe that my client was involved, but do you have any proof of this?" Sacha sat down next to Taz.

"We don't have any witnesses, if that's what you mean. Like I just told you, they're all dead. We do have several bullet casings that we retrieved from the crime scenes. Before we go any further, do you happen to own any dogs, Mr. Good?" asked Detective Bean.

Taz smiled and said, "Yes, I do. I have two Dobermans. Why?"

"I was just wondering, because at one of the crime scenes it seems that the victims were attacked by dogs. We'll know for sure once their autopsies are completed."

Taz started laughing and said, "So, you think I brought my dogs along with me to get revenge for my peoples? Come on, man! You gots to be kidding me! Look, you're reaching for straws and shit. I understand that you have a job to do, and I will do whatever I can to assist you. I have nothing whatsoever to hide. I want the guys that did this to my people caught and put *under* the jailhouse. Even though you coming to my home this early in the morning with these wild accusations should offend me, I'm not. So, if that's all, gentlemen, I have a funeral I have to start making arrangements for."

"Do you own any weapons, Mr. Good?"

Taz stared directly at Detective Bean and answered, "Yes, I do. I'm a registered owner of a 9 mm Beretta."

"Would you mind if we took your weapon back down to the station to have our forensics team check it out for any matches on the victims?"

"Just as long as you return it," Taz said as he got up from the sofa and went back upstairs and grabbed his gun. He came back downstairs with the weapon in his left hand and the clip in his right. He then passed the gun to Detective Bean and said, "Here you go."

After accepting the gun from Taz, Detective Bean smiled and said, "We'll be in touch, Mr. Good,"

With a laugh, Taz said, "Yeah, I bet you will. You two, have a nice day."

After the detectives left, Sacha said, "You shouldn't be mocking them like that, Taz. They could cause you a lot of problems if they choose to."

"Problems? Look, Li'l Mama. They don't have shit, and they know I know they don't have shit. Like they said, all of their potential witnesses are dead. They're tryin' to build a circumstantial case against me 'cause Bo-Pete and Wild Bill are my niggas. On top of the fact that somebody has heard a few rumors about our beef, that's it and that's all. They gots nothin', and I'm gon' make sure that it stays that way," Taz said before he grabbed the phone and called Bob.

When Bob answered the phone, he told him, "Look, dog, I know you're salty at me right now, and I understand that, but the shit is thick right

now, *G*. Them people just left my spot talkin'
like they knowin' somethin'. I really need you to
stand down, homey, for real."

"Yeah, the spot's hot, my nigga. I went on a
run last night and saw that for myself."

"You didn't put anything down, did you?"

"Nah, there was way too many of them black
and whites on the block. I came back to the pad
and laid it down."

"Cool. We'll finish this, *G*, but right now we
gots to kick it for a minute."

"What's up with Wild Bill?"

"They should be letting him out of the hospital some time this afternoon. Keno and Red are
goin' to scoop him while I start getting Bo-Pete's
funeral together. Might as well get ahead of the
game, 'cause ain't no tellin' how long they're
goin' to keep the body."

"Yeah, that shit is crazy. You know how homicide gets down. Who's goin' to take care of the
body?"

"Temple and Sons. You know they're the best
in the city. Ain't nothin' but the best for my
nigga. So, get that Armani out, 'cause we're all
wearing the same suit we're burying Bo-Pete in."

Bob smiled sadly and said, "Damn! I never
thought a day like this would happen to us, *G*.
We almost made it though, huh?"

"Yeah, almost. All we got now is us, dog, so we'll maintain like we're supposed to. Bo-Pete's family will be set for the rest of their lives. I'm about to get at Won now and have him take care of everything on the financial side, you know, change the accounts over to Bo-Pete's people and shit."

"I'm real tired, *G.* Go on and handle shit. Just make sure you keep me in the loop, dog."

"Gotcha."

After hanging up with Bob, Taz called Won. "What's up, O.G.?"

"What's going on, Baby Boy?"

"Bad news, dog . . . bad news. Bo-Pete's dead."

"*What?* What the hell happened?"

"It's a long story, O.G., so I'll give you the short version."

After Taz finished telling Won about everything that has happened, he ended with, "So you see, it's really all on me. If I would have laid that clown Cliff down from the beginning, this shit wouldn't be as fucked up as it is now."

"You can't blame yourself, Baby Boy. Shit like this happens sometimes. Don't stress yourself out too much behind this madness. I need you to remain focused."

"What's what on that other thing?" asked Taz.

Won sighed heavily and said, "To be honest, Baby Boy, I don't even have a fucking clue. I'm still stuck at square one. I'm going to make a few calls today and hopefully find something out."

"All right, get at me when you're ready. But, look, we need you to take care of Bo-Pete's money and shit. Everything goes to his moms and pops, since he didn't have any kids. Can you take care of that for us?"

"You already know that won't be a problem. Get back at me with their names as well as their socials, and I'll take care of everything. Make sure you let them know that there will be absolutely nothing to worry about as far as taxes or anything. But they will never be able to bring all of that money over here to the U.S. Explain to them that whenever they need any money, they will have to do a wire transfer through the Islands and their banks. As long as they do that, they'll be all right."

"All right, O.G. I'm about to take care of that right now. I'll get at you and let you know when the funeral will be."

"Make sure you do that, Baby Boy. Out!"

After getting off the phone with Won, Taz turned toward Sacha and said, "I need you to come with me over to Bo-Pete's parents' house. I don't think I can do this solo, Li'l Mama."

Sacha grabbed her man's hand and said, "Come on, baby. Let's go and get it over with."

Taz stood and gave her a tight hug as tears fell slowly down his face. *Damn!*

Chapter Twenty-one

This shit is in-fucking-credible! thought Pitt as he watched once again as Leo and Tru revived Gee.

They had been torturing Gee for over four days now, and the man still refused to break. Leo admired his strength, but Pitt was furious.

"This shit has to fucking stop! You have to break this fool, Leo! You fucking have to! If we don't get what I need, we'll never be able to move on that nigga Won!" screamed Pitt.

"I've thought of everything I could possibly do to this fool, Pitt. He's determined not to give up shit. He's not going to be able to hold out much longer. Shit, he should have been dead days ago," Leo said seriously.

When Gee heard Pitt mention Won's name, he smiled because he knew that once again the old man was definitely going to come out on top of the pile. *Won never loses,* he thought to himself.

Pitt sat in his seat steaming as he tried to think of a way to make Gee tell him what he needed to know. His thoughts were interrupted by the ringing of a cell phone. He checked his and saw that it wasn't his phone that was ringing, and so did Leo and Tru.

Tru reached inside of Gee's pants and pulled out his cell and passed it to Pitt, who answered it. "Hello. Hello? Hello?" Pitt smiled as he closed the cell phone and said, "Kill that piece of shit and put him out of his misery."

"But I thought we had to get that info you needed from him first," Leo said.

With a huge smile on his face, Pitt said, "We just did." He went and knelt next to Gee's tortured body and said, "Just before I kill your man Won, I'll make sure to tell him what a stand-up guy you were."

"Wha-what are you talkin' 'bout?" asked Gee.

"You know what I'm talking about, nigga. Won! He's the nigga that paid you to get at my peoples! You gave him to me even though you tried not to," Pitt said as he reopened Gee's cell phone and stared at the number that showed on Gee's caller ID screen. The number showing was Won's cellular number in Southern California.

"Don't feel bad. It's not your fault. That nigga fucked himself by calling your ass on his cell.

He's not that fucking bright after all." Pitt then slapped Gee lightly on his face and said, "See ya!"

Leo pulled out his 9 mm and shot Gee once in the back of his head.

Pitt grimaced and said, "Get someone out here to clean up this fucking mess. I gots shit to do."

Tazneema couldn't believe it. She was pregnant again! *Damn! I must be fertile as hell,* she thought as she threw the pregnancy test into the trash can. She had a smile on her face as she went into her bedroom so she could call Clifford and tell him that once again, she was pregnant with his child.

When Clifford answered his cell phone and heard the good news, he smiled and said, "We're going to make sure that everything turns out like it's supposed to this time, Neema. I can't believe that you got pregnant again so fast."

She laughed and said, "Well, it's really not that hard when you have unprotected sex, baby."

"I know, huh? That was stupid of me to say. But you know what I meant. I love you, baby."

"I love you too."

"When are you going to tell Taz and Mama-Mama?"

"As soon as I get off the phone with you. I'm not making the same mistake twice."

"Do you want me to come over? I can hit the highway and get back to the city in a couple of hours."

"Uh-uh. It'll be easier if I take care of this by myself this time, baby. I'll give you a call after I've told them. When are you coming back to the city?"

"Later on this week some time," Clifford lied.

"When is your interview?"

"Hopefully in a day or so. I'll know for sure later on after I talk to a friend of mine."

"Okay, make sure you keep me posted on what happens."

"I will, Neema. Bye, baby."

"Bye," she said and hung up the phone. She went into the kitchen, where her grandmother was preparing dinner. She sat down at the kitchen table and said, "Mama-Mama, I'm pregnant again."

Mama-Mama stopped stirring the pot of beans, turned around, faced Tazneema and said, "You had to go and be stupid again, huh? Girl, don't you know you're going to drive Taz crazy? What's wrong with you, Neema? Why must you continue to cause problems within this family?"

Mama-Mama had never spoken to Tazneema like this before, and she couldn't believe she'd heard what Mama-Mama had just told her. "How dare you accuse me of causing problems within this family! Just because I'm in love with my man and I'm having a baby by him doesn't mean that I'm causing any problems! You don't like Cliff, I understand that. Your son doesn't like him, I understand that too. What the both of you don't seem to understand is that y'all don't have to like him! As long as I love him, that's all that matters! I'm sick and tired of the both of you and the way y'all treat me! I'm no longer a child, Mama-Mama. The sooner you and your son realize that fact, the better off we all will be! I'm sorry for yelling at you, because you know I love you dearly, but I've had enough of this . . . this craziness! I'm going back to my place in Norman. This house has gotten too small for me now."

Mama-Mama stood in front of the stove and shook her head from side to side as she watched her granddaughter leave the kitchen. "That girl just don't understand. Her daddy ain't gon' let her be with that man, let alone have a baby by him. God, keep my family in Your hands, please. We're definitely about to need You and some of Your divine mercy," she prayed as she continued to stir her pot of beans.

After Tazneema packed her things, she said good-bye to Mama-Mama, jumped into her car and headed to her apartment she shared with Lyla out in Norman, Oklahoma, not far from the campus of OU. While she was driving, she decided she might as well go on over to Taz's house and tell him about her pregnancy while she had the nerve.

When she pulled into the driveway of her father's home, she noticed that her uncles were over there as well. She smiled, because even though they really weren't her uncles, she loved Bo-Pete, Wild Bill, Red and Keno as if they were blood relatives. Ever since she could remember, they had always made sure that she had whatever she needed. She jumped out of her car and went to go face her father's wrath.

Taz smiled at his daughter when he opened the front door and said, "What's good, Baby Girl? I see you're looking better."

As Tazneema stepped inside she smiled and said, "Yeah, and I'm feeling a whole lot better. How are you? I haven't heard from you in a while, so I decided to come over and see how you were doing," she lied.

"I wish I could tell you that I was fine, but that's not the case, Baby Girl," Taz said as he led her into the den, where everyone was.

After speaking to Red, Keno, Bob, Sacha, Gwen and Wild Bill, Tazneema asked, "What happened to you, Uncle Bill? Where's my Uncle Bo-Pete?"

Everyone else inside of the room turned and stared at Taz. Taz inhaled deeply and said, "Your Uncle Bo-Pete was killed a couple of days ago, Neema. He and Wild Bill got shot coming out of the club."

She screamed and ran into her father's arms and began to cry uncontrollably. "Who did this, Daddy? Who killed my Uncle Bo-Pete?"

As Taz held his daughter in his arms, he knew that he couldn't hold anything back from her. She had to know the truth about the man she loved. He just hoped and prayed that she wouldn't trip the fuck out on him once he told her what happened. He sighed heavily and said, "That nigga Cliff and his homeboys did it, Baby Girl. They been beefin' with us for over a month now. They tried to get us all one night at the same club, but they got Bill and Bo-Pete. Cliff and his Hoover homeboys."

She pulled from her father's embrace, glared at him and said, "What did you say? 'Cause I know I didn't hear you correctly."

"You heard me, Baby Girl. That nigga Cliff killed your Uncle Bo-Pete."

"Now, come on, Taz. You don't actually know for sure if Cliff is the actual person who pulled the trigger," Sacha said, trying her best to defuse a situation she knew was about to become volatile any second. She could see it in Tazneema's eyes.

"Even if the nigga didn't actually pull the fuckin' trigger, this entire war is behind him tryin' to take me out so that he could be with my fuckin' child. Go on with that shit now, Li'l Mama. You know damn well all of this shit is behind that nigga."

Tazneema shook her head from side to side and said, "No. I know for a fact that Cliff wouldn't do no crazy mess like this. He doesn't want any beef with you, Taz. He just wants to move on with his life. We've discussed this, and I know he didn't have anything to do with my Uncle Bo-Pete getting killed."

Taz shook his head in disgust and said, "What the fuck you mean, you've discussed this with him? You still been fuckin' with that nigga, Neema? Huh? After I told you not to go against the grain, you still been fuckin' with the nigga that has been tryin' to take me out? You gots to be outta your muthafuckin' mind!"

"Taz! Stop it! She's hurting enough as it is!" Sacha yelled as she stepped over to Tazneema who had sat down on the couch next to Gwen.

As tears fell slowly from her eyes, Tazneema said, "I love him, Taz, can't you understand that? On top of that, I'm pregnant again with Cliff's child. I'm having my baby, and I'm going to be with my man," she said.

"*You're what?* Didn't you hear anything I just told your crazy ass? That! Nigga! Killed! Bo-Pete! You just can't seem to understand what I'm tellin' you. That nigga ain't gon' be around to be no father to no fuckin' baby, 'cause as soon as this heat dies down in this fuckin' town, the hunt will be right back on for his punk ass! Do you hear me? He's a dead man, Neema! *D-E-A-fuckin'-D!*"

"So, it's been y'all who have been shooting all of those gang-bangers around the city? Me and Mama-Mama saw that stuff on the news the other day. All because you think Cliff is the one who killed my Uncle Bo-Pete?" Tazneema asked as she continued to cry.

"Think? *Think?* We're sitting here makin' fuckin' funeral arrangements for your uncle right fuckin' now! And you fuckin' ask me if I *think* that nigga of yours done this shit! You gots to be outta your fuckin' mind! Get this through your fuckin' head right fuckin' now! If you think that nigga will be around to be the father of your child, then you got another thing comin'! I raised you with the help of my mother and the men you see in this room right now, except for my nigga, Bo-Pete—rest in peace—and we can do the same for your unborn seed, Neema. But that child will *not* have that nigga Cliff as a father! 'Cause I swear to you, on your mother's grave, I'm going to kill that nigga before the month's out!"

Tazneema stood and calmly said, "If you kill my man, then you might as well kill me too. 'Cause I swear to *you*, on my mother's grave, that if you hurt Cliff, I'm going to try my very best to kill you!" Before Taz or anyone in the room could say a word, she grabbed her purse and left her father's home.

Taz sat down after Tazneema had left and said, "Well, I'll be damn!"

"Don't pay her any attention, dog. She's just too caught up emotionally right now," said Keno.

Taz shook his head no, and said, "Nah, dog, she's my child. I know her like a book. She's gon' ride with that nigga to the end."

"So, what are you goin' to do now?" asked Red.

Taz stared at everyone inside of the room for a full two minutes before he spoke. When he did speak, it was barely audible. "If she goes against the grain, I'll kill her myself. I've dedicated my life to take the very best of care of that girl, and I swore when I buried MiMi that I would always take care of her. But, I swear to God, if she rides with that nigga against me, I'm going to kill her, dog. Real fuckin' talk!"

Chapter Twenty-two

Pitt smiled as he waited for Cash Flo' to answer his telephone. *I'm about to get at that nigga Won something vicious,* he thought to himself as he impatiently tapped his fingers on top of his desk. When Cash Flo' came on the line, Pitt skipped the pleasantries and said, "Damn! What took you so damn long to pick up the phone?"

"What? Man, don't call me, questioning me on how long it takes me to answer my damn phone! What the fuck is wrong with you?" Cash Flo' asked, clearly agitated by Pitt's rudeness.

"Look, I got confirmation that it was that nigga Won who got at me. All I need for you to do is to give me the green light so I can handle my business," Pitt said excitedly.

"First off, I need to hear exactly what type of proof you have, and if I'm feeling that, then and only then will I give you the go-ahead."

Pitt smiled as he told Cash Flo, about Gee and everything that happened back at his torture house. After he was finished he said, "For a minute there I thought I was going to come up empty, but the cocky bastard called Gee's celly and made my fucking day!"

Cash Flo' was quiet for a few seconds as he absorbed everything Pitt had just told him. Then he said, "You really don't have all that much on him, Pitt."

"*What?* Come on with that shit, Flo'! You know damn well that's enough to green-light that nigga! You think it's a coincidence that Won would call that fool's cell too, huh? Don't do this shit, Flo'. You and I got that nigga dead bang."

Cash Flo' shook his head from side to side as if Pitt was in the same room with him and said, "You may be right, but I need to think on this shit a little bit more before I give you the green light. I've got to go out to the East Coast to holla at the dagos. They acting like they want a piece of the dope game all of a sudden. They see how profitable it's been for The Network lately, and now they want in. When I get back, I'll have a decision for you, Pitt."

"Decision? You mean you're actually telling me that there's a chance that you might not let me get with the nigga?" Pitt asked angrily.

"Like I said, I'll give you my decision when I get back."

"How long will that fucking be, Flo'?"

"You'll know when I call you, Pitt," Cash Flo' said before he hung up the phone in Pitt's ear.

"I can't fucking believe you, Taz! How in the hell could you forget to call me and tell me about Bo-Pete?" Tari screamed as tears streamed down her face. She sat down on Taz's couch in his living room and cried like a baby.

Taz stepped over to her and tried to console her. As soon as he was near her, he started crying himself. They sat there side by side and cried for over twenty minutes.

Finally, Taz shook it off a little and tried to regain his composure. "Look, Tee, we got all of the funeral arrangements made. All we're waiting for is the homicide detectives to give the go so they can release the body to Temple and Sons Funeral Home."

"Why haven't they done that yet? How long does something like that take?"

"Normally it's about a week or so, but sometimes it takes a Li'l longer."

"Okay. So all of this killing I've been reading about in the papers is behind Bo-Pete's death?"

Taz gave her a slight nod of his head and said, "Basically. You know it was that nigga Cliff and

his homeboys who got at us that night at the
club. If I would have popped that clown right
after he hit Neema, Bo-Pete would still be alive."

"You can't blame yourself, Taz. Too much shit
has been happening around here lately. There's
been entirely too much drama going on here in
the city. So, I guess it's safe to assume that Cliff is
no longer a breathing human being, huh?"

"Nah, that clown is hiding somewhere. We
ain't been able to get his ass yet."

"But you intend to, right?"

Taz stared at Tari as if she was crazy and said,
"What do you think?"

She sighed heavily and said, "I know. I just
can't get over the fact that Bo-Pete's gone. This
shit has me really tripping." As her tears started
to fall again, she said, "Let me go. Make sure you
give me a call whenever they release Bo-Pete's
body." She stood and kissed Taz tenderly on his
lips and left his home.

"Bitch, not only did I go with him, I was actually about to shoot somebody with him," Gwen
said as she held the cordless phone between her
shoulder and right ear.

"Stop lying, ho! You know damn well you
wasn't going to do shit!" Sacha yelled into the
receiver.

Gwen sat down at the dining room table and said, "Sacha, I'm not losing another man that I love. If Bob is determined to go out there and get revenge for his homeboy, then I'm going to be his ride-or-die bitch and be right by his side. If something goes wrong for him, then it's going to go wrong for me too."

"You love him that much, ho?"

"You damn skippy! But, anyway, since nothing happened, I've been praying like hell that he don't want to go back out there. Bitch, I was scared as hell!"

They started laughing, and then Sacha said, "Ho, you are too fucking much! Let me go. I have a court appearance to make. I'll give you a call when I get back to Taz's."

"All right, bitch," Gwen said and hung up the phone.

Bob, who had been listening to Gwen's entire conversation with Sacha, stepped back into his bedroom and sat down on the bed. *That woman really loves a nigga. I can't put her in that kind of situation again. What the fuck was I thinkin' about?* he asked himself as he laid back on the bed and started thinking about Bo-Pete and the past. *This shit has really gotten crazy. Taz is on the verge of losing it. If he's talking about hurting Neema, then I know the end of the*

*world is coming. That nigga Cliff has to die,
but is it worth Taz and his only child going at
it like some killas on the streets?* "Damn!" he
said aloud as he closed his eyes and drifted off
to sleep.

"I really need to see you, Cliff. When are you
coming back to the city?" asked Tazneema.

"I'm not sure yet, Neema. What's wrong, baby?"

"I need to talk to you, and it's very important.
Where are you staying? I could come out there if
I have to."

"What? Come on now, baby. You're in no
condition to be making this long drive to Dallas.
Why won't you tell me what's on your mind right
now?"

"I need to be with you when I talk to you, baby.
I have to look into your eyes to make sure that
you're not deceiving me."

"Deceiving you? What are you talking about,
Neema?"

"Do you really love me, Cliff? I mean, am I really the woman you want to be with?"

"Come on, Neema. You already know the answer to those questions."

"If I'm the woman you love, then come out
to my apartment in Norman. I need you to get

here as fast as you can. I'm only three hours or
so out of Dallas. You could make it here before
midnight if you left right now. I need you, baby.
I need you to confirm what my heart already
knows."

"And what is that, Neema?"

"Are you coming or not, Cliff?" she asked
firmly.

He sighed and said, "I'm on my way, baby."

She smiled into the receiver and said, "I'll see
you when you get here."

After Tari left Taz's house, Taz went downstairs to the gym and started to work out vigor-
ously. The harder he worked his muscles, the
heavier his heart felt. He was trying to punish
his body for the mistakes he felt he made. His
own daughter was going against him for a man
she felt loved her. One of his closest friends had
been murdered in the street because he waited
too long to handle what he normally would have
finished immediately. The only reason he paused
on killing Cliff was because of his daughter.
Now look at this shit! he thought as he pumped
his arms up and down, harder and harder. He
was bench-pressing two hundred and forty-five
pounds of solid iron. The burning sensation he

was feeling in his muscles was nothing compared to the hurt he was feeling inside his heart.

He heard a car pull into his driveway and smiled as he racked the weights he'd been lifting. He wiped sweat from his face as he left the gym to head back upstairs. Just as he made it to the next floor, Sacha was opening the front door to his home. He smiled and said, "Damn, Li'l Mama! Where you been? It's almost eleven!"

"I stopped over at Gwen and Bob's, and we ended up going out to dinner. I called you here and on your cell to see if you would want to join us, but you didn't answer either phone. Are you all right, baby?" she asked as she stepped over to him and kissed him lightly on the cheek.

"Yeah, I'm good. I was working out. I left my cell upstairs in the bedroom. Tari came by, and I told her about Bo-Pete. After watching her lose it a Li'l, I got depressed all over again and needed to work out some of my frustration."

"I understand. Are you hungry? I could make you something real quick if you want me to."

"Nah, I'm gon' go get me something after I take a quick shower. You go on and do whatever you got to do. I'm good."

"You sure?"

"Yeah, I'm sure."

"Taz?"

"Huh?"

"Go talk to your daughter. You have to put an end to this madness, baby."

He frowned and said, "I know, Li'l Mama. But the only way any of this will end is when Cliff is dead. That fact will never change. He has to die." He stepped past her and went upstairs to the bedroom.

Sacha shook her head from side to side as she followed her man upstairs.

Clifford was a nervous wreck as he pulled into Tazneema's apartment complex. When he'd left his room at the Westin, he drove around the city for close to the hour and forty minutes he needed to pass by before he drove out to the city of Norman. *What if she had Taz over there waiting to take me out? What if the police have gotten her to try and set me up? What if . . .?* These were the questions going through his mind as he sat in his car and stared up toward Tazneema's apartment. After five minutes of this, he took a deep breath and said, "I love her, and I know she loves me. She would never do anything to hurt me like that. I know she wouldn't." When he made it to Tazneema's front door, he shook all doubts out of his mind and knocked softly on the door.

Tazneema opened the door, smiled and gave him a tight hug and said, "Come on in, baby. Lyla isn't here, so we'll have all of the privacy we need."

Clifford let her pull him over to the couch and sat beside her and asked, "Now, what's so important that you made me drive all of the way back to Oklahoma, Neema?"

She stared into his eyes and said, "I wanted to know if you were responsible for my Uncle Bo-Pete's death, Cliff. Did you kill my uncle?"

Clifford was shocked by her abruptness. He was even more shocked at how calm she was. He stared directly back into those deep brown eyes of hers—eyes exactly like her father's—and said, "What? Come on now, baby. Do I look like a killer?"

"Answer my question, Cliff. I have to hear you say it. I have to see it in your eyes, baby. Please, answer my question. Did you kill my uncle Bo-Pete?"

Still staring directly at her, he said, "No. No, Neema, I did not kill your Uncle Bo-Pete."

"Did you have anything to do with him getting killed?"

"No."

"Did you know that your Hoover homeboys have been trying to kill my father?"

"For what?"

"I was hoping you would answer that question for me, Cliff. You see, my daddy has his mind made up that he's going to kill you. He feels that my Uncle Bo-Pete was either killed by you or your homeboys. Either way, he's holding you responsible."

"That's absurd! I don't deal with any of those Hoover homeboys, as you called them. Now, I do speak with some of my close comrades from back in the day, but that's about it. For Taz to even think I'd have something to do with a murder is absolutely ludicrous! I know you don't believe any of this craziness, Neema." Clifford stared at her for a minute and said, "You do! You actually think that I'd commit murder!"

Tazneema's heart began to literally melt at that very moment. She smiled at the man she loved more than anything in this world and said, "No . . . no, I don't, baby. I love you. I had to look into those gorgeous brown eyes so I could be sure my heart wasn't leading my brain. I've gone against my father for you, Cliff. I'll never leave your side, baby. Never!" she said and kissed him tenderly.

Clifford pulled from her embrace and said, "What did you mean, you've gone against your father, Neema?"

"He swore on my mother's grave that he was going to kill you, baby," she said with a sudden fury in her voice. "So I swore on my mother's grave that if he killed you, then I was going to kill him."

"My God! This is ridiculous! What the hell are we going to do to straighten out this madness, baby?"

She shrugged her shoulders and said, "I don't know. All I know is, I love you. I'm about to have our child, and no matter what, nothing and nobody is going to hurt my man without paying dearly for it. I'm my daddy's child. If he can kill, then so can I. Now, come on. Lyla won't be back for at least another couple of hours. I want to do it," she said with a sexy smile on her face.

Clifford shook his head and said, "You're something else, crazy girl!"

"But you love me, right?"

As he let her pull him toward her bedroom, he smiled and said, "Yeah, I love you. I love you more than you'll ever know."

Chapter Twenty-three

"So, she went back to her place, huh, Mama-Mama?" asked Taz as he turned his Denali onto the highway.

"Mmm-hmm. You really need to talk to that girl, Taz. She's acting out because she doesn't know any better."

"She's grown, Mama-Mama. I can't make her do anything that she doesn't want to."

"That may be true, but you can still try to talk some sense into her smart tail."

"I'm about to go out to her place now and see if I can do just that, Mama-Mama. I'll give you a call in the morning and let you know if I was able to do any good."

"Make sure you do that," Mama-Mama said before she hung up the phone.

Twenty-five minutes after he had gotten off the phone with his mother, Taz pulled into Tazneema's apartment complex. If he was fifteen minutes earlier, he would have bumped right into Clifford as he left Tazneema's apartment.

Taz jumped out of his truck and walked toward his daughter's place with a heavy heart. He knew she was going to stand firm on what she believed was right. *I hope and pray that I'll be able to convince her to see things my way because, if she doesn't, things are going to get ugly out here in Norman,* he thought as he knocked on her front door.

When Tazneema heard the knock at her door, she immediately assumed it was Clifford coming back for something. She ran to the door with just her thong and bra on. She opened the door and asked, "Did you forget something, baby?"

Taz stared at his damn-near naked daughter and said, *"What?"*

"Oh, shit! I'm sorry, Taz. Come on in," she said as she ran back into her bedroom to put on some clothes.

Taz stepped inside of her neat little apartment and asked, "Where is Lyla?"

"She's out! She should be back in a little bit though!" Tazneema yelled from her bedroom. "What brings you out this way at this time of the night?"

He glanced at his iced-out Cartier watch and said, "I know it's late, but I really need for us to clear the air, Baby Girl."

She came back into the living room and said, "Look, Taz. I love him, you hate him. He's my man, not your enemy. Cliff didn't have anything to do with shooting at you or my Uncle Bo-Pete's death. I know you don't believe that, but I do. Can you please let this go, Daddy? Please?"

He sat down on the couch and said, "Baby Girl, you know I will give you anything in this world. I love you more than words can ever express. You're all of my MiMi that I have left, Neema. But I can't and I won't let that nigga make it for the shit he's responsible for. He did it, Neema. I swear to you on your mom's grave, Baby Girl, he did it! He tried to get me, and he done Bo-Pete. For that he has to die. It's as simple as that. I don't want to lose you or the love we have for one another, but if you force my hand, Neema, I'll have no other choice but to do me."

"No choice about what? What? You're going to hurt me too, Taz? Are you that cold, Daddy?" she asked sarcastically. "You know what? You don't even have to answer that, 'cause I already know you are. Like I told you when I was at your house, if you get at my man, then expect for me to be getting at you. Now, if you'll excuse me, I'm tired and I'm going to bed now."

"You really don't understand, do you? That shit is crazy! Love's a bitch. I know this, and I realize that you're in love with that nigga. I respect that, just as I respect you for being loyal to your man. But by being loyal to your man, you're not being loyal to the one man who would do whatever it would take to make sure that you're taken care of for the rest of your life.

"I've done more in this lifetime than you could ever imagine, Neema. I've robbed, I've killed, and I've hurt a whole lot of people, Baby Girl. I did what I did to ensure that my only child would always be taken care of. You are set for the rest of your life financially because of the crazy-ass life I've chosen to lead, and you have the fuckin' nerve to stand there and tell me that you'll go against me! You can't even pay your half of the rent for this place! I pay your school bills, this apartment included, your expenses for clothes, food. Hell, I pay every fuckin' bill, you have! Me! Me, Neema! I pay for every fuckin' thing! And you think I'm gon' let you talk to me like I ain't shit?

"I could break your fuckin' neck right fuckin' now, and no one would ever know! I can't hurt you, Baby Girl. You're my blood, and I love you with all of my heart's love. So, for the last time, stay away from that nigga. He's a dead man as soon as I can catch up with his ass. After I do that nigga, if you still want to come get at me, you

know where to find me. I'll be waiting for you."
Taz stared hard at his daughter for another moment, shook his head sadly and left her standing
in her living room with tears falling down her
face.

The next morning Taz was lying in bed when
Detective Bean called and told him that he could
come and retrieve his weapon.

"Why don't you come and deliver it? After all,
you did come and get it," Taz said arrogantly.

"I'd prefer for you to come downtown to the
station, Mr. Good. I have a few more questions
I'd like to ask you," Detective Bean replied.

Taz laughed and said, "You know what? I
don't have anything else better to do. I'll be there
within the hour." Taz then hung up the phone
and took a quick shower. He dressed in his ev-
eryday gear, a pair of black Dickies with a white
T-shirt. After tying up the laces to his Timberland boots, he put his diamond grill in his mouth
and draped himself with the rest of his expensive
jewelry. He was all smiles as he went into his garage and hopped into his truck. *This shit is going
to be fun,* he thought to himself as he pulled out
of his garage.

***

Tazneema tossed and turned the entire night. She couldn't understand why her father was so confident that Cliff was responsible for her Uncle Bo-Pete's death. *Is Taz right? Did Cliff have something to do with it? Or is Taz trying to destroy my relationship with Cliff?* She asked herself all of these questions over and over almost the entire night. By the time she did fall asleep, she was bone-tired.

Now that she was awake, the questions still remained. *Did Cliff have anything to do with all of this mess? I love that man, and he loves me. He wouldn't lie to me. I'm not going to let you fuck up my relationship, Taz,* she thought to herself as she climbed out of her bed and went into the bathroom to take a shower.

Taz was talking to Mama-Mama on his cell phone as he drove toward downtown Oklahoma City. "I'm tellin' you, Mama-Mama, she's so caught up with old boy that she's not listening to me."

"Are you positive that that boy was the one who did this to Bo-Pete, Taz?" asked his mother.

"Yeah, I am. If I wasn't, I wouldn't move on that clown until I was, Mama-Mama. I don't want to cause my Baby Girl any pain, but I have no other choice. That fool has to go."

"I don't want to be hearing none of that, Taz! I understand that you're hurting, but so am I. That boy was like a son to me. You have a decision to make, Taz, and the sooner you make it, the better off you and Neema will be."

"What decision are you talkin' about? 'Cause I already done told you that clown has to go. I'm not changin' my mind about this, Mama-Mama. I love my daughter and she knows it, but if she chooses to go against me, then she has chosen her own fate." Before his mother could respond he said, "Look, I'm at the police station downtown. I'll give you a call later on Mama-Mama."

"What are you doing down there, boy?"

He smiled into the receiver and said, "Nothin'. I'm 'bout to have a Li'l fun, that's all."

"Fun? Oh, never mind. I got a funny feeling that I don't need to know what you're talking about. Be good, boy," Mama-Mama said and hung up the phone.

Taz closed his cell, stepped out of his truck and strolled confidently inside of the police station.

After a fifteen-minute wait, Detective Bean came out into the lobby, where Taz was waiting patiently for him and said, "Good morning, Mr. Good. Would you please come this way?"

Taz followed the detective into his office and took a seat in front of Detective Bean's desk.

Detective Bean stared at Taz for a moment and then said, "I know all about you, Taz. I've had some time to do some serious research on you and your past."

Taz smiled and said, "I figured you would. So, tell me, what you think? Pretty interesting stuff, huh?"

Detective Bean laughed and said, "That's funny. Yeah, you're an interesting individual, Taz. There's something that confuses me though."

"What's that?"

"You're a very wealthy man. Not only that, but you seem to have all of the right people behind you and your friends. How did a young man from the streets get into such a powerful position?"

"Sometimes when a person knows the right people, they can make certain dreams become a reality."

"I don't understand."

"I know. It wasn't meant for you to. Look, I'm here for my pistol. Can I have it back or what? I have a busy day planned ahead of me."

Detective Bean reached inside of his desk and pulled out Taz's 9 mm that he had inside of a plastic Ziploc bag. He passed it across his desk to

Taz and said, "One more thing, Taz. I know you and your crew did those Hoovers. To be honest with you, I really don't give a damn about those cowards. You live by the sword, you die by it. Just because you missed me on that one doesn't mean you'll always miss me. I'm very thorough. I don't miss too often."

Taz smiled and said, "Neither do I, Detective. Neither do I." He stood. "You have a nice day, Detective." Then he turned to leave Detective Bean's office. He stopped at the door, turned back and said, "I'm curious. Who informed you about me and my peoples?"

It was now Detective's Bean's turn to smile. He relaxed back in his chair and said, "Won's been around for a very long time, Mr. Good . . . a very long time."

Taz kept his poker face intact even though he was shocked as hell when he heard the detective mention Won's name. He smiled at the detective and asked, "Who's Won?"

Detective Bean burst into laughter and said, "Oh, you're good! You're very good, Mr. Good! Have a nice day. And, Taz, stay outta the way. It would be a shame for you to lose all that you've acquired over the years due to something as messy as this."

Taz stared at the detective for a full minute before finally turning and leaving his office. As soon as he was back inside of his truck, he called Won. When Won answered the phone, Taz said, "What's up with this Detective Bean out here in the city, O.G.?"

Won started laughing and said, "He's my cousin."

Taz gave a sigh of relief and said, "Yeah, well, you need to get your peoples off of my fuckin' back."

"I did. Why the fuck you think you had that meeting with him? He gave me a call a couple of days ago, asking me all types of shit about you. I gave him the semi-version of your life, and the rest is history. You don't have to worry about him. He's a teammate."

"You're something else, O.G. You know that?"

"Yeah, I know, Baby Boy. That's why my name is *Won!*"

Chapter Twenty-four

Taz, Keno, Red, Wild Bill and Bob were seated at the front of the church, staring at the closed casket that their lifelong friend was lying in. Each one of them was caught up in their own personal thoughts about Bo-Pete at that moment. They were dressed identically in black Armani suits, with black Mauri alligator shoes on their feet. Once Bo-Pete's casket was opened, everyone inside of the church would have noticed that he too was dressed as his closest friends were.

Sacha and Gwen sat in the pew right behind their men. Won was by their side, giving comfort to them both. Even though he too was hurting from this tragedy, he gave the appearance that he was in complete control of his emotions. He couldn't let his pain be seen by Taz and the others. If he did, he felt that Taz would lose it and all hell would break loose.

Just before Bo-Pete's family came inside of the church, Tari came and sat down beside Won. She was dressed in an all-black dress with matching pumps. She gave a nod toward Sacha and Gwen and then reached over the pew and gently rubbed Taz on his shoulders.

Taz turned around and smiled sadly at her, but said nothing. No words could express the pain he was going through at that very moment. Tari saw the pained expression on his face and couldn't stop the sudden flow of tears falling from her eyes. Taz turned back around quickly before he started bawling himself.

Bo-Pete's family was led into the church, and everyone inside of the building stood as the family was seated.

The reverend's sermon/eulogy was mostly about living right and doing the right thing. At least that's what Taz thought, until the reverend started screaming and yelling about violence and all of the senseless killings that had been going on all around them lately.

Though the reverend was bouncing all around the podium, Taz felt as if he was directing his sermon toward him. *I know this clown ain't shootin' his shot at me,* he thought as he continued to stare and listen to the reverend preach.

Then, as if the reverend had heard what Taz was thinking, he turned toward him and said, "Greed! Greed is what causes us to get together like this!" He yelled as he stood over the closed casket, "When men start controlling their urges for that almighty dollar, then and only then will we be able to avoid such tragedies as this one here!"

Taz turned toward Keno, shook his head from side to side and whispered, "I can't take too much more of this, dog. I'm goin' out to the truck. I'll be back when it's time for the final viewing." Before Keno could say a word to try to stop him, Taz was on his feet and on his way out of the church.

He was almost to the back of the church when he heard the reverend yell, "You can't run from your fate! Nor can you run from God! Change! Change is the only way to make things right!"

Taz stopped in his tracks and turned slowly back around so that he was facing the entire church. He saw his daughter sitting next to Mama-Mama and he smiled at the both of them. *I'm not lettin' this preacher man get to me,* he thought as he marched right back to his seat in the front of the church. After he was seated, he stared hard at the reverend, basically daring him to keep picking on him.

The reverend noticed and him and quickly directed his gaze elsewhere. After he finished his eulogy/sermon, it was time for friends and family members to say a few words about the deceased.

After a few of Bo-Pete's cousins and other relatives had spoken, Taz took a deep breath and stepped up to the podium. Once he grabbed the microphone, he stared out into the crowded church and said, "I've known Bo-Pete most of my life. We went to school together, we went on our first date with our girlfriends together, and we learned how to become men together. He always used to tell me that I'm too emotional and I need to learn how to control my temper. When this man died, so did a part of me. I'm not an overly religious person, but I do believe there is a God in Heaven. I pray that he forgives me as well as Bo-Pete for our wrongs in life. Because Bo-Pete's wrongs as well as mine coincide as one. Neither one of us should be considered as greedy men." He paused and glared hard toward the reverend before he continued. "We did what we felt was the right thing to do to take care of our families."

After that statement, Taz let his eyes scan the crowd, until they locked with Tazneema's. Then he continued, "There was nothing in this world that Bo-Pete wouldn't do for me and my family, just as there is nothing in this world I wouldn't do for his. That's not the way of greedy men. That's the love for one another! The respect! The loyalty! The honor! I'd gladly change places with my man lying inside of that there coffin," he said as he pointed toward Bo-Pete's casket. "But I can't. All I can do is live and let his memory give me strength to do the things that I feel I must do. I will do everything that needs to be done. That, I promise you, my dog . . . my brother . . . my friend!" Taz said as he stared at the gold-trimmed mahogany casket. He stepped away from the podium with his face wet with his tears. When he sat back down, Keno wrapped his arms around his shoulders and gave his friend some much-needed support.

Sacha was in tears also as she watched her man speak with so much passion. Gwen too was in tears as she stared at Bob, who was sobbing loudly. Wild Bill and Red, as well as Won and Keno, were all in tears also.

One of Bo-Pete's relatives came to the podium and started singing "Amazing Grace" as the morticians came to the front and opened the casket for the final viewing of Bo-Pete.

When Taz saw Bo-Pete's smooth, chocolate-brown skin look so pale with the makeup the morticians used, he lost it. "*No-o-o-o-o! No! No! No! God, no! Why you take my nigga? Why?*" he screamed over and over.

Keno tried to grab him, but he was too strong for him to hold.

Red stood up and grabbed Taz and said, "Come on, my nigga. Calm down. You're spooking everyone, *G*."

Taz took a few deep breaths and gave Red a nod of his head to let him know that he was okay. He then stepped over to the casket and stared at his dead homeboy. "I'm gon' get him, Bo-Pete! You know I got 'em, dog," he said as he bent forward and kissed both of Bo-Pete's cold cheeks. He then turned toward the family, walked over to Bo-Pete's mother and said, "I'm sorry for my behavior, Mrs. McClelland. Please forgive me."

With tears sliding down her face, Bo-Pete's mother said, "There's nothing to forgive, Taz. I know how much you and that boy loved each other. Don't you pay that preacher no mind, ya hear?"

Taz smiled and kissed her on her cheek and said, "Don't worry, I won't." He stepped back, so the family could have their final viewing of Bo-Pete.

After the casket was closed, Taz, Red, Bob, Keno and Wild Bill stepped over to the casket so that they could carry it to the hearse. Even though Wild Bill's right arm was still in a sling, he refused to let anyone stop him from helping carry his homeboy.

Once they had the casket inside of the hearse, they all went and got into their vehicles. Keno drove his Range Rover, Red and Wild Bill had come together in Red's Tahoe, Gwen drove Bob's Escalade, while Taz, Sacha and Won all rode in Taz's Denali.

Taz was climbing inside of his truck when Tazneema ran up to him and said, "Taz, can I speak with you for a moment? Please?"

He stared hard at his daughter and asked her, "Have you changed your mind, Neema?"

"No, but—"

Before she could finish her sentence, he stopped her with his hands and said, "Then please get the fuck away from me!" He started the ignition and pulled out of his parking space, leaving his daughter standing there with tears sliding down her cheeks.

Won, who didn't know what the fuck was going on, went ballistic. "What the fuck was that, Baby Boy? Why in the hell did you just speak to your child like that?"

"Let's talk about it later, O.G. I'm really not in the mood for it right now."

"*What?*" Won turned toward Sacha and said, "Would you please explain to me what the fuck is going on around here?"

"Later, Won. Just let it be for now, okay?"

"Okay? Hell nah, it's not okay! What the fuck is going on?"

Taz sighed heavily as he told Won everything that was happening with him and Tazneema. He finished just as they pulled into Trice Hill Cemetery.

"You can't—and I mean this, Baby Boy—you can't let this interfere with your relationship with your child. There has to be another way to handle this situation," Won said.

"If there is, I haven't thought of it, O.G. What? You want me to let that nigga make it or something?"

Won stared at Sacha for a brief second then to Taz he said, "Why not? You don't have to make it so damn obvious to your daughter. She's in love with the man, Taz, for Christ's sake! Give him a pass until we can think of a better way of handling this situation."

"Fuck, nah! That nigga is the reason we're about to put my nigga six feet deep!" Before Won could say another word, Taz jumped out of his truck and marched toward the hearse to help the others carry Bo-Pete's body to its final resting place.

Won and Sacha met up with Gwen and Tari, and they all walked toward Bo-Pete's graveside. Sacha knew that there was nothing that could be said to Taz. She hoped and prayed that maybe Won would have been able to talk some sense into him, but all of those hopes went out the window after the conversation she heard during their ride to the cemetery. She knew for certain now that Clifford was going to be buried himself real soon.

After the reverend finished with his final prayer, Taz and the rest of the crew stood over Bo-Pete's open grave. Each member of the crew said their good-byes in different ways. Bob pulled off his diamond-studded Cartier wristwatch and tossed it on top of Bo-Pete's casket and said, "Watch over us, G. I love you."

After Bob walked away, Red pulled out a picture of himself and Bo-Pete that was taken when they were vacationing in Cancun, and dropped it onto the casket and said, "You may be gone, my nigga, but you'll never be forgotten."

Keno took one of his two-carat stud earrings and tossed it onto Bo-Pete's casket and said, "This life ain't gon' be the same without you, G. I love you, homey."

With tears sliding down his face, Wild Bill took off his Presidential Rolex watch and tossed it onto the casket and walked away. He was too choked up to even speak.

Finally, Taz pulled out his favorite Jesus piece and platinum chain and tossed it onto the casket and said, "Hold me down, dog. Hold me down."

They waited and watched until three of the cemetery's caretakers came and started shoveling dirt over Bo-Pete's coffin. Once they were a quarter of the way finished, Taz turned toward the crew and said, "Come y'all. Let's bounce."

"Are we rollin' back to the church to eat with the family?" asked Keno as he loosened his silk tie.

Shaking his head no, Taz said, "Nah. If I get too close to that wack-ass preacher, I just might sock his ass. Let's go to my spot and get faded."

"Yeah, I'm wit' that!" Wild Bill said as he wiped his eyes.

"Bust out the XO, nigga, 'cause it's about to be a long muthafuckin' night!" Bob said as he led the way back toward their vehicles.

As Taz followed the crew back to their trucks, he paused and looked over his shoulder and said, "I got 'em, Bo. I got his ass, G. Real talk."

Chapter Twenty-five

The remaining crew members, plus Won,
Tari, Gwen and Sacha, were having a good time
getting drunk and listening to each member of
the crew as they took turns talking about something funny concerning their fallen comrade. Katrina and Paquita had been invited to their little
get-together also. Taz felt that since they were
kind of close to Red and Keno, they were worthy
of knowing where he rested his head. Therefore,
he welcomed them into his home.

"All right! All right, y'all, hold up. I got one. Do
y'all remember when we had those goofy-lookin'
twin niggas hemmed up at their dope spot on the
East Side?" asked Keno.

"You mean them fag niggas from Prince Hall?"
asked Red.

"Nah, not them fools. Them niggas didn't give
us a fight at all. I'm talkin' 'bout those fools who
didn't want to tell us the combo to they shit.
You remember, Taz. You was like, 'Fuck it! Let's

bounce!' 'Cause we had already popped they weak-ass crew comin' in."

"Oh, I know who you talkin' 'bout. The umm . . . umm . . . what was they fucking names? Oh! Mick and Mike, or was it Mikey and Mike? Some shit like that," Taz said and sipped some more of his XO.

"Yeah, them clowns. Anyway, remember when I got mad and was about to pop 'em?"

"Yeah, and Bo-Pete stopped you."

"That's right! Do you know the reason why he stopped me?"

"'Cause the spot was hot and we had to get the fuck outta there!" Wild Bill laughed from the other side of the room.

"Nah, nigga. That nigga Bo-Pete was cool with them fools. He didn't want to hurt them 'cause he said y'all used to be on the same football team back at John Marshall and shit."

"Yeah, they was, but I wasn't even thinkin' 'bout no shit like that. We was hungry, and we did what we did 'cause that was our thang," Taz said as he sat down next to Sacha.

"I know, but you didn't care if we let them make it or not. Remember how hot Bo-Pete got at me when I told him to take his soft ass outside to the truck while I pop them clowns?"

"Yeah. That nigga wanted to do you somethin' for real," answered Red.

"That's right. Y'all got into it big time after you smoked them fools. Bo-Pete was mad at your ass for about a month behind that shit," Bob said as he rubbed Gwen's thigh.

"So tell me. What's the point of this story?" asked Won.

"The point is, my nigga was a good nigga. He had a good heart. Me, I was on some Eazy-E ruthless shit. They saw our faces so they had to fuckin' go! But not my nigga Bo-Pete. He felt they wouldn't try to get back at us, so he wanted to give them a pass. That was one good nigga right there for real!" slurred Keno.

The room fell silent for a few minutes as everyone started thinking about how much they missed Bo-Pete. Taz broke the silence and said, "Come on, y'all. Let's go get something to eat. I'm fuckin' starvin'."

"Yeah. Let's hit up one of your spots. At least that way we'll be able to eat for free!" Bob started laughing.

"Look at this clown! All those chips and he wants to get a free fuckin' meal! Niggas will always be niggas!" Red said as everyone started laughing.

Won stepped over to Taz and said, "I gots to be going, Baby Boy. I got a flight to catch out of Tulsa in a couple of hours. Let me talk to you for a minute."

Taz took Won upstairs to his bedroom and started to change clothes. As he was getting undressed, Won told him, "I don't know what's what on this last mission. Shit ain't going according to plan, so I really need for you to stay on point for me. If something goes wrong, I want you to promise me that you will take care of things that need to be taken care of."

After Taz slid into a pair of black Dickies, he asked Won, "What are you talkin' about, O.G.? Don't be gettin' at me with no riddles. That's not for me and you. What's up?"

Won sighed, and for the first time in a long time he showed someone that he was worried. "I don't know, Baby Boy. I think Pitt done got the upper hand on me this time. I haven't heard from one of my peoples in a minute, and when I got at him, I could have sworn that Pitt answered his phone."

"So, you think that nigga Pitt got at your peeps?"

"I don't know. I think so though. Flo' is shaking me, and the rest of the council is being real tight-lipped, like they know something is about to pop off. But, look, I'm gon' keep it straight with you. If something happens to me, you will inherit everything that I have. You're like the son I've always wanted, Baby Boy, and I love you that much. But you gots to promise me that you won't try to get revenge on any member of the council."

"What are you talkin' about, O.G.? I don't even know who the council is."

"Listen. When everything is everything, you will then understand the meaning of this conversation. You will have a decision to make, and I'm banking on you to make the right one. If something happens to me, Pitt will be responsible. Don't worry about that nigga though. He's a slipper."

Taz smiled and said, "Yeah, and slippers fall."

"Exactly."

"But, on the real, what's poppin', O.G.?" Taz asked seriously.

"It is what it is, Baby Boy. Only time will tell how this one is going to fall. You just make sure that you continue to stay ready. If things go as planned, I'm going to need you to be ready. If they don't, you're still going to have to be prepared to handle shit. Remember this—whatever you decide, you will have my blessing. If and when the time comes, you'll understand everything I've just told you. All of the hard work we've put in was for this sole purpose. I don't want to fail. You know I've never lost, but I got a funny feeling I just might lose this one. If that's the case, I want you in the position that I've been striving for all of these years."

"The position of power you told me about?"

"Exactly." Won gave Taz a tight hug and said, "We can't change fate, Baby Boy. If it's meant to be, it will be. Always remember, I will always love you and that crazy-ass crew of yours."

"Come on with that shit, O.G.! You're spookin' a nigga. We've already lost Bo-Pete. I don't think I can stand another loss that heavy."

"Losses are a part of life, Baby Boy. You can handle it. You're built for the long haul. I knew that the first day I saw you. There's one more thing I want you to do for me."

"What's that?"

"Start thinking things through more thoroughly. You handled the situation with Neema ass backward. I realize it was because of your pain and anger behind Bo-Pete. She's your only child, you should have considered her feelings in this mess."

"I did. That's why I waited to deal with that nigga, and look what happened because of me waiting."

"Still, you should have finessed the situation instead of exposing your hand. Now you're on the verge of losing the love of your only child. If something happens to that fool right now, even if it's an accident, there would be nothing you could do or say to prove your innocence to Neema. She would blame you, no matter what."

"So, what should I do now, O.G.?"

"Call her and let her know that you love her, and even though you're not feeling dude, you're willing to let this pass simply because you're hurting too damn much behind the loss of Bo-Pete. Explain to her how deeply you feel for her and her well-being. Show your seed that the love you have for her is stronger than any revenge plot. Make sure that you're sincere enough to convince her you're being real with her."

Taz smiled and asked, "And after I've convinced her that I'm sincere?"

"You already know. Smoke that nigga! He has to be punished for our loss. But make sure you have a solid alibi, not only for the people, but for Neema as well." They hugged each other again quickly, and Won said, "All right, I'm out. I'll give you a call in a few days if I've learned anything. If you don't hear from me, then that means I've went dark and I'll holla when the time is right. I have to take care of a few loose ends out in Texas, but I will get at you when the time is right."

"What if something goes left? How will I know what's what?"

"You'll be notified," Won said as he turned and left the bedroom.

***

Later on that night after enjoying a pretty pleasant evening with his friends, Taz and Sacha were lying in bed, talking about their future. "Which room are we going to turn into the baby's room, Taz?" Sacha asked as she stretched and slid into his arms.

"It don't matter to me, Li'l Mama. Whichever one you want."

"I was thinking about the guest room right next to us. I want my baby to be as close to me as possible, all of the time."

He laughed and said, "*Your* baby? What about me? Ain't he gon' be mine too?"

She laughed and said, "Why do you keep referring to the baby as a *he*? What if it's a she?"

Taz shook his head from side to side and said, "No way, Li'l Mama! I know for sure it's goin' to be a boy."

"What makes you so positive about that, Mr. Taz?"

"'Cause my son is replacing Bo-Pete," he said somberly.

"Is that the name you've chosen for him if indeed we do have a son?"

"Yep. Reginald Good—Li'l Bo-Pete," Taz said with a sad smile on his face. "Do you have a problem with that, Li'l Mama?"

"Nope. I like it, baby. I really do. Can I ask you a question though?"

"You know you can. What's good?"

"When are we going to make this engagement official and do the damn thing? I'm ready to become Mrs. Good."

"You know, I was thinking about that too. Do you want to wait until after the baby is born, or are you ready to make it happen this summer?"

She smiled and said, "This summer is fine with me!" They laughed and shared an intense kiss with one another. Afterward, Sacha said, "Umm, you know you done got me horny with all of that sweet tongue you just gave me."

He pulled at her transparent thong and said, "Well, let's take care of that then!"

Chapter Twenty-six

The next morning when Taz climbed out of bed, he noticed that Sacha had already left for work. He smiled as he thought about her and how freaky she had been during their lovemaking. *That girl be trying to put it on a nigga,* he thought as he went downstairs to get himself something to drink.

As he sipped on some orange juice, he decided to give Neema a call and do as Won suggested. He grabbed the cordless phone off the kitchen counter and dialed his daughter's number. When Tazneema answered the phone, he said, "Hey, Baby Girl. What you up to?"

"Nothing. Just getting ready to go back to school. It feels so strange since I've been out for so long. I have a lot of catching up to do."

"Yeah, I bet you do. You'll be all right though. Look, Neema, I'm not goin' to play any games with you. I hate that nigga Cliff. I hate the fact that you fell in love with him also. I hate it even more that you're goin' to have a child by him. But all of the hate I have is nothing compared to the love I have for you, Baby Girl. I could never intentionally cause you any pain. It took for me to bury Bo-Pete to realize that this shit is just not worth it. Please understand that I'm not changing the way I feel about him, 'cause that will never change, because whether you believe it or not, he did have something to do with the death of you uncle."

"Taz—"

"No, wait, Neema. Let me finish. Like I was sayin', the love I have for you is stronger than any hateful feelings I have for Cliff. Keep him away from me and my home. He's not welcome. Do that, and I promise you that I'll never do him nothin'."

"What about the others? How do they feel?"

"We all love you, and we've all come to this conclusion last night," he lied. "You mean the world to us, and we don't want to cause you any pain. Plus, Keno said he feared for his life 'cause you was wolfin' some high-powered gangsta shit!"

Tazneema laughed as tears of joy and relief slid down her face. "I love you, Daddy! Thank you! Thank you so very much!"

"I love you too, Baby Girl. Now, gon' and finish gettin' ready for school. If you need anything, give me a holla."

"I will," she said, and hung up the phone feeling real good inside.

After Taz hung up the phone, he smiled because he knew that Won would be proud of how he just rocked his daughter to sleep with his manipulation. Because there was no way in hell that nigga Cliff would still be breathing by the end of the summer. *After me and Sacha do our wedding thang, that nigga is good as dead,* he thought to himself as he downed the rest of his orange juice.

Keno slapped Katrina on her thick behind and said, "Girl, you better get your ass up! You're goin' to be late for work."

She rolled to the other side of Keno's California king-sized bed and said, "Come on, boo. Let me sleep a li'l longer, 'kay?"

Keno laughed and said, "For real, for real, I don't give a damn if you never went to work again. It ain't like you need the money. Fuckin' with me, you straight."

His statement made her open her eyes. She turned and faced him and asked, "What does that mean, Keno? You trying to take care of me or something?"

"Yeah, it's time for a nigga to settle down and start a family and shit. You with somethin' like that?"

Katrina smiled and happily asked, "Are you trying to wife me, Keno?"

He returned her smile and said, "Do you wanna be wifey?"

She frowned and said, "You can't answer a question with one, Keno!"

"Yes, I'm tryin' to wife you. Will you marry me, Katrina?"

"Yes! Yes! *Yes!*" She screamed as she rolled into his arms and kissed him passionately. "I love you, Keno! I love you so much!"

Keno didn't know how much he had actually cared about Katrina until that very moment, because he said the three words he never thought he would ever tell a woman. "Yeah, Mommy, I love you too. So, you gon' quit your job and shit now?"

She pulled from his embrace and said, "Uh-uh. I'm going to finish school and keep on working. What I look like, just living off my man? I'm gon' bring something to the table too. I'm a *real* woman, Keno. Not some leech."

Keno laughed and said, "Mommy, if I thought you were anything less than a real woman, you would have never gotten as close to me as you have. My wifey don't have to do no work if she don't want to. I'm in a position to make sure that your every dream can come true. Your every want and desire can and will be fulfilled. All you have to do is tell me what you want, Mommy. Real talk."

Staring deeply into Keno's brown eyes, Katrina said, "I believe you, baby, but all I want from you is your love and devotion."

"You got that, Mommy."

"What about the game, Keno? Are you going to stop hustling?"

Keno laughed and said, "Hustling? What makes you think I'm a hustler?"

"Come on, baby, don't play me like that. Look at all of this," she said as she waved her arms around Keno's bedroom. "This big-ass mini-mansion you're living in, the fat Range Rover, the six hundred and all of them expensive low riders that you have in your garage, not to mention all of the expensive jewelry and stuff. I'm not lame to the game, baby. I just want you to be smart enough to get out while you're way ahead of it, that's all. I don't want to become your wife just to lose you one day to jail, or like Bo—well . . . you know what I'm saying."

Keno pulled her toward him and said, "Listen to me, Mommy. I'm not goin' to nobody's jail, and I don't plan on leaving this Earth anytime soon. You don't ever have to worry yourself about none of that craziness. I'm here for as long as you want me to be. As for the hustling, that shit is funny. I don't get down like that. I'm a legit businessman. I have more shit than I can even begin to explain." He jumped off the bed and stepped quickly toward his dresser. He opened one of the drawers, pulled out a black bankbook, went back to the bed and handed it to Katrina and said, "Look at this, Mommy, and tell me if you think a hustler could do it this big."

Her eyes damn near popped out of their sockets when she saw the seven figures inside of Keno's bank account. She was speechless as she saw how much money he earned yearly.

"You see, Mommy, I ain't no damn hustler. Everybody out there thinks we're dope boys or some shit like that. They're so far off that it's crazy, and that's exactly how we like it. Let niggas in the streets think we're dope boys or whatever. As long as we keep everyone in left field, we'll always stay one step ahead of the game. So, don't worry about a thang. Once you become wifey, everything in my life will finally be complete. You with that?"

"Am I! Come here!" she said as she pulled his face to hers and kissed him deeply.

After their kiss, he asked her, "So, are you goin' to work today? Or are we going to go get your wedding ring?"

She smiled and said, "Yeah, I'm going to work. You're going to go get my wedding ring, baby. I want you to pick what you want me to have on this finger," she said as she wiggled her ring finger in front of his face.

"Your wish is my every command, Mommy," he said as he started laughing. *Damn! This love shit feels pretty good,* he thought to himself with a smile on his face.

Katrina frowned and asked, "What's so funny, Keno?"

"I can't believe I just said some corny-ass movie shit like that."

She playfully slapped him on his face and said, "That was not corny, Keno. That was the sweetest thing you've ever said to me."

"Yeah, it may be, but that was still some corny-ass shit," he said as he quickly ducked another blow from his fiancée. He grabbed her around her waist and pulled her close to him and said, "I'll be as corny as I wanna be for you, Mommy, 'cause you're about to be wifey."

With a bright smile on her face, Katrina said, "That, I am, baby. That, I am."

After Katrina had gotten dressed and left for work, Keno called Red and told him what he had done.

Red started laughing and said, "Nigga, stop lyin'! I know you didn't! Not you!"

"I did it, dog. As a matter a fact, I'm about to get dressed and go pick her out a tight-ass wedding ring right after I get off the phone with your ass," Keno said proudly.

"That's cool, my nigga. Congratulations."

"Thanks. What you got goin' on for the day?"

"Shit. I might go scoop Paquita up and take her out to lunch or something. Other than that, my plate's empty. We need to be gettin' back on our regular schedule for real. We haven't worked out in a minute."

"Yeah, I know. But with Wild Bill out of commission and Bob still laid up, I guess Taz just ain't been feelin' it, ya know?"

"Yeah, this shit is crazy, dog. I still can't believe all of the shit that's happened. Bo-Pete's gone, dog. He's fuckin' gone!"

"I know. All we can do now is finish what we started, and live on for him, G. His peoples is straight, so it ain't like he didn't bless the game."

"That's one way you can look at it. But from my eyes, I'm like, why didn't the game bless my nigga? Bo-Pete didn't deserve that shit, dog."

"I feel you. But, look, I'm in a pretty good mood right about now. I'm not tryin' to get back all depressed on the day that I've officially surrendered my playa card. I'll holla at ya later, my nigga. I'm about to go buy a wedding ring."

Red laughed and said, "My bad, dog! Gon' and do you, my nigga. Get at me when you've finished handlin' your business."

"Out!" Keno said and hung up the phone and went into his bathroom to take a shower so he could start his day.

After Taz finished getting dressed, he called his mother and explained his conversation with his daughter. When he was finished, Mama-Mama said, "Humph! She believed all of that, huh?"

Taz smiled into the receiver and thought, *I can fool my daughter, but I damn sure can't fool my Mama!* But to her he said, "Why wouldn't she? I meant it, Mama-Mama. I want nothing but the best for Neema. You know that."

"Yes, I do know that, but don't you think for one minute that I believe you're not going to do something to that boy! I know you better than you think, Taz Good! You are not the type to let things go. And if your silly-ass daughter was thinking straight, she would be able to see through the bullshit you're pulling her through. I have one question for you: What are you going to do after you finally do whatever you have planned for that boy, Taz? And don't you dare lie to me, boy!"

He laughed and said, "Whatever's goin' to happen won't be my fault, Mama-Mama . . . at least that's how it's goin' to look."

"Mmm-hmm. I figured that much. Bye, boy! I got my food on the stove."

"Bye, Mama-Mama," Taz said and hung up the phone laughing.

After taking a quick shower and getting dressed, he called Sacha at work to see if she wanted to go out to lunch with him. Sacha's receptionist told him that she was out of the office and that she would be back around one. Since it looked like he was solo for the day, he picked the phone back up and called Bob.

Bob answered the phone on the first ring and said, "What's really good, my nigga? You must have read my fuckin' mind, 'cause I was just thinkin' 'bout your ass."

"Yeah! What's poppin', *G*?"

"Please—and I mean *please*—come and rescue me from this overbearing woman of mines! She's driving me fuckin' batty in this house, dog!"

Taz started laughing and said, "Yeah, well, that's good for your ass. Gwen needs to stay on top of your ass."

"That's the fuckin' problem! She won't get off a nigga! She's turned into some kind of fuckin' sex maniac! I'm tellin' you, G, I'm not even fully healed, and she's tryin' to fuck my brains out! You know a nigga loves the pussy and all, but damn! A nigga needs a fuckin' break sometimes!"

Taz heard Gwen in the background scream, "What kind of man runs from some good pussy, Taz?"

Taz laughed so hard that tears started forming in his eyes. "Damn, my nigga! It's like that?"

"You fuckin' right, it's like that! Come and get a nigga, dog. You're the only one she'll let me bounce with. She said I'd run over Red, Keno or Wild Bill and get into some shit. She's comfortable if you come scoop me though. For some reason she feels you can control 'The Bob.'"

"All right, look. Get dressed, and I'll be over there in about thirty minutes. We can go get somethin' to eat and go check out a few rental houses out in Midwest City. I checked my e-mails a li'l while ago, and saw that a few new listings have been posted."

"That's cool, *G.* Anything, and I mean *any-thing,* to get me away from this house is fine with me!" Bob said, relieved.

"You scared-ass nigga! You better hurry up, Taz, 'cause I might just change my mind and pull out my whips and handcuffs!" yelled Gwen in the background.

Taz hung up the phone and was in tears as he grabbed his keys and went into the garage.

Taz and Bob had just left from checking out their fourth rental house out in Midwest City. They were now on their way to get some lunch when Taz got a call from Sacha on his cell phone. "What's good, Li'l Mama?" he asked when he answered it.

"I just got back to the office, and I saw that you called. Why didn't you call me on my cell?"

"I didn't want to disturb you. I thought you might have been busy or somethin'. Have you had lunch yet?"

"Nope. I was hoping you'd take me some-where so I could get my grub on. I'm starving."

"You're always starvin', Li'l Mama." Before she could reply, he said, "I know, I know. You're eating for two."

She laughed and said, "You got that right, buddy! So, are you taking me and your child to lunch or what?"

"Yeah, I'll feed you two. Better yet, you three! Bob is with me. We've been out in Midwest City checking out some rental houses that recently came up for sale."

"Bob? Where's my girl at? Don't tell me he done shook my nigga!" Sacha said, trying to sound as 'hood as she could.

Taz laughed and said, "Nah, she let him roll with me for a li'l while. Really, it was more of an escape for Bob. Your girl has been tryin' to fuck him to death."

"*What?* Never mind. Forget I asked."

"I'll put you up on it in a li'l bit. We'll be there in about fifteen minutes. I'm gettin' on the highway now."

"Hurry up. I want me some ribs from Tony Roma's."

"All right, greedy. I'll be there in a minute," he said, and closed his cell phone.

Taz, Bob and Sacha were enjoying their meal of barbeque ribs, baked beans and potato salad, when Red called Taz and told him about Keno asking Katrina to marry him.

"Is that right? That's way out. I'd never think that nigga was the marrying type," Taz said as he continued to munch on his rib tips.

"Yeah, I know, but it looks like that nigga is for real. When I talked to him earlier, he told me that he was on his way to go pick her up a ring and everything. That nigga is definitely serious. I got Wild Bill with me now. We're about to roll over to that nigga's spot and check out how much money he done spent on his future wifey."

"Y'all niggas are that bored, huh?"

"Yeah. It ain't shit else to do. I was tellin' Keno earlier that we need to get back to working out and shit too. We've gotten way off schedule."

"I know. Let's get together around seven and get back on it."

"That's straight. Did Won speak about finishing up everything while he was here?" asked Red.

"Yeah. He told me to make sure that we stay ready. He also told me that he thinks things may have went left on him."

"What? What's up with that?"

"I'm not knowin', really. I'll put y'all up on it when we get together for our workout. Ask that li'l nigga, Wild Bill, if he can put any weight on that sore shoulder of his."

After Red asked Wild Bill Taz's question, Taz heard Wild Bill say, "Fuck you, nigga! I can still out-bench your ass with a weak shoulder!"

Taz laughed and said, "Now that's what I'm talkin' 'bout! All right then, my niggas. I'll holla in the morning. Tell that nigga Keno I said he will be gettin' clowned when I see his ass. I ain't forgot how he tried to clown me when I told him I asked Sacha to be wifey."

Red started laughing and said, "All right, dog. I'll—*What the fuck!*"

"What's up, G?" Taz asked with alarm.

"Somethin's wrong, dog! Keno's front door is wide the fuck open, and there's a body layin' in the doorway, my nigga! Hold on for a minute," Red said as he and Wild Bill jumped out of his truck and ran toward Keno's front door.

When Taz heard Red scream, "Ah, hell nah! Hell nah!" He knew that he had lost another close friend. Fuck!

Chapter Twenty-seven

After Taz and Bob dropped Sacha off back at her job, Taz drove like a bat out of hell toward Keno's home.

"I'm tellin' you, dog, we gots to put an end to that nigga Cliff! He's fuckin' tryin' to kill all of us!" Bob yelled from the passenger's seat.

"He's dead, dog! That nigga is dead to-fuck-ing-night! I can't believe this shit! How in the fuck was he able to find out where Keno's spot was?"

"Do you think ol' girl might have put them niggas up on it?"

"Nah, Katrina don't strike me as a broad like that. But we'll still check into it later though. I ain't puttin' nothin' past nobody right now," Taz said as he pulled into the long, circular driveway that led to Keno's mini-mansion.

Police cars, as well as an ambulance, were parked in the driveway as they climbed out of Taz's truck. Taz saw Red talking to Detective Bean, and quickly rushed over toward them. Once he was standing in front of the detective, he asked, "Where's the body? I want to see my nigga!"

"This is a crime scene, Taz. You'll do more damage by trying to take a look at your friend," Detective Bean said as he stood in front of Taz.

Taz frowned at the detective and whispered through clenched teeth, "Where is my homeboy's body?"

Detective Bean sighed heavily and said, "Follow me."

Taz, Red and Bob followed the detective toward the front door of Keno's home. There were several police officers, as well as other detectives standing and moving around.

Taz stepped to the doorway and saw a body covered with a white sheet. He stepped to the body, knelt next to it and pulled the sheet back. Tears fell slowly from his eyes as he stared at Keno's dead body. He could see one of the bullet holes that had killed his man. Keno had been shot three times at close range with a small-caliber pistol. He could tell because of the size of the bullet-holes. After wiping his face, he replaced the sheet over Keno's body, stood and stepped out of the house.

Wild Bill, who had been on his cell trying to get in contact with Katrina, saw Taz walking toward his truck and said, "Dog, what the fuck are we gon' do now?"

Taz stared at Wild Bill for a moment then said, "Right now, I'm goin' home, G. Y'all take Bob back to his spot for me. I need to be by myself for a Li'l bit."

Before Wild Bill could say anything in response, Taz saw a blue Nissan Maxima pull into the driveway. Katrina jumped out of her car and ran toward the front door of Keno's house, screaming, "No-o-o-o-o! No-o-o-o! He asked me to marry him today! God, no-o-o-o! We're getting married!"

With tears sliding down his face, Taz said, "Go take care of her, G. I gots to get the fuck outta here." He turned and stepped quickly to his truck and left the scene of a crime that had just broken his heart.

Taz drove from Keno's home straight to his mother's house out in the country. As soon as he walked inside of the house, Mama-Mama took one look at him and knew something was wrong. She stood and asked, "Who's been killed, Taz?"

Taz stared at his mother with tears falling from his eyes and said, "Keno. That nigga done killed my man, Mama-Mama! Out of all of us, that nigga killed my man! Please, Mama-Mama! Please tell me that you know where that nigga lives!"

Mama-Mama sat back down on the couch and shook her head sadly as she said, "I've never known where that boy's house is. And if I did, you know I wouldn't tell you, Taz. You have to let this stuff go, boy."

"Let it go? *Let it go?* How in the hell can I let this go when that nigga keeps on killin' my niggas? That man has to die, Mama-Mama! Can't you see that?"

Tears started falling from Mama-Mama's eyes as she fully understood what her only child was telling her. She couldn't believe Keno was dead. She'd practically raised him along with Taz. "Oh, Lord, please stop this madness!" she prayed aloud.

Taz went and sat down next to his mother, wrapped his arms around her and gave her a tight hug. "I'm sorry for yellin' at you, Mama-Mama, but it feels as if I'm losing my mind. I can't take too much more of this. I've got to put an end to that nigga, and the sooner the better."

"But what about Neema? You know what this is going to do to that girl, Taz."

"Yeah, I know, but what about the rest of us? Sooner or later, that nigga and his Crip homeboys are going to get lucky and get me, Bob and Wild Bill. I'm tellin' you, Mama-Mama, this is the only way. That man has to die!"

***

Sacha went to Taz's house after she got off of work, and went straight into his den. She turned on the television and watched the news as the reporter talked about Keno's murder. She sat down on the sofa and said a silent prayer: *Please, God, don't let Taz get too crazy behind this.* As she prayed, she knew that her prayer was in vain, because there was nothing and no one that could stop Taz from getting his revenge for Keno. That thought scared her more than anything in this world. She grabbed the phone and called Gwen.

As soon as Gwen answered the phone, she said, "Bitch, you do know that all hell's about to break loose, don't you?"

"Yeah, I know, ho. Them niggas are 'bout to go crazy," Sacha said as she relaxed back on the sofa.

"Do you know what happened?"

"Uh-uh. Me, Taz and Bob were having lunch at Tony Roma's when Red called Taz and told him that something was wrong at Keno's house. Taz dropped me off back at the office and left to go over to Keno's. I just came home and turned on the TV and saw that they don't have a clue as to what happened to him."

"Humph! Them TV people might not know what happened, but I do! Them Crip niggas did this shit! Bob is going to go so crazy behind this shit!" Gwen yelled, totally frustrated.

"Bob? Ho, Bob's not going to be half as bad as Taz is. The shit is really about to hit the fan. I can't believe this shit either."

"Believe it, bitch, 'cause it damn sure is true!"

After sitting and talking to his mother for a few hours, Taz decided that it was time to get at Tazneema, so he grabbed the phone and called his daughter. When she answered the phone, he said, "What's up, Baby Girl?"

"Hi, Taz," Tazneema said as she sat down on her bed.

"I'm not goin' to waste time with this, Neema. There's somethin' I need to tell you, and you're not goin' to like it."

"What's wrong now, Taz?"

"Your Uncle Keno was found dead at his house this afternoon."

"Wha—what are you saying? Wh-who did this?" Before Taz could answer her questions, she had slapped her hand over her mouth and screamed into her palm. She knew what her father was about to say, and she didn't want to hear it. "Please, Daddy! Don't tell me that you think Cliff did this to my Uncle Keno!"

Taz inhaled deeply and said, "He did. I know what I told you about tryin' to accept that nigga, Neema. At that time I meant it. But now, shit has changed. That nigga won't stop until he has all of us lying side by side up at Trice Hill. He's got to go," he said, and hung up the phone in his daughter's ear.

Tears were streaming down Mama-Mama's face as Taz gave her a kiss on her salty cheek and said, "I'll talk to you later, Mama-Mama."

Mama-Mama was too choked up to speak. She gave him a nod of her head and watched her only child as he left her home, on his way most likely to commit a murder.

As Taz was leaving his mother's house, Taznee-ma was calling her man to warn him. Clifford answered his cell and listened to her as she screamed at him. "You have to stay out there in Dallas, Cliff! My daddy is going to kill you if you come back to the city!"

"What are you talking about, Neema? Calm down!" Cliff said as he got off of the bed in his hotel room at the Westin in downtown Oklahoma City.

"Someone has killed my Uncle Keno, and my daddy thinks that you are that someone!"

"What? That's preposterous! You know damn well I'm not even in the city right now, Neema!" Cliff lied.

"I know, but my father doesn't."

"Well, why didn't you tell him?"

"He didn't give me a chance to. He hung up on me before I could tell him. Just make sure that you stay where you are until I can get a chance to talk to him, okay?"

"That's bullshit! I'm sick and tired of this shit! I'm on my way back to the city now. I'll give you a call when I hit Norman."

"Please, Cliff! Stay where you are, at least one more day. Give me a chance to talk to my daddy."

"No, Neema, it's time we put a stop to this madness right now," Cliff said, and he hung up the phone. He grabbed his keys, wallet and cell phone as he left his hotel room. As he was riding the elevator down to the lobby, he dialed H-Hop's cell phone number. "I can't believe that nigga got at Keno! "Clifford said to himself as he waited for H-Hop to answer his phone. When he got H-Hop's voice mail, he left him a quick message: "Get at me, cuz. We gots to talk. Hit me on my cell," he said, and closed his cell phone. *This shit is about to get hectic real quick like,* he thought as he stepped off of the elevator.

By the time Taz pulled into his driveway, Sacha was a nervous wreck. She just knew that he would be out hunting for Cliff all night long. She gave a sigh of relief when he walked into the bedroom. She jumped off of the bed, ran into his arms and said, "Taz, baby, I'm so sorry. I'm so sorry about Keno."

He held on tightly to his fiancée and said, "It's real fucked up, Li'l Mama . . . real fucked up!" He gave her a kiss on her forehead and said, "Come on, let's lay down for a minute." He pulled her back toward the bed and slipped off his Timberland boots.

Once they were comfortable, he said, "I've been driving around the city for the last few hours, thinking about all types of shit. This shit with Won, what's happened to Keno, you, and everything else that's been goin' on in my crazy-ass life. I'm tellin' you, Li'l Mama, I'm a cursed nigga. Everyone that comes into my life seems to always end up getting hurt."

Shaking her head no, Sacha said, "That's not true, baby. It just seems that way because of Bo-Pete and Keno's untimely deaths. You're not cursed, you're just going through some rough times right now, that's all."

"Rough times, huh? Li'l Mama, in less than a month I've lost two of my closest friends—two men who were like brothers to me. I lost one woman who I loved more than anything in this world because of my arrogance and stupidity. Can you imagine how it feels every time I look at Tazneema and see her mother's features? Can you imagine how it feels to know that I'll never be able to tell my niggas how much I really loved them? Can you imagine how my relationship is going to be with my daughter after I kill the nigga she's about to have a baby by? Can you? Huh? You can't sit there and tell me I ain't cursed, Li'l Mama. The life I chose to live has caused all of this pain! All of this is my fuckin' fault! I accept that, because that was the hand I was dealt. I'm not a quitter, nor am I ever goin' to let another nigga beat me at this gangsta shit. So, the first thing in the morning, I want to go down to your office and redo my will. I have one already written through your firm. I want to make a few changes just in case somethin' goes left."

"What are you talking about, baby?"

He stared deeply into her eyes and said, "Won has always taught me to be ready, and that's exactly what I'm doin' now. I'm stayin' ready for whatever."

"But why?"

"'Cause I'm 'bout to go all the way out, Li'l Mama. All the fuckin' way out!" Taz said as he turned flat on his back and closed his eyes.

Tears slid down Sacha's face as she watched the tears slide slowly down the face of her man. *Damn!*

Chapter Twenty-eight

After riding through his old neighborhood a few times looking for H-Hop, Clifford decided to go on and head out to Tazneema's apartment. He left word with a few of his homeboys to tell H-Hop to get with him as soon as possible. As he drove toward Norman, he was still wondering where the hell H-Hop was. More importantly, how in the hell did he get at Keno? "Damn! We gots to hurry up and smash that nigga Taz now! If we don't, he won't stop until I'm a dead man," he said aloud as he made a right turn into the city of Norman.

Tazneema was so happy to see her man that she didn't know what to do. She grabbed Clifford around his waist and led him into the bedroom.

Lyla was sitting at the kitchen table studying as they went into Tazneema's bedroom. "Damn, that was rude! She didn't even have time to stop and let that whack-looking clown speak! The dick can't be that good!" she said as she went back to her studies.

Inside the bedroom, Tazneema and Clifford were kissing each other as if this would be their last time ever being intimate with one another. After a few minutes of this, Clifford pulled from her embrace and said, "Whoa! What's gotten into you, Neema?"

"I love you, baby, and I'm so scared that my daddy is going to hurt you. Why couldn't you do as I asked you and stay out in Dallas?" she said as she sat down on the end of the bed.

Clifford sat next to her and said, "Because, I haven't done anything, Neema. Why should I hide from Taz when I have absolutely nothing to hide for? Whomever killed Keno has nothing to do with me."

"Are you sure? Are you positive that it wasn't some of your old homeboys, Cliff?"

"I can't honestly say that right now, but I am looking into it. I'll know for sure after I talk to my homeboy, H-Hop. As of right now, I'm speaking from my gut, because I don't feel that any of my people had the resources to be able to get at someone like Keno. So relax, baby. Everything is going to be all right."

"How can you say that and be so sure, Cliff? Haven't you understood anything I've told you? Taz is going to try his best to make sure that you no longer exist. He's not playing, baby, and he damn sure doesn't give a damn about how I feel anymore. My Uncle Bo-Pete, and now my Uncle Keno . . . I'm positive he's about to go on a rampage. Any and everybody who gets in his way is going to be in some serious trouble."

"I understand what you've told me, Neema, but what can I do? Run from your father for the rest of my life? I haven't done anything to him or any of his friends. Once I've found out for sure whether or not any of my homeboys had anything to do with this mess, I'm going to put an end to this craziness."

"How are you going to do that, baby?"

"I'll call a meeting with your father and explain the situation to him."

Tazneema started laughing and said, "You have to be playing, 'cause ain't no way in hell Taz is going to go for some shit like that. Do you really understand what kind of man my daddy is? You obviously don't, because if you did, you would know that trying to arrange a meeting with him would be like you signing your own death certificate!"

Clifford smiled and said, "I'm no fool, Neema. Nor am I trying to put myself six feet under anytime soon. When it's time for us to meet, we'll meet somewhere I'll know I'll be completely safe. I still have some powerful friends in the city, baby. They'll make sure that I'm protected while I present my case to Taz."

"If you say so, baby. Just please, don't think for an instant that he's going to let you make it, 'cause I could hear it in his voice, he wants your head."

"Don't worry about that mess. I got it under control," he said as he pulled her into his arms again. After sharing another intense kiss, he smiled and said, "Is it cool if I spend the night with you, baby?"

Tazneema smiled, pulled off her T-shirt and slid back onto her bed and said, "I was hoping you'd say that. Now, come here and give me some of that big old thang!"

Red, Wild Bill and Bob came over to Taz's home early the next morning, feeling defeated. The pain of losing yet another close friend was weighing heavily in their hearts. Taz let them inside and led them into the den.

Precious and Heaven were lying in front of the pool table when the four men entered the room. Taz smiled at his beloved Dobermans and said, "Go play!" Both of the dogs jumped to their feet and silently left the den.

Bob smiled and said, "I don't think I'll ever get used to how them dogs understand you so well, G. That shit is crazy for real."

"It cost me a grip and a lot of time with them, but it was well worth it. They'll never let me down, dog," Taz said as he sat down on the sectional sofa. "All right, we already know who did this shit, and we already know why. What's fuckin' with me is, how in the hell did they get that close to Keno?"

"Yeah, I've been thinkin' the same shit," said Red. "I mean, the Ones said he was tapped three times in the back of the head. How the fuck could someone other than one of us get that close to him? I called Katrina's job. She arrived at work exactly when she said she did, so that scratches her, G. Who else could get close enough to him to be able to tap him in the back of the dome? That's the million-dollar fuckin' question."

"Fuck it! It's done, dog. Our nigga is out. We gots to lay the rest of them fools down now. Them niggas ain't playin', so we might as well turn this shit right back up until we get our man," Wild Bill said angrily.

"I agree. Them niggas gots to go, dog," added Bob.

"We might as well get onto that nigga, H-Hop. He's our best bet at gettin' at Cliff. Once we take them two, this shit should be over. Them other youngstas ain't tryin' to let this shit carry on."

"How can you be so fuckin' sure, Taz? Them niggas might be ready to ride or die for their losses too. Fuck this shit! Let's take it to every last one of them niggas! Fuck Hoover! They all die!" screamed an emotional Bob.

"Come on, my nigga. I'm feelin' your pain, but we can't be stupid with this shit. We know who the beef is with, and we're goin' to take it to they ass. But overdoin' it won't do any of us any good. It'll only hurt us in the long run. We gots to play this shit smart. Let's get onto that nigga, H-Hop's spot later on tonight and see if we can get a line on where Cliff rests his head."

"Yeah. So once we find that out, we can take that nigga's head smooth off!" Red said menacingly.

"Exactly!" Taz said as he stared at his friends.

Clifford woke up when he heard his cell phone beeping, indicating that he had messages on his voice mail. He slipped out of Tazneema's bed and put on his boxer shorts and pants. He tiptoed lightly into the bathroom and closed the door so he wouldn't wake either Tazneema or her roommate, Lyla. After he relieved himself, he opened his cell and checked his messages. He had three, all of which were from his homeboy, H-Hop. He quickly dialed his apartment number and waited for him to answer his phone.

After the fourth ring, H-Hop finally answered. "What's up, cuz? Why the fuck are you callin' me this fuckin' early?" he asked.

"Where the fuck have you been hiding, cuz? I've been trying to get at you to see what's what with this shit."

"What's what with what? What the fuck are you talkin' 'bout?"

"Listen. My girl told me that her daddy is on the hunt for me, loc. We gots to hurry up and out that nigga, cuz. We can't be wasting no more time on his homeboys. We gots to get that nigga Taz. He told my girl that there is nothing and no one that's going to stop him from getting at me, so you know he's going to try and get at the homies again."

"I know, huh? Where you at, cuz?"

"I'm out here in Norman at my girl's pad."

"Nigga, you layin' up with that broad?"

"I'm good out this way."

"How the fuck you know she ain't called that nigga Taz and told him you over there?"

Clifford laughed and said, "That's the last thing I gots to worry about, cuz. Neema loves my dirty drawers. She'd never do me dirty like that, cuz."

"Nigga, you slippin'."

"As long as she never finds out about what we did to that nigga, Bo-Pete, she'll always be in my corner. I'm telling you, she'll go against her daddy for me, cuz. She loves me that fucking much. That's why we gots to hurry up and handle that nigga."

"Whatever, cuz. Look, get at me later so we can come up with somethin'. I'm about to lay it back down. That bitch I was chillin' with out in Midwest City damn near sucked a nigga dry. I gots to get me some fuckin' rest!"

"All right, cuz. I'm going to stay out this way until the sun sets. Then I'll come over to your pad. I'm about to go get me some early-morning pussy real quick, then I'll lay it down for a while."

H-Hop started laughing and said, "Cuz, you just as gone for that young broad as you say she is over your ass."

"Yeah, loco, you might be right. I do love her. I really don't want to hurt her or cause her any kind of pain, but her daddy gots to go," Clifford said seriously.

"You fuckin' right, cuz! I'll holla," H-Hop said, and he hung up the phone.

After Clifford closed his cell phone, he tiptoed out of the bathroom and back into Tazneema's bedroom. He didn't notice that Tazneema's roommate, Lyla, was standing right outside of the bathroom door.

After Red, Wild Bill and Bob left, Taz went upstairs and watched Sacha as she got dressed for work. He smiled as he saw the slight lump showing in her stomach. *Damn! I'm about to be a daddy again! This shit has got to stop. I can't keep livin' like this,* he said to himself as he continued to watch his fiancée.

Sacha turned, and for the first time she noticed that he was watching her. She said, "Are you all right, baby?"

"Yeah, I'm good. I'm just sittin' here thinkin' about how my nigga won't ever get to meet his future nephew."

She smiled sadly and said, "You mean his niece?"

Taz returned her smile and said, "Nah, I meant what I said, his nephew. Come here, Li'l Mama."

Sacha stepped over to where he was sitting, sat down on his lap and gave him a hug. He put his right hand on her stomach and began to rub it lightly and said, "I love you, Li'l Mama. When everything is everything, I think it's time we got the fuck outta the city and try somethin' new."

"Something new like what, baby?"

He shrugged his shoulders and said, "I don't know. I was thinkin' about some shit that Won got at me about. What do you think about movin' out to the West Coast?"

"California?"

"Yeah. You think you could do somethin' like that with me?"

"Baby, I'll go wherever you want me to. As long as I'm with you, I have no doubt that I'll be taken care of and completely happy."

"But what about your career? You haven't even been a partner at your firm for a full year yet."

"I don't care about that anymore, baby. All I want is for you to be happy with me. I can get a job, or even open up my own firm once we're settled out West. So don't let me stop you from making whatever decisions you need to make. I'm behind you one hundred percent." They kissed each other passionately. Then Sacha pulled from his embrace and said, "Now, let me go. I have a court appearance at ten."

He smiled and said, "All right, Li'l Mama. I got some calls to make and some more shit to handle later on. If I'm not here by the time you get off, hit me on my cell. It might just be a late one for me tonight."

She stared at her man and said, "Be careful, Taz."

Taz stared right back at his heart and soul and said, "All the time, Li'l Mama. All the time."

Tazneema got up a little after 9:00 A.M. to find Clifford sound asleep right next to her. She smiled as she thought about their early-morning sex session that they had a couple of hours ago. She climbed out of bed and went into the bathroom to get ready for her ten o'clock class. By the time she finished showering, she felt as if she was ready to take on the world.

That feeling changed quickly after she had a discussion with Lyla. As Tazneema was leaving the bathroom, Lyla came up to her and urgently said, "Come into my room for a minute. I know something that I think is very important to you."

Tazneema followed her roommate into her bedroom and watched as she closed the door behind them. "What's got you all spooked, girl?" she asked as she sat down on Lyla's bed.

Lyla took a deep breath and said, "Girl, you know I know how much you love Cliff, right?"

"Yeah, and?" Tazneema asked, slightly agitated.

"You know I would never do or say anything to hurt you, right?"

"Stop with the fucking questions, Lyla, and tell me what you have to say."

"All right. Dang! This morning, I was on my way to the bathroom, and I saw that the door was closed. I had to pee bad, so I waited outside of the door for whomever was in there to finish. I heard Cliff talking to someone on the phone. I looked at the bottom of the door and didn't see the phone cord, so I assumed he was on his cell phone. Anyway, he was talking to someone, and he told them that, and I quote, 'As long as she never finds out about what we did to that nigga, Bo-Pete, she'll be in my corner, cuz.' He then started talking about hurting your father."

"*What?* Are you sure, Lyla?"

"Come on, *T*! It might have been early in the morning, but I know what I heard. He said something about how he really loves you, but your daddy has to go. He kept saying 'cuz' a lot, like he's a gang member or something. Just before he hung up the phone, he said that he was about to go get some early-morning pussy, then he was going back to sleep for a while. Did you two do it this morning?"

"That's none of your business, girl!"

"I mean, if you did do it, then you know what I'm telling you is the truth. Your boyfriend is out to hurt your father, *T*. What has Taz done to Cliff?" Lyla asked with a puzzled look on her face.

Tazneema wanted to cry. She wanted to let her tears wash her face, not because she was physically hurting, but because she was ashamed of herself. She actually believed Cliff and all of his lies. She went against her flesh and blood for that man. Though she tried her best, she wasn't able to control her tears as they slowly slid down her face. She stared at her friend and said, "Tell me again everything that you heard, Lyla. Don't skip anything. This is very important." Tazneema wiped her eyes and listened closely to every word that her roommate said. Her pain had now turned into anger as she thought about her father. *I went against the grain, Daddy, and I'm so sorry!* she thought as she continued to listen to Lyla as she told her about Clifford's early-morning telephone conversation.

After Sacha left for work, Taz grabbed the phone and called Won out on the West Coast.

He knew it was early out there, but he needed to talk to his O.G. When Won answered his phone, Taz wasted no time in telling him about Keno's murder. After he finished, he took a deep breath and said, "We're handling this shit tonight, O.G. I gots to have this fool before he hurts someone else close to me."

"Yeah, you need to handle this as soon as possible. I didn't think that clown was that 'bout it," Won said as he wiped his teary eyes.

"To be honest with you, neither did I. Look, I just wanted to put you up on everything. Don't trip. I gots this end."

"I know you do, Baby Boy. Make sure that you take care of yourself, and remember what we talked about."

"Yeah, I got you. Is everything cool on your end?"

"As of right now, things are good. I'll know more soon. Cash Flo' is out on the East Coast taking care of some business. That nigga Pitt has been laying low, so that tells me that he's waiting for some reason or the other. Don't worry about me though. You just do what needs to be done. If you ever get at me on this line and I don't answer, that means either I went dark, or I'm no longer breathing. Either way, you will be notified of the next phase of the game."

"Come on with that shit, O.G.! I'm not tryin' to hear that shit!"

"It is what it is, Baby Boy. I love you. Out!" Won said, and he hung up the phone.

Taz hung up the phone and called Tari at her job at Mercy Hospital. She screamed so loud that he thought she was having a heart attack after he told her what had happened to Keno. He tried his best to calm her down, but she kept screaming over and over, "No! No! No! No!"

Finally, one of her coworkers took the phone from her and came on the line. "I'm sorry, but Tari is having problems right now. Can she call you back?" asked the coworker.

"Tell her that Taz said to call him as soon as she's regained her composure."

"I'll do that, sir," she said, and hung up the phone.

"You're a dead man, you punk-ass nigga!" Taz said aloud as he got up and went into the kitchen to get himself something to drink.

Just as he was pouring himself a glass of orange juice, his cell rang. He went back into the den and grabbed his phone, flipped it open and said, "Yeah!"

"Taz, I need for you to take me to Tulsa today. I have to get out of this city for a while," said his mother.

"When do you want to leave, Mama-Mama?"

"I just got off the phone with Christy and Derrick. They told me that I could come stay with them for as long as I liked. I don't plan on being out there for too long 'cause I want to be here for Keno's funeral."

"All right, Mama-Mama. Go on and get yourself ready. I'll be out that way in an hour or so."

"Okay, baby. Bye," Mama-Mama said before hanging up

Taz sat down and thought about having to make funeral arrangements for Keno for the very first time. He couldn't believe that he was going to have to do this shit all over again. All of the sudden, he slapped his forehead, quickly grabbed his cell and redialed Won's number. When Won answered, Taz said, "I forgot to ask you if you could take care of Keno's ends for me, O.G. He don't have any family other than us though. I think he has an aunt somewhere out in Cali, but I'm not sure."

"Don't panic, Baby Boy. I got you. I'll have all of his ends transferred into your account. That way, if you find his peoples you'll be able to look out for them."

"That's good lookin', O.G."

"You know I gots y'all. Now, let me bounce. Out!"

"Out!" Taz said, and closed his cell phone. Just as he was setting his phone down, it began to ring. He reopened it and saw that it was his daughter calling. He sighed and said, "What the fuck does this crazy-ass girl want?" He took a deep breath and prepared himself for another argument with his only child. "Hello."

"Daddy, we need to talk," Tazneema said seriously.

Taz pulled the phone away from his ear and stared at it as if it had done something to him. *Daddy? I know she don't think she's goin' to be able to sweet-talk me outta not taking that nigga Cliff!* he thought. But to his daughter, he said, "What's good, Neema? What do we need to talk about now?"

Tazneema stared at Clifford's sleeping form and said, "I can't really talk about it right now, 'cause I'm late for class," she lied. "What will you be doing later on?"

"I'm about to take Mama-Mama to Tulsa. She's goin' to spend a few days with Christy and Derrick. She's trippin' off of what happened to Keno."

Tears welled into Tazneema's eyes as she said, "I am too, Daddy. I am too. I want you to know that I'm so sorry for not believing you. I should have known better. You have never lied to me. I should have never gone against the grain. Please forgive me, Daddy!"

Taz pulled the phone away from his ear again, because he knew he was really tripping out now. He put the phone back to his ear and asked his daughter, "What's brought on this sudden change of heart, Baby Girl?"

"Mama-Mama always told me that whatever goes on in the dark will always come to the light sooner or later."

"Yeah, yeah, I understand all that. What does that got to do with this situation, Neema?"

"You were right and I was wrong, Daddy. Just leave it at that."

"All right, I'll accept that. Now, does this mean you'll assist me and tell me where that nigga Cliff lives?"

Tazneema stared at Clifford as he continued to sleep soundly and said, "Yeah, I'll tell you, Daddy. Call me when you get back from Tulsa."

"You understand what's goin' to happen to him, don't you, Neema?"

"Yes, Taz, I understand perfectly. As you and my uncles like to say, 'It is what it is.'"

He smiled into the receiver of his cell phone and said, "Exactly!"

Chapter Twenty-nine

Pitt was all smiles as Cash Flo' gave him what he'd been waiting a very long time for—permission to murder Won.

"I've spoken with no one about this, Pitt. I thought it would be better this way. So if you miss, you're on your own. You know Won is not to be taken lightly. The only reason why I'm giving you the green light is because I feel that Won is up to something, and that something just might jeopardize my position within The Network. So, handle your business, Pitt. Efficiently and effectively."

"Gotcha," Pitt said, and hung up the phone. He then pressed the intercom button on his desk and told his secretary to call Leo and Tru and tell the both of them that he wanted to see them as soon as possible. He then relaxed in his chair and smiled. *I got your ass now, Won. It took me over fifteen muthafuckin' years, but I got your ass now!* he thought as he fired up one of his Cuban cigars.

***

"Cliff, would you mind meeting me out at Mama-Mama's house later on?" Tazneema asked as she slipped on a pair of loose-fitting capri pants.

"Why? What's up, baby?" he asked lazily as he stretched and climbed out of bed.

"I'm putting an end to this stuff today. The only way I'll be able to do that is if I can convince Mama-Mama that you didn't have anything to do with the death of my uncles. Mama-Mama's real old-fashioned. She believes that if a person can look another person in the eyes and deny the charges that are against him, then he's either telling the truth or is a very good liar. If you come over there with me and help me present your case, I truly feel that we'll be able to get her on our side. And, believe me, we need her on our side."

This woman really does love me, Clifford thought, and then said, "What time do you want me to be there, baby?"

As Tazneema was putting on her Nike running shoes, she said, "I'll be out of my last class by two. Then I'm going over to my daddy's house to talk to him before I go on over to Mama-Mama's house. So, meet me there around four."

"Are you sure you want to go over to your father's alone? I could go with you, Neema."

And you'd be a dead man as soon as you stepped through the fuckin' door, you slimy bastard! she thought to herself as she grabbed her school bag. "No, I have to talk to him alone, baby. If you came with me, all there would be is a bunch of yelling and arguing. Once we have Mama-Mama on our team, we'll all meet and talk this thing through. I feel that's the best way to go about this situation."

Cliff stepped over to where Tazneema was standing, gave her a hug and said, "Whatever way you want to handle this, baby, is fine with me. The sooner we get this mess cleared up, the sooner we can move on with our lives." He then gave her a soft kiss on her lips and went into the bathroom to get dressed. If he'd suddenly stopped and turned around, he would have seen the look of complete disgust and contempt Tazneema had on her face.

"That's right, Mama-Mama. Neema agreed to tell me where that fool lives," Taz said as he continued to put Mama-Mama's bags inside of his truck.

"What made her change here mind about this, Taz?"

He shrugged his shoulders and said, "I don't know. I'm just glad she did. Now I can put an end to all this shit."

"Watch your mouth, boy!" Mama-Mama scolded.

"Sorry about that, Mama-Mama. But you know what I mean. That man has caused us all nothin' but grief since he came into our lives."

"Lord knows what you're saying is the truth, Taz. But taking that man's life is another sin that you're going to have to answer for one day, baby. God is a loving and forgiving God, but you're pushing Him, baby, pushing Him real hard."

After making sure his mother was comfortable inside of his truck, Taz started the ignition and said, "Whether God forgives me or not will have to be determined at a later time, Mama-Mama, 'cause that nigga Cliff gots to go."

Mama-Mama closed her eyes and said a quick prayer for her only child: *Please keep Your hands on my son, Lord. He's only doing what he feels is right. Though You and I both know he's about to commit a sin against one of Your Commandments, please don't abandon my baby. Please watch over him for me, Lord!*

Sacha was sitting inside of her office, talking to Gwen on the telephone. "Ho, I'm telling you, this shit is really about to get off the hook. Taz hasn't even been acting angry about Keno's death. That tells me that he's at the point of no return. Cliff and the rest of his homeboys are in some very deep shit."

"That's putting it mildly, bitch. Bob is so mad, that he hardly slept at all last night. I had to give him one of my top-notch blow jobs to drain him for him to close his eyes for a little while."

Sacha started laughing and said, "You nasty ho! You would have done that whether he was mad about Keno or not!"

"I know that, bitch. What I'm saying is, my baby is real fucked up too behind this shit. If Taz is going to go crazy, you better fuckin' believe Bob is too."

"And so are Red and Wild Bill. I just hope and pray that nothing else happens to any of them. God forbid someone else loses their life behind this craziness."

"The only one who's about to bite it now is that nigga Cliff. If your man don't kill him, then it's going to be mines, Red or Wild Bill that does. Either way, he's outta here," Gwen said seriously.

"You ain't never lied, ho. Let's hook up for lunch later on, 'kay?"

"I might as well. I'm not trying to be around this house all damn day by myself. Meet me at the Red Lobster on Northwest Expressway around noon."

"I'll see you then. Bye, ho!"

"Bye, bitch!" Gwen said, and hung up the phone.

After Taz dropped off Mama-Mama at his cousin's home in Tulsa, he quickly got back onto the highway and headed back toward the city. His only thoughts were on how and when he was going to kill Cliff. *I want to punish that nigga real slow,* he thought as he drove in silence. *Nah, better yet, I might feed his ass to the hogs out at Mama-Mama's house while he's still breathing. That nigga has to feel the type of pain I'm feeling behind losing my niggas. Yeah, nice and slow. That nigga is goin' to die nice and slow!*

By the time Tazneema had gotten out of her last class, she was hyped for what she was about to do. *That nigga fuckin' lied to me all this time. He took complete advantage of me and my feelings for his punk ass. I forgave the bastard for shooting me. I continued to love that man even after my father and uncles warned me to leave him alone, and he crossed me like I was noth-*

ing to him. Humph! Well, now, nigga, you're nothing to me. I'm my daddy's daughter, you coward muthafucka! You cross a Good, then you die, you bitch-ass nigga! Tazneema thought as she climbed into her car and headed out to her father's home.

She prayed that Taz wouldn't be home when she made it to his house. If he was, that would interfere with her plans. She crossed her fingers as she got onto the highway.

When Taz made it into the city limits, he picked up his cell, called Red and told him to get with Wild Bill and Bob and meet him at the Outback Steakhouse in Edmond. After hanging up with Red, he called Tari at work. He was told that she had taken the day off, so he quickly hung up and called her at her house. She sounded so weak and weary when she answered the phone, he felt as if he was being stabbed in his heart. He took a deep breath and said, "What's good, my snow bunny?"

"Hi, Taz. What are you up to?"

"Shit, I just got back from taking Mama-Mama out to Tulsa so she could visit with some relatives. I'm on my way to the Outback to meet with the homies. Why don't you meet us out there? We gots some shit to discuss."

"I'm really not in the mood, Taz. I can't get Keno off of my mind. It hurts, Taz, it really hurts!"

"I know, Tee, but you gots to shake this shit off for the time being. We're about to bring the end game to that nigga, and I know you're wanting to be a part of that."

Shaking her head no as if Taz was standing in the same room with her, she said, "No, Taz, I don't. This stuff has to end, I know, but I don't want any part of it."

"I understand."

"Have you heard from Won? I've tried to call him, but I keep getting his voice mail."

"Is that right? I spoke with him earlier, and he told me that if I called and didn't catch him, then he went dark and he'll be in touch."

"Is everything all right with him?"

"To tell the truth, Tee, I don't even know."

"Great! That's fucking great! Look, I'm about to try to get some sleep. I've been up all night looking at old pictures of us all. I'm so depressed I feel as if I'm losing my mind, Taz."

"Do you want me to come out there and kick it with you for a Li'l while, Tee?"

"Go on and take care of this madness first. After everything is everything, then come and spend some time with me. I need to get some sleep right now. Don't worry about me. I'll be all right by the time you get out here."

"All right then, Tee. I love you."

Those words put a smile on her face as she said, "I love you too, Taz." After she hung up the phone, she grabbed her 9 mm pistol, jacked the chamber back and watched as the single bullet popped out of the chamber.

Taz would never know that he had called just in time to save Tari's life.

Tazneema smiled as she jumped out of her car and ran toward the front door of Taz's home. She pulled out her keys and quickly opened the front door. She saw Heaven and Precious as they watched her punch in the security code to the alarm system. After the alarm was deactivated, she stepped over to the Dobermans and said, "Hey, babies! You guys miss me?" Both of the dogs began to rub their wet noses against her open palms. After playing with them for a few minutes, she said, "Okay, guys, protect me." Heaven's and Precious's ears became alert as they silently stepped away from her.

Tazneema then went downstairs to her father's indoor gym, and went directly toward the equipment closet, where he kept all of his weapons. He didn't know she knew about his arsenal. *Hell, he doesn't know that I know a lot of things about his lifestyle!* she thought to herself as she grabbed a small .380 pistol and a full clip of bullets. She snapped the weapon back and slid a live round inside of its chamber. She smiled and put the gun inside of her purse, quickly closed the door to the equipment room and went back upstairs. She went into the kitchen and saw that the dogs' water bowls were empty. After refilling them, she went and grabbed a bottled water out of the refrigerator and left her father's home, ready for the next phase of her mission.

Tru and Leo arrived at Pitt's office an hour after Pitt's secretary had summoned them. Once they were seated, Pitt said, "All right, this is how it's going to go down. That nigga Won is about to try to shake the spot, but I gots eyes on his ass, so it's all good. We're about to catch a flight down south to L.A. and handle his punk ass real quick like. It's a must that I get some information from that nigga before we out his ass. Once I got what I need and he's done, you two will have another mission to complete."

"And what's that?" asked Leo.

"I want y'all to fly out to Oklahoma City and out Won's li'l country-boy crew. Those country muthafuckas are the niggas that have been putting down all of those licks against The Network."

"How did you find out about them?" asked Tru.

Pitt laughed and said, "Money can get you whatever you want in this world, my nigga. I learned that from that nigga Won. Not only do I know the names of those niggas, I know where the daughter and the mother of the head nigga reside. I want them bitches to pay for even thinking that they could get away with fucking with The Network. So, come on. We gots a flight to catch."

Back in Oklahoma City, Taz was the first to arrive at the Outback Steakhouse. He was seated and had just ordered himself a glass of XO when Red, Bob and Wild Bill entered the restaurant. After they were seated, Taz told them what Tazneema had told him. "I wanted to wait until we were all together before I made the call to her to get the address on that clown-ass nigga."

Wild Bill smiled and said, "We're here now, nigga! What the fuck are you waitin' for? Make the call!"

Taz laughed as he pulled out his cell phone and called his daughter's cell. When she answered her phone, she said, "Hi, Daddy."

"What's up, Baby Girl? You good?"

"Yep, I'm just fine."

"That's cool. I need that address, Neema. It's time for me to handle this shit."

"Okay. Can you meet me at Mama-Mama's in about an hour?"

"Yeah, I can do that. Is everything all right?"

She smiled and said, "Everything is everything, Daddy. I'm your daughter, and whether you know it or not, you taught me well."

Taz raised his eyebrows as he stared at his cell phone. Then he asked, "What exactly is that supposed to mean, Neema?"

She laughed and said, "You'll see, Daddy. Just make sure that you meet me at Mama-Mama's house in one hour."

After she hung up the phone, Taz told everyone what she had just told him. When he was finished, Bob said, "Dog, you don't think she's goin' to try to do some shit to you, do you?"

Taz took a sip of his drink then said, "For her sake, I hope not."

Chapter Thirty

As Tazneema waited for Clifford to arrive, she began to have doubts about what she was about to do. *I should just wait for my daddy to get here and let him handle this mess. I'm no killer,* she thought as she stared at the gun she held in her hand. Before her doubts could totally consume her, she heard Cliff's car as it pulled into Mama-Mama's driveway. She took a deep breath, put the gun back inside of her purse and set her purse back down on the coffee table. She then went to the front door and watched as he climbed out of his Mercedes 500 CLS.

Cliff smiled at her as he strolled confidently toward her. When he made it to the door, he said, "Hey you!"

They shared a kiss, much to Tazneema's dislike. She pulled away from his embrace and said, "Come on inside. Mama-Mama went to the store. She ran out of something. She's cooking dinner."

"That's cool. You know I love your grand-mother's cooking," Cliff said as he entered the house and took a seat on the sofa. "So, have you had a chance to talk to her yet?" he asked.

She shook her head no and said, "I was wait-ing for you to get here so we could do it together. It's very important that we convince her that you had nothing to do with my uncles getting killed." Tazneema stared at him hard after she made that comment. She wanted to see if he was really that good a liar, as well as a cold-blooded killer.

Cliff smiled a confident smile and said, "There's no need for convincing when you're telling the truth, baby. Your grandmother will know that we're not lying to her. The truth is exactly what it is . . . the truth. I didn't have anything to do with either of your uncles' murders, baby. It's as simple as that."

This nigga is really good, Tazneema thought as she said, "I'm glad that you're here now, baby. Now we can put this mess behind us." She checked her watch and thought to herself, *Taz should be on his way right about now. Either I'm going to handle my business now, or leave it up to my daddy.* She shook her head as she made her decision. *This is for my uncles!* She reached inside of her purse, pulled out the .380 and pointed it directly toward Clifford's head and said, "You're a fuckin' liar and a coward, Cliff! You did kill my uncles, and you're still plotting to kill my daddy! How the hell can you tell me that you love me and still hurt me this way? Answer that for me, Cliff, before I kill your sorry ass!"

Cliff jumped out of his seat when he saw that Tazneema was dead serious, and said, "Come on, Neema, baby! You know damn well I didn't have anything to do with killing your uncles! Hell, I wasn't even in town when Keno was killed! That should be enough proof for you right there! Come on, baby. Put the gun down so we can wait for Mama-Mama to get back so we can talk this out."

She laughed and said, "Nigga, Mama-Mama is out of town. The only person we're waiting on is my daddy. And you and I both know what's going to happen to your ass when he gets here. You might not have killed my Uncle Keno, but that wouldn't have stopped one of your gang-banger friends from doing it. Either way, it's *your* fault, Cliff. And to think I loved your sorry ass!"

"*Loved?* Come on, Neema. You know you still love me. Just like you know damn well that I didn't do what you're accusing me of. You've let your father's influence over you finally get the best of your judgment. You know me. You know

I'm no killer, baby. Come on, let's talk this out sensibly."

For some reason, Clifford's words irked her to no end. She felt ashamed—ashamed of being manipulated, used and made a complete fool of. These feelings caused a fury to swell inside of her so cold that she didn't even realize that she was pulling the trigger to the pistol that was gripped tightly in her right hand. She shot Clifford seven times right in the middle of his chest. Her first shot was what killed him though. It was a direct hit to his heart.

As he fell back onto the sofa, he had a look of shock on his face as he grabbed his chest in an effort to stop the flow of blood that seeped from his body. He died with his right hand over the hole in his heart.

Tazneema calmly went and checked his vital signs to make sure that her job was complete. Afterward, she got to her feet and pulled Clifford's body onto the floor. "Mama-Mama would kill me if I'd gotten any blood on her sofa," she said aloud as she went into the hallway closet to get a sheet to cover Clifford's dead body.

Just as she returned to the living room and put the sheet over the body, she heard Taz's truck pull into the driveway. She quickly stepped to the door and smiled as she watched her father and her three uncles come running toward the door with their weapons in their hands.

When Taz made it to the front door, he asked, "Where's that nigga at, Baby Girl?"

Tazneema stepped aside so that Taz and her uncles could enter the house. She said, "There he is, Daddy." She pointed toward Clifford's covered body and continued. "I went against the grain, Taz, but I fixed my mistake."

Taz stared at his daughter in disbelief and asked, "What the fuck have you done, Neema?"

She smiled at her father and said, "What I had to do."

Red went over to the body, pulled the sheet back and said, "Well, I'll be damned! She done got the bastard!"

Bob started laughing and said, "Like father, like daughter for real!"

"Shut the fuck up, Bob! This shit is fucked up!" Taz yelled as he turned back toward his daughter. "Get the hell outta here, Baby Girl! Take your ass back to Norman, and don't you dare mention this shit to nobody, do you hear me?"

Now that the realization of what she'd actually done had sunk in, she became very nervous all of a sudden. "Are you going to take care of this, Daddy?" she asked in a voice that was of a little girl instead of an eighteen-year-old young lady.

Taz nodded and said, "I've taken care of you all of my life, Baby Girl, and I'm not about to stop now. Go on and let us take care of this shit. I love you, Tazneema."

She smiled and said, "I love you too, Daddy." She grabbed her purse and left the house without so much as a good-bye to any of her uncles.

Red smiled and said, "Well, at least this clown-ass nigga is out of the way."

"Yeah, you're right. Come on. Let's take care of this fool. Then we can go get at that other nigga, H-Hop," Taz said as he grabbed Clifford's body and lifted him onto his broad shoulders.

"So, that nigga gots to go too, huh?" asked Wild Bill.

"You fuckin' right! He's the last piece to this fucked up puzzle, dog. Once he's done, it's a wrap."

"What are we goin' to do with this fool's body?" asked Bob.

Taz smiled and said, "We gon' feed him to the hogs."

"Da-a-a-a-amn! That's fucked up!" Wild Bill said with a sadistic smile on his face.

Taz carried Clifford's body outside to Mama-Mama's backyard and set it down right beside the hog pen. He turned toward Red and said, "Look. This is how we're goin' to get down. After we dump this nigga to the hogs, you and Bob go take his car somewhere in the city and dump it. Me and Wild Bill will go sit on that nigga, H-Hop's spot. If we can get his ass, then we'll move on him. If not, I'll get at y'all later on. Either way it falls, at least we're more than halfway through with this shit."

"Yeah, thanks to Neema," Red said with a smirk on his face. "That's straight crazy, G. We couldn't get to this nigga, but Neema could."

"It was easy for her, though. She had a line on the fool. That nigga was slipping, because he was in love and didn't see it comin'. Oh, well! It's a done deal now. Here," Taz said as he went into Clifford's pants pocket and pulled out the keys to his Mercedes. He passed them to Red and said, "There should be some gloves in the garage. Go check and see. That way, y'all won't leave any prints on that nigga's shit. Now, help me throw this piece of shit to the hogs."

"Gladly," Red said, and helped Taz throw Clifford's lifeless body over the fence and into the hog pen.

Mama-Mama's four humongous hogs squealed loudly as they began to tear into Clifford's dead flesh.

***

Tazneema was scared, yet she was calm as she drove toward her apartment in Norman.

Just as she was passing the City of Moore, she decided to make a quick stop. She got off the highway exit and headed toward Tari's home. When she pulled into Tari's driveway, she smiled when she saw her peeping out of the living room window. She quickly cut off her car and went to the front door.

Tari smiled when she opened the door, and said, "Well, well! What a lovely surprise! How are you doing, Baby Girl?"

They shared a brief hug, and Tazneema said, "I'm fine, Tee. I was on my way back to my place and I thought I'd drop by to holla at you for a minute."

"Come on in here, girl, and tell me what's on your mind."

Tazneema followed Tari inside of her home. After they were seated in the living room, Tazneema said, "Ain't too much going on. I just wanted to talk to you for a few, that's all."

Tari smiled at her and said, "Mmm-hmm."

"Mmm-hmm what?" Tazneema asked with a smile on her face.

"Girl, you're just like your father. Whenever you two have something on y'all's mind, y'all get to talking about how you just want to talk for a little bit. So save it, Neema, and spit it out. What's on your mind?"

Tazneema smiled again, shook her head from side to side and said, "I don't want to have this baby, Tee. Could you take me somewhere so I can get an abortion?"

"Whoa! Are you sure about this?"

"I'm positive. I don't want to have anything that will remind me of that sorry, lying-ass nigga Cliff!" she answered angrily.

"Watch your mouth, young lady! You know how I feel about that *N* word!"

"Sorry, Tee," she said sheepishly. "Anyway, will you take me to get one?"

"Does your father know about this?"

"Nope. But do you really think he'll mind?"

"I guess not, huh? All right, let me make a few calls, and I'll get back to you in a day or so."

"Thanks, Tee. I knew I could count on your help," Tazneema said sincerely.

"I have one more question though. How is Cliff going to feel about you killing his child?"

Tazneema stared at Tari for thirty seconds, and finally said, "Ask my daddy."

Chapter Thirty-one

Taz and Wild Bill were sitting inside of Taz's truck in front of H-Hop's apartment building. Taz smiled as he pulled out his cell phone and quickly dialed Red's cell. When Red answered, Taz asked him, "Where are y'all at now?"

"We just left Arcadia. We're on our way back to the city now. What's good?"

"That nigga H-Hop's car is parked in front of his spot. We're about to go on and do this nigga. Do y'all want us to wait for y'all or what?"

"Nah, go on and do that clown and get this shit over with, G."

"I'll get at y'all when we're on our way back to my spot," Taz said, and closed his phone and said to Wild Bill, "Let's go do this bitch, G."

Wild Bill smiled as he checked to make sure that he had a live round chambered in his 9 mm, and said, "You know it!"

They jumped out of the truck and calmly walked toward H-Hop's apartment building.

When they made it to H-Hop's apartment, Taz put his ear to the door and listened. He heard some rap music playing, and he could tell someone was walking around inside. He glanced toward Wild Bill and gave him a nod, directing him to kick in the door.

Wild Bill, though small in height, was a very powerful man. He stood in front of the door and gave it a solid kick right next to the doorknob.

Taz stepped inside of the apartment with his gun pointed directly toward H-Hop, who was standing at the open refrigerator door. The shocked look on his face told Taz all he needed to know. *This clown-ass nigga is alone, and he's about to die alone,* he thought as he slowly stepped toward the kitchen.

Wild Bill stood at the door and kept an eye out for any unwanted company.

When Taz made it to the kitchen, he told H-Hop, "You already know what time it is, so turn around and drop to your knees, nigga."

Realizing that he had been caught slipping, H-Hop inhaled deeply and said, "Fuck you, cuz! I may be 'bout to die, but I'll be damned if I'm gon' go out like a coward! Do what you got to do, cuz, 'cause I ain't gettin' on my knees for no nigga!" he screamed defiantly.

Taz admired him for his courage. For that, he decided that he would at least let his family be able to have an open casket at his funeral. Instead of shooting him in his face like he had originally planned, he smiled as he shot H-Hop twice in his heart. He then turned and left the kitchen without a backward glance. As he made it to the door, he told Wild Bill, "It's over, my nigga. Come on, let's get the fuck outta here."

Pitt, Leo and Tru's flight arrived at LAX, and they were picked up by some of Pitt's people in Southern California. Once they were inside the back of the limousine, Pitt asked the driver, "Has that nigga Won left his home?"

"No, sir. He's been home the entire day," the driver answered as he eased the limousine into the heavy Los Angeles traffic.

"All right, this is what I need you to do. Make the call to my associates and let them know that I said they have the green light to proceed, but not to take any action against Won. He is not to be harmed. Secure his home until we get there."

"Understood," the driver said, and picked up his cell phone and did as he was told.

Pitt sat back in his seat and smiled. "By the time we make it to Won's home, everything should be secured. When we get there, I'll get the information I need. After that, I'm going to enjoy killing that bastard."

"What? I thought that was our job," said Leo.

"Yeah! Since when did you start gettin' your hands dirty?" asked Tru.

"Won is a major player within The Network. He has been for a very long time. Even though he let his thirst for power blind him, he's still a man of respect and tremendous integrity. He played the game his way. But he underestimated another man with the same amount of integrity though. He has to die by my hand, and my hand only," Pitt said, and fired up one of his Cuban cigars.

Back in Oklahoma City, Taz and the rest of the crew were all sitting in his den, replaying the day's events.

"I still can't believe that Neema did that nigga, dog," Bob said as he sipped his Absolut Vodka and cranberry juice.

"Yeah, that shit is crazy. But it is what it is. Now, all we have to do is put my nigga to rest properly and try to move on with our crazy-ass lives," Taz said, and downed the rest of the XO he had in his glass.

"What about Won? Is this shit over with him or what?" asked Red.

"To be honest, dog, I don't even know. All we can do is sit back and wait on that one, G. The last time we spoke, he told me that I'd be contacted one way or the other."

"One way or the other? What the fuck is that supposed to mean, my nigga?" asked Wild Bill.

Taz shrugged his shoulders and said, "Your guess is as good as mine, dog." Before he could say anything else, he heard Sacha as she came into the house. "Look, let's get together tomorrow and work out. We might as well try to get back on our regular routine."

"Dog, what about Bo-Pete and Keno? Shit ain't never gon' be regular no more," Bob said somberly.

"I know that's right, G. But you know what I mean. Right now, I'm about to chill with wifey and let her know that everything is everything. I can't be havin' her stressed the fuck out while she's about to have my second shorty."

"All right then, 'Foolio!' We'll see you in the morning," Red said, and he led the rest of the crew out of the den and out of Taz's home.

After the crew was gone, Taz poured himself another shot of XO and went upstairs to the bedroom. He smiled as he entered the room and saw

Sacha sitting on the edge of the bed, taking off her stockings. "Damn, you look sexy even when you're doing the simplest things!"

She smiled and said, "I don't feel sexy. I feel tired and hungry."

"Do you want me to make you something to eat, or do you want to go get something?" he asked as he stepped to the bed and sat down next to his fiancée.

Sacha smiled and said, "I've already ordered a pizza. It should be here any minute."

"A pizza? You and your cravings! Well, I guess pizza it is then."

Sacha stared at her man for a full minute then asked him, "What's on your mind, baby?"

He returned her stare and simply said, "My niggas. I'm never goin' to be able to tell either one of them how much I really loved them. They're gone, Li'l Mama. They're gone," he said as he wiped a tear from his eye. He sipped the drink in his hand and continued. "It's over, Li'l Mama. That nigga Cliff and his homeboy have been dealt with. It's over."

She let his words register deep within her before she spoke. "I don't know whether to be happy or upset, baby. I'm glad this mess is finally over with, but I'm sort of upset because of the pain Tazneema is going to have to endure once she finds out about Cliff's death."

Taz smiled and said, "Don't worry about her. She'll be good. As a matter of fact, I need to call her to make sure she's straight. She's had a pretty busy day today."

"What do you mean by that, Taz Good?"

Taz started laughing, and told her exactly what had happened earlier at his mother's home.

Sacha couldn't believe what she was hearing. When he was finished, she stared at him to see if he was really telling her the truth. After staring into his brown eyes for a couple of seconds, she shook her head from side to side and said, "Well, ain't that something! But what about the baby, Taz?"

He shrugged his shoulders and said, "Let's see." He picked up the phone and dialed his daughter's apartment.

Pitt was smiling as he climbed out of the limousine, followed by Leo and Tru. The limousine driver was talking to some of Pitt's hired help as Pitt was led into Won's vast estate. Pitt's team had been able to secure all of Won's security with very little difficulty. Since Won's mansion was so secluded, it wasn't difficult at all for his people.

As Pitt entered Won's home, he was amazed at how calm he felt. Victory was his, and he was loving every second of it. The leader of Pitt's team led him into Won's office, where Won was being held.

When Won saw Pitt, he smiled and said, "I was wondering when you'd arrive, Pitt. I guess I've finally lost, hmm?"

Pitt smiled and said, "Yeah, you finally lost the game, old boy. Look, I'm not going to take a whole bunch of time with this, Won. There're some things I need to know before we can finish up this mess."

"And what is that?" Won asked as he calmly relaxed back in his chair.

"Where's the work, Won? I want to know exactly where the drugs are at. I know you didn't dump them. If you had, I would have gotten your ass years ago. So, the only other possibility is that you got all that work stashed real fucking good."

Won smiled and asked, "Are you sure about that, Pitt? I move more work across the board than anyone else in The Network. It could have been real easy for me to move it without tipping my hand."

"But you didn't' do that. You stashed it until you got ready to make your power move. That's what all of this shit is about, you and your fucking power trip. So stop playing games and give me the information I need, Won."

"Or what? You're going to kill me?" Won started laughing and continued. "That's funny, 'cause I can only assume that you're here to do that anyway."

"I'll tell you what. I'll spare your li'l clique in Oklahoma City if you just go on and give me the whereabouts of the work. It's either that, or they all die—even that pretty li'l daughter of your boy Taz," Pitt said with a devious smile on his face.

With his poker face intact, Won asked, "Taz? Who's that?"

Pitt laughed and said, "Good! Very good, Won, but not good enough. I've done my homework thoroughly. That country-ass clique you got has robbed The Network. For that they have to go. If you do me this justice, I can find it in my heart to let them make it."

Won sighed heavily and said, "What guarantees do I have that you'll honor your word, Pitt? I could give you the information you desire, and you could still kill my peoples. I might as well take the location of the drugs with me to my grave."

"I swear on my mother's grave, as well as the oath we both took when we helped form The Network so many years ago, that if you give me the location of the work, your people in Oklahoma City will be spared. That's about all I can do for you, Won. Like you said, you are about to die," Pitt said seriously.

Won shrugged his shoulders slightly and said, "I guess I'm going to have to take your word on this, Pitt. The work is out in Austin. My people out that way have it secured in a warehouse. I'll need to make a call to let them know that everything is good, or they'll never let you get near that warehouse."

Pitt smiled brightly, gave a nod of his head toward the telephone that was on Won's desk and said, "Make the call."

Won grabbed the phone and quickly dialed the number to his main man out in Austin, Texas. When the line was answered, Won said, "Hey, Charlene, what's good? Is Snuffy around?"

"Yeah, here he is, Won," Charlene said, and passed the phone to her man, Snuffy.

Snuffy accepted the phone from her and asked, "What it do, big homey?"

Won laughed and said, "Not much. Look, I need for you to pass along what you got put up for me. My people will be contacting you soon."

"What? Are you serious, big homey?"

"Very. It is what it is, Snuff, so make sure you take care of this for me. My people's name is Pitt. Give him everything he asks for. Your account has already been taken care of, so you and Charlene will be straight."

"I gots you, big homey, and don't worry. You know I'm gon' handle my end of this shit for you."

Won simply said, "I know you will," and he hung up the phone. He reached across the desk, grabbed a pen and a piece of paper, wrote down Snuffy's number in Austin and passed it to Pitt and said, "There you go. All you have to do is give him a call and make the necessary arrangements."

Pitt put the piece of paper into his wallet and said, "Thank you, Won. You're a top-flight nigga all the way." He then pulled out a chrome 9 mm with a silencer attached to it and asked, "Have you taken care of your affairs, Won?"

Won stared directly into Pitt's eyes and said, "Everything is in order. I'm ready for the next part of the game. I'll see you when you get there."

Pitt smiled sadly and said, "I won't be coming for a minute, but hold me down, baby." He pointed his gun at Won and shot him three times in the heart.

Won took all three shots with three grunts, reclined back in his chair and died with what looked like a smile on his handsome face.

"Even in defeat the cocky bastard has a lotta class. Come on, you two. We gots more shit to handle," Pitt said.

"Are you really gon' let them fools in Oklahoma make it?" asked Tru.

Pitt showed that devious smile again and said, "Fuck, no! Them niggas gots to die. You know my word ain't shit!"

"But you put it on your mom's grave and shit," Leo said with a frown on his face.

"That bitch never gave a damn about me, and I damn sure ain't never gave a damn about her. As for that oath shit, nigga, this ain't no *La Cosa Nostra* shit. This is The Network, the Black Mafia for real! We do shit how we want to do shit. I'm at the top of the pile now. I can do or say whatever the fuck I want to. First, we're going to Austin to secure that work with my peoples in San Antonio. Then we're going to hit Oklahoma City, so you two can earn some of this muthafuckin' money. Now, come on. Like I said, there's work to be done!"

Chapter Thirty-two

Three days after Won's murder, Taz was sitting in his den talking to Bob, when he received a call from one of his attorneys at Whitney & Johnson. "What's good, Peter?" he asked as he relaxed on his sectional sofa.

"I just received some papers marked 'Urgent,' along with a DVD for you from a law firm out in L.A."

"What's it about?"

"From what I've read, it looks like a will for a William B. Hunter."

"William B. Hunter? I don't know anybody by that name. Are you sure it's for me, Pete?"

"Positive. Whoever he is, or was, made sure that the attorney in L.A. sent this to me. Are you busy? If not, why don't you come on down and check this out?"

Taz checked the time on his watch and said, "All right, I'll be there in about thirty minutes. Is Sacha around?"

"Yes. I just saw her heading to the boss' office."

"Good. Let her know that I'm on my way down there, and that I want her to join us for this meet."

"Will do, Taz. See you in a little bit," Peter said, and hung up the phone.

Taz set the phone down and told Bob, "Dog, some shit has come up. I'm gon' need you to get with Red and Wild Bill so y'all can go make the funeral arrangements for Keno. Detective Bean called me this morning and told me that they were releasing the body today."

"All right, I got you. What was all of that about?"

"I'm really not knowin'. I'm about to find out though. Give me a holla after y'all made all of the arrangements."

"Bet!" Bob said as he followed Taz out of the house.

By the time Taz made it to Whitney & Johnson's law firm, Sacha was waiting for him inside of Peter's office. He smiled as he stepped inside and said, "What's good, Li'l Mama?"

"Hi, baby." Sacha stood and gave him a kiss.

Taz reached across Peter's desk, shook his hand and said, "Now, tell me exactly what the hell is goin' on here, Pete."

Peter once again explained how he had received the paperwork and the DVD that was sitting on his desk. Afterward, he said, "If you don't know who this William B. Hunter is, then I guess we need to watch this DVD in order to figure this mess out, Taz."

"Put it in then. I got a heavy plate today, and I don't have any time to waste."

Peter inserted the DVD into his portable DVD player, pressed the play button and turned it so that Taz and Sacha were able to look at the screen. As soon as Taz saw a picture of Michael Jordan slam-dunking a basketball over John Starks of the New York Knicks, he inhaled deeply and said, "Stop it!"

"What's wrong, Taz?" asked Peter.

"I said stop it, Pete!"

Peter did as he was told. He sat back in his chair and stared at Taz with a puzzled look on his face.

Sacha knew that something was terribly wrong, because Taz's smooth brown complexion seemed to pale right before her eyes. She put her hand on his shoulder and asked, "What's wrong, baby? Do you know who this person is now?"

Tears fell slowly from his eyes as he nodded his head yes.

Pitt, Leo and Tru arrived at Austin's Bergstrom International Airport a little after 5:00 P.M. Pitt had arranged for a vehicle to be waiting for them when they arrived in Texas. As usual, there was a stretch limousine parked in front of the arrivals terminal. The limousine driver was standing at the rear door of the limo, holding it open for Pitt and his men, who got inside of the car.

Once the luxury vehicle pulled away from the curb, Pitt pulled out his cell and called Snuffy. As soon as Snuffy answered the phone, Pitt said, "This is Pitt. I'm in town. When and where can we meet so we can handle what needs to be handled?"

"I'm out in San Antonio right now, but I'll be back in a few hours. Does it matter whether it's daylight or not?"

"Not really. I just need to check and make sure that everything is there. After that, it's all about transporting really."

"All right then, check this out, *G*. Why don't you go get a room and hit me after you're checked in and shit. I'll make some calls and see if my girl Charlene can come and scoop you up and take you over to the warehouse."

"I'd prefer to deal with you rather than your girl."

"Hold up, partna! Charlene is my ace. She rolls with me on everything. Won told me to take care of you, and that's exactly what I'm gon' do, ya dig? You ain't gots to worry 'bout wifey. She's with the team."

"Whatever!" Pitt replied sarcastically.

"Like I was sayin', after you get checked in, hit me back up and I'll see what we can do about making everything go down tonight."

"All right. I'll call you after I get to a room," Pitt said, and hung up the phone on Snuffy. He then leaned toward the front of the limousine and asked the driver, "Are there any decent hotels around here?"

The driver smiled and replied, "Yes, sir, there's an AmeriSuites right up the street on Ben White Boulevard."

"Good. Take us there and then you can be on your way. I'll give you a call when your return is needed."

"Yes, sir," the driver said as he navigated the huge car toward the Ameri-Suites Hotel.

Taz sat in the chair inside of his attorney's office in a daze. He couldn't believe that Won was actually dead. He shook his head sadly and said, "Look, I'm sorry for yelling, Pete. This shit is just too much for me. Do me a favor though."

"Anything, Taz. You know that," Peter said from behind his desk.

"Do what needs to be done with the paperwork. I trust you and your judgment completely. Right now, I've gots to get up outta here. I need that DVD though. If need be, I'll get it back to you. I have a feelin' that what's on it was meant for my eyes only."

"Of course, Taz. Anything you say. I'll give you a call in a couple of days, after I've taken care of everything."

Taz stood and said, "Thanks, Pete." After shaking his attorney's hand, he turned toward his fiancée and said, "I gots to go get some air, Li'l Mama. Can you come join me for a minute?"

Sacha checked her watch and saw that she had a few minutes to spare before going to her court appearance. She smiled and said, "I have ten minutes before I have to run over to the courthouse, baby."

"That's cool. Come on," Taz said, and led her out of Peter's office. Once they were outside of the building, he stopped by his truck and said, "This is too fuckin' much, Li'l Mama! Too fuckin' much! I feel as if I'm losin' my fuckin' mind!"

405 Gangsta Twist 2

Sacha put her arms around her man and held him tightly for a moment then said, "It's Won, isn't it? Won is William B. Hunter."

Taz sighed heavily and said, "Yeah. Yeah, Li'l Mama. Another loved one of mines is gone. Won is resting in peace."

"But how?"

With a shrug of his shoulders, he said, "Ain't no tellin'. He knew somethin' was goin' to go down because he's been warning me for a minute now."

"Warning you?"

"Basically lettin' me know that I'm goin' to have to prepare to take on somethin' new."

"What does that mean, baby? You're confusing me."

"I'll know more after I look at this," Taz said as he held up the DVD in his right hand. "I expect to be told everything that I'm goin' to need to know on this here DVD. So let me bounce. We'll go over everything when you come home later on."

"Okay, baby," she said, and gave her man a hug and a kiss. "I love you, Taz."

He smiled and said, "I love you too, Li'l Mama." He watched as she went back into the office building. Then he turned and climbed into his truck.

Once he was comfortable, he inserted the DVD into his DVD player and said, "Screens one and two, please!" The DVD player was then activated by his voice command. The picture of Michael Jordan slam-dunking the ball over John Starks showed on the two front TV screens inside of the truck. As Taz pulled out of the parking lot and into the light mid-morning traffic, the two screens slowly changed into a picture of Won.

Later that evening, after Pitt had checked into the AmeriSuites Hotel and had gotten himself comfortable, he called Snuffy back and told him where he was staying. "Do you know where it's at? It's not too far from the airport."

"Yeah, you're about ten minutes away from where we're going to meet in the morning," Snuffy said as he smiled at his wifey, Charlene.

"In the *morning!* I thought we were going to do this shit tonight!"

"Man, ain't no way in hell you're going to be able to move that much shit this late at night."

"Who said anything about moving it tonight? Look, you're doing way too much damn thinking. All I need is to see the product and make sure that everything is everything. After that, everything else will be taken care of. So, you need to come and pick me and my peoples up and take us to wherever this fucking warehouse is!"

"All right then, big-time! Calm down! My bad! Like I told you, you're about ten minutes away from the warehouse off of Highway 71. I'm like twenty minutes from you now, so give me ten to fifteen minutes then come outside of the hotel. How many people you got with you, boss?"

"There's three of us total."

"That's cool. Be looking out for me and wifey. We'll be in a red Escalade."

"Hurry up!" Pitt said impatiently, and once again hung up on Snuffy.

Fifteen minutes after hanging up in Snuffy's ear, Pitt, Leo and Tru were standing outside of their hotel, still waiting for Snuffy and his wifey. Just as Pitt was pulling out his cell phone to call Snuffy again, Leo said, "Here comes a red Escalade now, Pitt."

Pitt turned and smiled when he saw the red truck had come to a stop in front of them. His smile brightened at the sight of a tall, brown-skinned woman with legs that seemed to never stop, and an ass that could make a grown man cry.

Charlene stepped up to Pitt and said, "Would you like to sit up front with my man, or would you like to ride in the back with your friends?"

"Yeah, the back's cool. That way, I can keep my eyes on you!" Pitt said flirtatiously as he followed Charlene back to the truck.

Once everyone was inside of the vehicle, Snuffy pulled away from the curb and said, "What it do, boss?"

"Everything is everything, my man. How long has the product been at this location?"

"Won used to have a lot of shit brought here every other month or so. It's been a minute since he's gotten down like that though. This is his main spot in town. No one knows about it but me and my baby. Ain't that right, boo?" Snuffy asked Charlene.

Charlene smiled and answered, "That's right, baby."

"Do y'all know exactly how much work is there?" Pitt stared at Charlene.

The both of them started laughing, and after they seemed to regain their composure, Charlene said, "Baby, ain't that much countin' in the fuckin' world! Won always told us to make sure that we kept everything in order for him, and that's exactly what we did. What we look like, tryin' to count all of that damn dope?" she said.

Snuffy pulled into the parking lot of a large warehouse and turned off the ignition to the truck. He then said, "Here it is, boss. The building is locked tighter than a virgin's twat. Here're the keys to the two locks, as well as the security code to the alarm system." He then passed the

keys and a piece of paper with the alarm code
written on it to Pitt.

After Pitt accepted it from Snuffy, he said, "All
right, why don't you let your girl take me inside
and show me the work? I'll leave my boys here
with you."

Snuffy shrugged his shoulders and said, "Go
on with the man, *mami*. The quicker we get this
over with, the quicker we can go do us, ya feel
me?"

Charlene smiled at Snuffy and said, "I got you,
baby." She grabbed her purse and stepped out
of the truck, followed closely by Pitt. She led the
way to the warehouse, and when they made it to
the main entrance, she told Pitt, "You gots the
keys, baby. Open it up."

Pitt stepped in front of her, unlocked both of
the locks on the door, and stepped inside. He saw
the control panel for the alarm system blinking
on his right, so he quickly stepped over to it and
punched in the seven-digit code to deactivate it.
He smiled when he saw that the alarm was deactivated, and asked, "Where's the fucking lights?"

"Over to your left," Charlene said as she pulled
a silenced 9 mm out of her purse and took aim
exactly where she figured Pitt would be standing
when the lights came on.

When Pitt turned on the lights, he almost pissed on himself when he saw Charlene pointing her gun at him. "What the fuck is that for, Charlene?" he asked nervously.

"You don't know? Nigga, did you really think that you could kill Won and get away with it?"

"Come on with that shit! Won ain't dead! What the fuck is wrong with you?" he lied convincingly.

Charlene started laughing as she shook her head from side to side. She then said, "You are somethin' else, Mister Pitt!" She quickly glanced down at her watch then said, "Since we got a li'l time until Big Junior gets here, I'll break it all down to you real quick like."

"Who the fuck is Big Junior?"

"He's Won's only living relative. He's the man who's going to take your life."

"*What?* Come on with this shit, Charlene! Stop playing!"

"Playing? That shit is too funny right there, for real! But check it. When Won called my boo and told him to turn over everything to you, that was the code that you were to be killed. We were to kill whoever came to get this work. Won was prepared for you years ago, buddy. It really hurts me to know that he's no longer with us, but it makes my heart feel real good to know that me and my man did our part just as he expected us to."

Pitt stood in front of Charlene with a look of disgust on his face. He couldn't fucking believe it. That nigga Won had still beaten him. Before he could say another word to try and talk Charlene out of this mess, his eyes grew as wide as saucers when he saw Leo and Tru being led inside of the warehouse by Snuffy and two other men.

Snuffy smiled and said, "Baby, these Cali boys is somethin', ain't they?"

"Uh-huh. I just got finished explaining to Pitt here what Won told us about him."

"Good. Let's get this shit over with," Snuffy said coldly.

"Wait! Don't you realize that I can make the both of you richer than either of you ever imagined? I'm the second in charge of The Network! Whatever you ask of me, I can give it to you. Don't be stupid, Snuffy. You'll be able to have whatever you want."

"If I let you go?" asked Snuffy.

Pit bobbed his head up and down and said, "Yes, if you let me go."

Snuffy and Charlene started laughing, and so did the other two gentlemen who had remained silent up until that moment.

"Dog, don't you realize that Won has already made it possible for me and Charlene here to have anything we want in his world? Why would we want to have a plug with the second-in-charge of The Network, when I'm about to have a direct link with the number one man of The Network?"

"What? Cash Flo' would never fuck with any of you guys! I'm telling you, you gots to listen to what I'm saying here!" Pitt yelled.

"Cash Flo'? Who the fuck is Cash Flo'?" asked one of the men who had accompanied Snuffy when he brought Leo and Tru into the warehouse. "Taz is about to be the next head of The Network. My Uncle Won planned on taking over himself, but since thangs went left for him, it's meant for Taz to be the man. You kilt my uncle, and for that, Mister Pitt, you gots to die by my hand!" Big Junior said as he smiled at Pitt.

Big Junior stood a little over six foot three inches, and was fucking huge. He could easily pass for a defensive lineman or a lean-ass linebacker. His muscles rippled all through his white tee.

Pitt looked as if he had already been shot by one of the guns aimed at his heart. "Ta-Taz! That country nigga in Oklahoma City?"

Big Junior nodded his head and said, "Yep! In a few weeks, he's about to take complete control of The Network."

"Never! Cash Flo' won't stand for that shit!"

Big Junior shrugged his huge shoulders and said, "If you say so. But check this out. We got thangs to do, and I'm sure Snuffy and Charlene have made plans for the evening."

"That's right, dog. Me and wifey tryin' to go get our freak on!" Snuffy said with a laugh.

Big Junior pulled out his silenced 9 and said, "Oh, I almost forgot. Uncle Won told me to tell you that he'll be waitin' for you in hell!"

Before Pitt could speak, Big Junior shot him two times in the head. He died instantly.

Snuffy turned toward Leo and Tru, and in his best Tony Montana impersonation, he asked, "You two want a job?"

Both Leo and Tru nodded their heads up and down eagerly, grateful their lives were being spared.

Charlene laughed and said, "Quit giving these niggas false hopes." Then she shot Leo and Tru right between their eyes. Their bodies fell to the floor instantly. She smiled at Snuffy and said, "Come on, 'Tony.' Let's get out of here!"

Snuffy smiled and asked, "But what about them?"

Big Junior said, "Don't trip. Major gots some of y'all's peoples from the twenty-one on their way to handle the cleanup. Let's ride!"

***

With tears sliding down his face, Taz stared at Won's image and listened to what he had to say. Won had a sad smile on his face as he spoke to the camera.

"If you're watching this DVD, Baby Boy, then I guess I've finally lost the game. Don't worry, though, 'cause if I lost, then that means you've won. Listen, and make sure that you do exactly as you're told, if, in fact you do decide to roll with what I'm about to propose to you.

"Pitt was able to pick up the pieces, and he obviously got to me before I could get to him. So, that means that by the time you get to watch this DVD, he too should have come to his demise. You will be receiving a call from my peoples with confirmation of this act. You then will also be notified of the position of power that is awaiting you out here on the West Coast."

"As you can see in my Will, I've left everything I have to you and Tazneema. But that's not all. I would be very pleased with you if you took over and became the head man of The Network. Everything is in order. All you have to do is give my man Snuffy the word that you have agreed to be the next head of The Network. After that, Cash Flo' will be eliminated, and the position of the most powerful Black criminal organization

in the U.S. will belong solely to you. I know this is a shock to you, Baby Boy, but take your time before deciding which way you're going to go. I designed this for the both of us. Either it was going to be me or you who ran The Network.

"Since I've come to my demise, I'm hoping that you'll carry on my dream and take this position. If not, I still want you to know that I have always loved you as my son, and I will forever be watching over you . . ."

Won paused and stared at the camera then said:

"Follow your heart on this one, Baby Boy. Out!"

The picture on the screen faded out slowly into another picture of the great Michael Jordan, only this time it was a picture of him standing with all six of the NBA championship trophies that he'd helped the Chicago Bulls win during his stellar career.

By the time Taz made it back to his house, he watched Won's DVD three more times. He couldn't believe what he had done for him. Now, the questions remained. What the hell was he going to do? Should he take the position as head of The Network? Or should he leave all of that shit alone and try to move on with his crazy-ass life? A decision had to be made. He just didn't know what the fuck he was going to do. *Life's a bitch, ain't it?* he thought as he climbed out of his truck and entered his home.

Chapter Thirty-three

It was the night before Keno's funeral. Taz was glad that Wild Bill, Red and Bob had decided not to have a wake. *I don't think I would be able to go through seeing my nigga in that coffin more than once,* Taz thought as he relaxed on his bed.

For the last few days, Taz kept himself busy by going over all of the financial matters of Won's estate. Won left him and Tazneema over sixty million dollars, including his big-ass boat and properties all over the West Coast. Everything was to be divided evenly between the two of them. That put a smile on Taz's face as he thought about how Tazneema was going to react when she found out that she was now an extremely wealthy young lady.

His smile quickly turned into a frown when he thought about her having that nigga Cliff's child. He reached and grabbed the phone and gave his daughter a call. When Tazneema answered the phone, she sounded a little funny, so he asked, "What's up, Baby Girl? You all right?"

"Not really, Daddy, but I'll be fine. I just need to get some rest, that's all," she said as she held onto her stomach.

"What's wrong? You sick or something?"

She took a deep breath and said, "I just got back home from having an abortion, Daddy."

"You what? What made you do that, Neema?"

"I didn't want to have that man's child. He was the devil, Daddy. I couldn't see myself bringing a child into this world that could possibly have that man's lying ways inside of him or her."

"Why didn't you tell me? I could have gone with you."

"I had Tari take me. I didn't think you'd be too comfortable with me going through that process."

"Are you sure you're okay? Do you need me to come out there?"

"I'm fine, Daddy. Tari's here, and she refuses to leave until I've eaten something and have fallen asleep. So relax."

Taz smiled and said, "Whatever, Baby Girl! Put that white girl on the phone."

Tazneema smiled and said, "You are too crazy, Taz! I'll see you tomorrow."

"All right, Baby Girl," Taz said somberly as he thought once again about having to attend his best friend's funeral in the morning.

Tari accepted the phone from Tazneema and said, "Don't you start with me! She made me promise not to tell you about any of this. It was her decision to make, Taz," she said seriously.

"Would you be quiet, snow bunny? I ain't mad at you or her. On the real, I'm kinda glad she did it, but a part of me wished she didn't. Does that make any sense?"

Tari laughed and said, "Yes, it makes perfect sense, silly! You're human, Taz. Don't worry though. The doctor told us that everything went fine. She's going to feel a little sluggish for a few days, but she's going to be A-okay. How are you doing?"

"I'm good, I guess. What about you?"

"I'm trying my best to accept all of this death. It's hard, baby . . . it's real hard."

"Yeah, I know."

"Why didn't Won want us to bury him properly? That was so damned unfair of him."

"You know he always had to do things his way. He requested to have his body cremated and his ashes spread out over the Pacific, so I had his attorneys take care of everything. Do you want to fly out to Cali with me to take care of the ashes?"

"I need a vacation, so why not? Can we do some thangs while we're out that way?" she asked devilishly.

"Tari!"

"All right! Damn! Can't a girl at least try?"

They both laughed.

"All right then, I'll see y'all tomorrow. I'm about to chill out for a li'l bit. Sacha should be here any minute."

"Tell her I said hello. I'll talk to you later," Tari said, and hung up the phone.

As if on cue, Sacha came into the bedroom, followed by Heaven and Precious. When Taz saw them enter the room, he smiled and said, "What's good, Li'l Mama?"

After slipping out of her pumps, she said, "Not much. Just tired as hell." She climbed onto the bed next to him, put her head on his chest and asked, "How are you holding up, baby?"

As he slowly stroked her long, jet-black hair, he said, "I miss him, Li'l Mama. I miss my man so much, it's killin' me slowly. I don't know how in the hell I'm gon' be able to look at him in a fuckin' casket. I don't think I'm gon' be able to take that shit."

Sacha closed her eyes as she listened to Taz speaking with so much pain in his voice. Her heart rate seemed to increase as she thought about all of the pain she had caused the one man that she would gladly give her life up for. For the thousandth time, she tried to convince herself to tell Taz the truth about how Keno was killed, but she just couldn't bring herself to do it. She couldn't tell her man, her fiancé, her heart, that she had killed his best friend because Keno had murdered her twin brothers so many years ago. Taz loved her, she was confident of that fact. But she wasn't willing to put their love to that ultimate test. This secret was going to have to go with her to her grave.

She raised her head, looked at her man and said, "Don't worry, baby. I'll be right by your side. I know it's going to be hard, but you know he's in a much better place now. He's with Bo-Pete and Won, and you know all three of them are watching over you."

Her words put a sad smile on his face as he thought about all three of his friends. "Yeah, they'll be watching over us all."

Before he could continue, they were interrupted by the telephone ringing. Sacha reached over Taz to answer it.

"Hello . . . May I ask who's speaking? . . . Just a moment please," she said. She handed the phone to Taz and said, "It's someone named Snuffy from Austin, baby."

Taz accepted the phone from her and said, "I was wondering when he was goin' to call." He put the phone to his ear and said, "What's good?"

"Everything is everything, my man. Do you know who I am?"

"Yeah, I know. I've been expecting your call."

"Do you have an answer for me yet? Or do you need some more time?"

"I have a question."

"Holla at your boy then."

"Has Cash Flo' been taken care of yet?"

"Do you want the grimy details?" Snuffy answered as he rubbed Charlene lightly on her left breast.

"Nah, I'm good. I just wanted to know. So, everything is all on me now, huh?"

"Yep. So, what's it gon' be, *G*? Do you want to accept this position or what?"

Taz stared at Sacha as she rested her head on his chest and asked, "Can one man handle that much power?"

"Won felt that you could handle it, and I've never doubted that man in all of our years dealing with one another, *G*. And I'm not about to start now. I think you can handle it," Snuffy said seriously.

Taz took a deep breath before answering Snuffy's question, because he knew it would change the direction of his life, as well as everyone else's around him. Wild Bill, Red, Bob, Sacha, Tari, Mama-Mama, Tazneema and Gwen's as well. If he moved to the West Coast to run The Network, they were all coming with him. There was no way in hell he would have it any other way.

"Yeah, I'm with it, Snuffy. I gots to carry the torch for my man. Won wanted it this way, so I gots to roll with my nigga's wishes. It wouldn't be right if I didn't."

"Exactly! I'll notify the rest of the counsel. When do you want to have our first official meeting?"

"What? You're part of the council?"

Snuffy smiled and said, "Dog, that was me and my wifey Charlene's blessing for being loyal all of these years. We would have gladly given our lives up for Won, dog. Now, that same loyalty belongs to you, Taz. We'll die for you if we have to. Real talk."

"That's good lookin'. Check it. Set it up with everyone else for next week out in Cali. We'll take Won's boat out and spread his ashes over the Pacific like he wanted. Afterward, we'll put the wheels of this ride in motion."

"Gotcha!" Snuffy said, and hung up the phone.

After Taz replaced the cordless phone back on its base, Sacha looked up into his eyes, smiled and asked, "So, we're going to California, baby?"

Taz smiled at his fiancée and said, "Yeah, we're all moving to the Wild, Wild West!"

ORDER FORM
URBAN BOOKS, LLC
78 E. Industry Ct
Deer Park, NY 11729

Name: (please print):_____

Address:_____

City/State:_____

Zip:_____

QTY	TITLES	PRICE
	16 On The Block	$14.95
	A Girl From Flint	$14.95
	A Pimp's Life	$14.95
	Baltimore Chronicles	$14.95
	Baltimore Chronicles 2	$14.95
	Betrayal	$14.95
	Black Diamond	$14.95

Shipping and handling-add $3.50 for 1st book, then $1.75 for each additional book.
Please send a check payable to:
Urban Books, LLC
Please allow 4-6 weeks for delivery

ORDER FORM
URBAN BOOKS, LLC
78 E. Industry Ct
Deer Park, NY 11729

Name: (please print):_____

Address:_____

City/State:_____

Zip:_____

QTY	TITLES	PRICE
	Cheesecake And Teardrops	$14.95
	Congratulations	$14.95
	Crazy In Love	$14.95
	Cyber Case	$14.95
	Denim Diaries	$14.95
	Diary Of A Mad First Lady	$14.95
	Diary Of A Stalker	$14.95

Shipping and handling-add $3.50 for 1st book, then $1.75 for each additional book. Please send a check payable to:

Urban Books, LLC

Please allow 4-6 weeks for delivery